EYES LIKE BLADES

TOM HADLEY

TOM HADLEY

This is a work of fiction. While reference may be made to
actual events or existing locations, the names, characters,
places, and incidents are either the product of the author's
imagination or are used fictitiously.
Any resemblance to any actual persons, living or dead,
or business establishments is entirely coincidental.

TOM HADLEY
asserts the moral right to be
identified as the author of this book.

Acknowledgements

Many thanks to my team of eagle-eyed beta readers: Janet, Katie, Sharon and especially Rob, without whose help and advice this book would not have been possible. Thanks too to my designer, Katie Birks for the fabulous cover.

1

Late one November evening in Bournemouth

George slowed the car to a halt about fifty metres before the house, noting the vehicle parked further away on the other side of the road. Neither car would be visible to any of the numerous surveillance cameras in which the owner had invested so much of his money.

It was an imposing enough house, he thought, but in such an affluent Bournemouth neighbourhood, it didn't exactly stand out. Most of the time, only the family lived there. It was rare for the owner himself to stay overnight, but George liked to keep tabs on anomalies. You never knew when such nuggets of information might prove useful – as tonight.

Nothing to be done now but wait and George was very good at waiting, which was probably as well since, at times, he seemed to do little else. On this occasion, however, he was obliged to linger only a few minutes before a figure emerged from a footpath beyond the house and got into the parked car. Though George wasn't close enough to hear the engine start, when the car headlights flashed twice, he gave a grim smile of satisfaction. So, it was done. But God only knew what would happen next. He just had to hope that he ended up on the winning side.

2

Christmas Eve in Slough

Waiting alone at 1am on a deserted platform at Slough railway station might make some 28-year-old women nervous, but not Liv Fisher. She wallowed in the cold, gloomy darkness because she was truly more comfortable out of the light. The light brought with it a plethora of visual detail which she could really do without. Exceptional vision was the reason she was a lifelong fuck-up. So, yeh, darkness had become her friend.

Irritatingly, the information screen above her flickered, while a hollow, distorted voice announced the imminent arrival of her train. On time, as it happened. Not that it mattered much since there was nothing especially enticing to return to in her tiny, empty flat. Not even a hungry cat awaited her there.

She was glad of her long, sleek, leather coat though, because Christmas Eve was proving to be a chilly night. Years ago, the coat had cost her an alarming chunk of income. Now, though the black hide was irreparably worn in places, she was still just as fond of it as the day she first slipped it on. Perhaps because it recalled more hedonistic times when she wore little else - literally. But those heady days were left far behind when she started a proper job. If teaching PE was a proper job. Still, this evening her tenure even of that post was looking particularly tenuous.

Working out your rage at a 24-hour gym could only distract you for a time. And just now, there was plenty of rage swirling around in Liv's head. Closing her eyes, she reflected that, if today's hearing went against her, they'd sack her. And since, even before her recent suspension, her rent was in arrears, the outlook was bleak. Bleak enough that when she got back to Reading she'd seek out her favourite bar and administer a serious anaesthetic of gin. The Orange Lobster would still be open – just about.

Though her eyes were shut, Liv sensed the instant she was no longer alone. Reluctantly, she raised her eyelids a little and saw that, sure enough, a man had wandered onto the far end of the platform. His arrival caused her no anxiety. He was just a man. If it came to it, Liv reckoned she could still handle any man. Even if it was a well-built one, wearing a flat black cap and a long grey coat. Unbidden, a bitter thought reminded her that it was a long time since she'd 'handled' any man.

No sooner had she allowed her eyelids to drop again, than a shadow flitted across her. A smartly-dressed woman had strolled across the platform to stand a mere metre away. Some people did that. A hundred metres of platform to wait on and the woman in the pale coat, with sparkling eyes and pinched features, had to put herself only a Covid breath away.

'Black cap', Liv noticed, was now walking slowly towards the two women. Curiosity, safety in numbers, or perhaps just the vain hope of a nocturnal chat up?

To her right, another traveller shambled into view. A pale, dishevelled youth with glazed, vacant eyes and lank hair which morphed into a dark brown T-shirt. By the time 'black cap' joined the small cluster of humanity, it was getting positively crowded. If they huddled any closer together for warmth, they wouldn't find a willing ally in Liv.

As if on cue, the woman sidled nearer.

Muttering: "For fuck's sake...", Liv glared at her, before easing away to maintain her distance. Liv didn't like people getting too close. For several more minutes the four strangers remained there with their collective mist of warm breath rising into the chill air.

Since waiting had never been one of Liv's strengths, she was relieved when, in the distance along the line from Paddington, a tiny pinprick of white light appeared. As it grew steadily larger, 'black cap' started to engage the other woman in conversation. Clearly, the man was a trier. Since the locomotive was still all of a hundred metres away, he was more than likely positioning himself to follow the woman onto the train to complete his pick-up. A sound plan - if neither original nor subtle.

While the train was slowing, a station announcement blared out to confirm that this was indeed the train from Paddington which stopped, after several other soulless destinations, at Reading. Liv, eyes still comfortably half-open, took a step forward up to the faded yellow line which warned of the platform's edge. She was quietly relieved when the other woman didn't follow suit. But, as the train slowed further, her shadow edged nearer again. Close enough for a small hand to press against the centre of Liv's back.

Even before alarm bells sounded in Liv's head, the pressure increased and the woman reached across to seize Liv's arm with her other hand. Just as Liv tensed for a struggle, she was hauled roughly aside and two sharp popping sounds came from behind her. The woman launched herself forward and, twisting around as she fell, lunged for Liv's coat. As her desperate fingers clawed at the leather, Liv instinctively thrust out a hand to catch her. But she was already far out of reach.

Staring back at Liv, with wide bright eyes, she plummeted out onto the tracks below. She opened her mouth but, before the scream was more than a thought, it was obliterated by a two hundred ton locomotive crushing the life out of her.

Liv, her own eyes fully open, couldn't stop her brain from processing heavy engine parts eviscerating a human body. She had witnessed senseless death before, but never one illustrated in such fine and horrifying detail. Whoever the woman was, she didn't deserve such a fate. In that moment, before her eyelid shutters slammed down, Liv was in shock. So much so that she didn't notice that 'black cap' was gripping her arm. Once she did, her eyes darted open to deliver an acid-laden glare.

"Sorry," he muttered, releasing his hold. "I, er, thought she was going to take you with her..."

Recalling the hand pressing against her spine and the final lunge for her coat, Liv suspected he might just be right. But how had he reacted so fast? No-one moved that fast – unless they were expecting trouble. Her forensic attention was now focussed upon him alone. Short black hair, flecked with grey. Pale blue eyes set in a stubbled, but otherwise unremarkable, face. His grey overcoat, rather tired and old-fashioned, matched perfectly with the dirty grey trainers. So, who was he?

"How did you know what was going to happen?" she demanded.

"Lucky guess," he replied.

Just for an instant, his eyes met hers before he turned away to walk briskly towards the rear of the platform. It was the briefest of interactions, but enough for Liv to suspect that he was not just some random stranger. Somewhere, somehow, she had seen those eyes before. But while she was reflecting upon that little revelation, he was gone.

"A bloody suicide," remarked the pale-faced youth moodily.

"Yeh, suicide," agreed Liv, still wondering.

Suicide, the ultimate ego trip: final, brutal and utterly selfish – and yet...

Why, if the woman was so hell-bent on ending her life, had she, in that last instant, worn such an astonished expression. Why the urge to scream in shocked outrage · and the last-minute outstretched hand? Because, what did she expect would happen if she jumped in front of a fucking train? If you're set on doing it, sister, at least own the moment and do it alone.

It was the unlucky train driver Liv reserved her sympathy for. The poor sod didn't have a prayer of stopping and now he'd carry the woman's death around with him. And death, as Liv knew only too well, could weigh even more heavily than a locomotive.

Since the train, now stationary, would not be moving on anytime soon, she prepared herself for a long, cold night. Eventually, the transport police would come and interview them all and then the track would have to be cleared of the grisly remains. If she was lucky, the railway company would provide a replacement bus for the passengers but, even if it did, there was certain to be a prolonged delay.

The train driver, she observed, was working his way back through the carriages to inform his passengers that they would have to get off and await alternative transport. The disappointing, though hardly surprising, news was greeted by a cocktail of snarled complaints and muttered abuse. Kick a man when he's down, why don't you?

But she'd seen enough – more than enough. So, while she was waiting on a not very comfortable bench, Liv's eyes were firmly shut as she worked through in her mind what to tell the police. A description of the woman prior to impact was easy enough: medium height, blonde hair, flat chest and thin face – none of which would be discernible from what remained of her on the track. She was wearing a light-coloured raincoat – beige, Liv thought – and had appeared perfectly at ease when the train rolled in. Yeh, right up to the moment when she'd pulled at Liv and then catapulted herself off the platform.

Already, Liv was struggling to sequence the events and that almost never happened to her. The woman pressed her from behind... leapt forward... reached out to her... 'blackcap' intervened and held onto Liv... the woman threw herself forward onto the tracks. But there must have been something else because, why did she stop pushing at Liv and hurl herself into oblivion? Liv knew she was missing something. Yeh... the two kind of snapping, popping sounds. What made that sort of a noise? Almost like someone flicking a big switch on and off.

For several minutes she manipulated the images in her head, seeking a thread to link them all. Because she knew that, all too soon, the fine detail which seemed so clear now would fade to nothing.

"Where you bound for then?" Unnoticed, the pale-faced youth had sat down beside her.

"Piss off," growled Liv.

"Only asking," he complained.

"Ask someone else."

With a shrug, he left and she returned to her examination of what she had seen. How her brain stored the deluge of images it received, she could never fathom. All she could do – something she had done a thousand times before – was try to hold on to some of them. In her head she imagined them stacked like containers on a dockside but only the most recently stored could ever be opened.

Reliving the fatal moments was brutal, especially when she sharpened the focus of every frame in search of an anomaly. With the woman turning over and twisting around in mid-air, it was difficult to be certain. But... there it was: a piece that didn't fit. Two red splodges on the back of the woman's pale coat which suggested something other than suicide.

People always told Liv that she overthought things, but it was hard not to when every hour of every day, she absorbed so much grinding optical detail. On this occasion at least, she felt pretty justified in doing some serious overthinking. How could she tell the police that a stranger in a black cap had taken her arm lest she was dragged over? And then, for good measure, he'd loosed off two silenced shots at the woman? Because, what was that all about?

Perhaps she was being a tad ungrateful, but 'black cap' appeared to have taken very extreme measures to help a complete stranger. Except, she had seen those eyes before. Probably just once and, unlike her recently deceased mother, she didn't have a facility to remember what she saw for very long.

Inevitably, the chat all around her was about the 'suicide', along with the resulting delay, inconvenience, etc, etc. Liv attempted to shut out the random chatter while she opened her eyes to a narrow slit, to search again for 'black cap'. Though she scanned the entire length of the platform, observing a thousand things she really didn't want to know about the milling throng of passengers alighting from the train, there was no trace of her saviour. But was he truly a saviour, or was he perhaps a brutal killer?

From the moment 'black cap' appeared, he'd ignored Liv completely and focussed on the other woman. So, had his intention all along been to kill the poor woman? If so, then Liv's survival might just have been serendipitous. It would certainly explain why he left so fast – and why his victim looked so shocked. Yet, having said that, there was little doubt that the woman had tried to push Liv under the train. The question remained then: did he always intend to kill the woman, or did he act solely to protect Liv? And, if the latter, why?

He had vanished now anyway and she didn't think he'd just popped out for a piss. But his disappearance presented her with an awkward dilemma. When interviewed by the police, should she mention him, or not? If she expunged him from her account, she was covering up a crime. But a crime that appeared to have saved her life. On balance, she concluded that she couldn't mention 'black cap' at all without opening a very large can of worms.

A sudden shiver swept through her but not from the cold, nor even the notion that she had just come close to death. No, what really freaked her out was that someone actually appeared to want her dead · and it was a very long time since that had happened. When she worked through the legion of people that she had recently pissed off, she could only come up with one possibility, but even that seemed far-fetched. True, she had caused some serious grief for that one pupil and his family. But then, didn't a rapist deserve to be a little fucking hassled, at the very least? Even so, an attempt to kill her seemed over the top since she was the one facing the sack.

Slow to arrive in the first place, the police were even slower getting around to interviewing the only two genuine witnesses – in the absence of 'black cap'. So when, in the end, a replacement coach dropped her off at Reading station, it was just after 4.30am. Sadly, the Orange Lobster had closed long before but, thankfully, a certain all-night convenience store happened to be on her way home. Well almost.

Supporting such outlets was socially important, she told herself. Otherwise they'd no longer exist. And besides, the bottle of red wine she purchased was purely medicinal. After the whole chaotic mêlée of probably losing her job and then witnessing a grisly death on a railway line, she was going to need some assistance getting to sleep. Consuming copious quantities of alcohol was her tried and tested method of blurring the images and expunging the visual minutiae which would otherwise smother her.

Only when she was entering her flat, did she remember that the coming day was not going to get any better. In fact, the coming day had already come and, several hours later, she had an appointment with a sodding lawyer. For all of her twenty-eight years thus far, Liv, deeply distrustful of all 'establishment' figures, had avoided lawyers as if they carried some fatal contagion. Of course, in recent years, some of them certainly had, but they were hardly alone in that. There was no logic to her antipathy because, as far as she knew, she had never been screwed over by one. But, hey, better to err on the safe side.

This particular lawyer had been hounding her for weeks but she had deliberately and, she thought, quite skilfully, staved off meeting him. At the time, Christmas Eve had seemed sufficiently far away to ignore. Except that now it wasn't. She had a fair idea what it was all about because he first got in touch with her a few days after news of her parents' sudden deaths appeared in the papers. But shit, if there was one topic of conversation that Liv didn't want to be a part of, it was one that involved her parents. And now, somehow, that formerly distant appointment was scorching towards her like a drone-launched missile.

Yeh, Christmas Eve had started very badly, but she feared it was only going to nosedive from there.

3

The sleek black Mercedes lingered, illegally parked, outside the station building, engine idling softly. As the lone rear seat passenger watched the entrance, he listened out for the wail of a siren but heard nothing. Probably too soon for the transport police, he decided. But, when a figure in a black cap and overcoat emerged from the station entrance, he sat forward slightly.

"That fellow, George," he said to his driver. "I'm sure I know him from somewhere."

"Me too," agreed George, "but I can't place him, boss. Don't think he wanted to be seen."

"Follow him while I go and find out if it's done," ordered his employer.

Switching off the engine, George got out and set off after the man in the flat cap. A few moments later, his employer sauntered into Slough station noting, with distaste, how grubby the whole edifice was. It took him less than a minute to establish that there had been a suicide and not much longer to ascertain that the person he expected to be smeared along the track was still very much alive. Not wishing to linger, he walked briskly out to his vehicle, where he found George waiting.

"Got his car number," reported George.

"What if it's a rental?"

"It isn't," George assured him. "All done inside?"

"No, not all done. Not done at all, I'm afraid. So, there's no need to wait because Brigid won't be coming."

"Right," said George, starting the engine.

"Tomorrow, I'd like you to find that fellow in the flat cap," instructed the passenger. "Watch him and, if you see him with the daughter, take him out."

"And her?" enquired George.

"Yes, obviously her too."

4

Rochester, Minnesota in the USA, five weeks earlier

All her life, Hal's mother, Alice, had worked several jobs but it had never been enough to provide more than a subsistence upbringing for him and his brother, Brad. Abandoned by the twins' father before they were even born, Alice had given them all she could until her long, grim struggle with illness began.

How frail she'd looked in those last slow months, thought Hal. Ravaged by cancer and weakened by the relentless pain, there was not an ounce more fight left in her. To him, it was a relief when the end came, because no-one should have to endure so much agony for so long - nor should a son be condemned to watch his mother simply waste away. If they had better healthcare insurance, she could have afforded more palliative care but, as it was, the money had drained away much faster than Alice's will to live. Since, in her desperate poverty, she had long ago signed away her paltry life insurance, there was barely enough money to pay for her daily care, let alone any actual treatment.

Having just left the army, Hal had used most of his accumulated pay to service her medical bills. But, soon enough, the cash had run out. His brother, Brad had nothing in the way of savings since most of the trickle of income from his ailing tech business was consumed by the rent of his New York apartment. 'New York apartment' sounded plush but Hal knew that, in reality, it was a tiny box with a bed, a stove and a can, deep in the South Bronx.

Alice, Hal reflected, despite all the shit that life had tossed in her direction, had been a stellar mother. It was typical of her that, early on in her illness, she had signed up to donate her body to medical science right there in Rochester in the hope that her boys might be spared the expense of a funeral.

Though Hal had done difficult tours in Afghanistan and the Middle East – and seen some bloody action there – he had found Alice's illness difficult to live with and couldn't bear to stay by her bedside to the bitter end. He had witnessed plenty of killings, but this slow-burning fuse of death was different. Brad, the elder son by two minutes, had, God love him, shouldered that final burden. There was much to be done in those last days so, Hal volunteered to sort through their mother's few remaining cherished possessions. That was hard but, far harder was transporting her body to the clinic.

"What if they don't take her?" Brad had enquired at the last minute. "In the small print, it says they reject some donors."

Since Hal had never read any small print before in his life, he took Brad's word for it. As ever, Brad just needed some reassurance.

"It'll be fine," Hal told him, though he too found the concept of 'whole body donation' rather unnerving. It sounded perfectly fine until applied to someone you loved. Still, however unsettling, it was what she'd wanted. Once her body was delivered, the two brothers found themselves standing alone outside the clinic, unsure what to do next. But, of course, all that was left to do was to go back to their separate lives. Brad returned to New York in a last-ditch attempt to revive his flagging business, while Hal went back to the sofa he occupied in the apartment of a fellow veteran.

Before the final stages of their mother's illness, the brothers had spent little time together. Hal might be Brad's twin but the two men were wired very differently. Hal was as even-tempered as Brad was eccentric. Yet, despite their often remarked upon differences, Hal still felt a strong bond between them – a bond forged throughout a childhood of penury.

As soon as Hal was old enough, he had joined the army – but there was nothing selfish about his decision. Knowing that his mother had struggled to raise her boys on the low income she gleaned from several cleaning jobs, he decided that leaving home was the best way he could help her out. Of course, Alice never saw it that way and, he knew, never really forgave him for leaving.

Being in the army and going to Afghanistan, changed Hal. He went there with a deserved reputation as something of a laconic, easy-going guy. When he returned, there was anger in him. Things he had seen over there, comrades he had lost... a lot had happened that he could never talk about to Brad – or anyone else who wasn't a 'vet'. While the brothers tried to rekindle their former affinity, their mother's long struggle was drawing inexorably to its wretched end.

Hal, struggling to find work, was poor company and his burgeoning grief only fed the rage which already threatened to consume him. Underpinning that rage was the lifelong belief – shared by both brothers – that abandonment by their natural father was the root cause of all the family's troubles. Brad had long ago shoved it to the far reaches of his mind and buried it by working every hour he could on his business, As he told Hal, when the subject came up, there was no sense in pointing the finger at a man they didn't even know. But while Hal was sorting through his mother's effects, he found an old photo of a young man with the word Hal scrawled on the back. But Hal knew it was not his face staring back at him. He and his brother had looked at the photo sometimes when they were kids, wondering why this other Hal had deserted them.

5

Somewhere a muffled, but persistent, alarm was sounding. Inexorably, it was hauling Liv out of her drunken stupor, which was irritating. There was a lot to be said for spending the rest of her life under a duvet because then her relentless eyes would never have to see anything ever again.

As usual, it was her own fault. She should have silenced that sodding alarm clock more effectively weeks ago when she was first suspended from work. But apparently, slapping it wasn't enough to persuade it to shut the fuck up. Now it railed on at her, prodding at her consciousness with its savage, repetitive, little bleeps. But Liv could be a determined opponent. She waited it out and then went back to sleep.

Later, a bleary-eyed glance at her phone suggested it might already be after the middle of the day. But which day? Christmas had passed in such an alcohol-fumed blur that she had no clear recollection of where she'd been or what she'd done. Because drinking large quantities of alcohol and keeping your eyes shut a lot of the time could get you into all kinds of shit.

When a scary thought struck her, she stretched a wary arm across the bed, wondering if she might find another warm, comatose body laid out beside her. It was a relief - tinged with a trace of disappointment - to discover that no-one appeared to have accompanied her home.

At the back of her mind she had a sort of feeling that there was a reason for the alarm sounding. Aside from just to annoy her. But, if there was, it remained elusive as she hauled herself out of bed and under a lukewarm shower. She really should nag her landlord about the hot water – or, more accurately, the lack of it. On the other hand, he would then take the opportunity to remind her about the overdue rent. So, cool showers it would have to be, even if it did make her long hair rather more difficult to manage.

Eventually, she discovered that it was around mid-afternoon - or breakfast time, as she now liked to call it. It was another hour before she remembered missing the lawyer appointment on Christmas Eve. But hey, what was the rush when her parents were already dead? Late on Christmas Eve afternoon, when Liv thought she had dodged the lawyer's bullet, the cunning bastard had called her to reschedule. Seriously, who was still working that late on Christmas Eve? The trouble was that Liv couldn't exactly remember now when the rescheduled appointment was, though the 27th sounded possible.

Breathing a little easier, she considered how she should spend the remainder of Christmas Day. Struggling to recall when she'd last eaten, she glanced at her mobile as if it might jog her memory. The phone was helpful to a degree because it told her it was 4.17pm. It also told her it was 27th December, which surely couldn't be right, could it?

What, she wondered idly, had happened to Christmas Day? No, scrub that, where had Boxing Day gone? She might have spent much of her time down at the Orange Lobster. But then... she might have been anywhere. No matter how much she thought about it, she was forced to accept that Christmas, as an actual period of time, was entirely lost to her.

The better news was that, if it truly was the afternoon of the 27th, then the re-arranged appointment with the lawyer had already been and gone. Again. Savouring a delicious moment of relief as a potential headache was magically removed, she decided that it was close enough to 5pm for a drink. Drinking would dull her wits once more, stop her noticing, thinking, worrying, obsessing...

Over the past decade and a half, she had proven that red wine was habit-forming – not to mention spirits. So, showing admirable restraint, she shunned the red stuff and opened a bottle of white. She felt virtuous right up to the moment that she drained a second bottle and crawled back into bed.

The next day she was awoken by a bright dawn – far too bright. Sitting up in bed, she realised that she was still wearing her clothes from the day before – or was it the day before that? Swaying sideways, she rolled inelegantly off the bed and hit the floor. Getting up so early was much overrated and she seriously considered clambering back under the covers. What she needed was coffee. A small bucket of it would probably do the trick. But before she managed to locate any coffee, her phone vibrated and its lit face glared at her. Angry and insistent.

It was an unfamiliar, unidentified number calling her – although, since she had no friends, every number was pretty unfamiliar · except the school office. Not that they would be calling her any time soon. Reaching for the phone, she contrived only to knock it off the small bedside cabinet and groaned when it continued to vibrate as it crept across the floor.

"Hold still, you crazy little bastard," she groaned, as she attempted to snare the runaway.

When she did finally succeed in answering it, she found it was the lawyer's office. But, of course, she should have known... Unable to stifle a loud sigh, she followed it with a groan of apology for missing her second appointment. Perhaps, she suggested, it could wait until after the New Year? But no, apparently it couldn't and the word urgent figured frequently in the course of the brief conversation. There were, apparently, matters to sort out in the wake of her parents' death which she, as their only surviving relative, was required to deal with.

Just then, however, dealing with staying upright seemed more than enough of a challenge. But, albeit grudgingly, Liv agreed to attend their office at 11am the following day. It was bloody typical of her parents, who had offered her sod all while they were alive, to make unreasonable demands upon her once they were dead.

In a bleak mood, she wrote off the rest of the day until it was late enough to drown herself at the Orange Lobster. But there, even after a succession of strong gins with only a trace of tonic, she still couldn't forget what had happened in the past week or so. Not just the sword of fate that hung ominously over her employment status but, rather more worryingly, the apparent attempt upon her life. In the wake of her unpromising dismissal hearing, she ought to be planning for the worst, but simply couldn't face it.

What depressed her most was that, despite her recent trouble at the school, she'd truly believed that, as a PE teacher, she had found her niche in life. True, the girls could be right bitches sometimes but she thought she'd done OK. At least until the whole 'rapegate' saga. If she lost her job over that, what else was there for her? A judgement like that would hang over her like a gigantic turd. She'd struggle to find another teaching post of any description. Perhaps, after all, it would have been better if she'd been dragged off that railway platform and smeared along the cold, unforgiving rails.

Despite spending a long, morose evening, the following morning she made an effort to rise early. She managed to shower, brush out her hair and dress in good time to go to the lawyers. But, just as she was about to leave the flat, some mail arrived – the first since Christmas. Slithering through the letter box, a single envelope with the school crest upon it dropped onto her doormat. Shit, that was quick. The witch who chaired the governors must have posted it before the blood was even dry on her signature. Liv had prayed it would be held up a bit longer in the Christmas mail. A vain hope though in an age when hardly anyone sent cards anymore.

For several minutes, she stared at the letter, unwilling even to pick it up in case that implied an acceptance of her fate. Then, remembering her appointment, she decided that, whatever the letter said, it could wait a few hours. So, donning her dark glances, she went out, giving the door a satisfying slam. Though her habitual shades softened the glare a little, her eyes were still hooded as she stalked out into the street. The immediate result was that she almost collided with a passerby and, from then on, she took a little more care. Slowing her breathing, she struggled to counteract a feeling she guessed was somewhere in between cold turkey and terminal alcohol poisoning.

Travis, Travis and Humboldt occupied an expensive-looking brick building in Reading's market place. No longer housing a market, it had become a busy thoroughfare on weekday mornings for large, noisy buses and rude people in a hurry. Reporting to the glossy, highly-polished desk in the foyer, she faced a receptionist, whose faint, apathetic smile suggested that Liv's efforts to look presentable had not proven entirely successful.

When Liv gave her name and asked for Travis, Travis and Humboldt, she was airily directed - without any words, or even eye contact - to the third floor. The forefinger of an outstretched hand, with immaculately painted nails, on the end of a wholly uninterested arm, pointed towards the lifts. Frowning, Liv briefly considered polite restraint but she was really not in the mood to be especially tolerant.

"Thank you, dear," she told the receptionist. "Perhaps you could make use of all that time you're not spending being helpful to visitors by – oh, I don't know, maybe removing the stick wedged up your arse."

Without pausing, she left the wide-eyed receptionist and swept over to the lifts where her righteous momentum was brought to a somewhat disappointing halt because there was no lift waiting. Unfazed, Liv fixed an icy smile and continued on past the lifts and up the stairs. To her chagrin, her fitness was called into question long before she arrived at the third floor. Reaching out for support from the gleaming, stainless steel handrail, she shuttered her eyes a little to limit the distractions.

At the third floor landing, a spotty, bespectacled youth in a suit greeted her with a bored expression that suggested he'd been afflicted by the same personnel training package as the receptionist. When he ushered her into an office, she expected him to leave because clearly he was doing some sort of youth work experience. However, the fresh-faced boy lawyer proceeded to sit down opposite her.

"I'm Tom Reynolds, Ms Fisher," he began. "But please, call me Tom."

Not Travis, Travis or Humboldt then…

"You've been rather elusive, haven't you?" chided the young man posing as a lawyer.

That was true enough because her parents' private aircraft had dropped out of the sky back in November.

"But let me assure you from the outset," continued 'call me Tom', "how sorry we are here at Travis, Travis and Humboldt for your loss-"

"Don't be," interrupted Liv, "unless you actually crashed their plane. And, if you did, thanks a lot for that. You can rest assured I've not sustained any 'loss' at all."

"Right... I see," he said, frowning – presumably at her lack of grief. "Er, perhaps you could remove your sunglasses?"

"No."

"Keeping up a cool image, eh?" ventured her host.

"Yeh, icy," replied Liv. "But no, I just have very... very sensitive eyes..."

"Right. Let's take a look at what needs to be done, shall we?" suggested Tom, clearly eager to move on.

"Oh, do let's, *Tom,*" she agreed, abruptly gushing fake enthusiasm.

Though wrongfooted again by her manner, he pressed on, perhaps in the vain hope that the tone of their meeting could only improve.

"Obviously we don't handle your late parents' affairs here," he explained, "being as they live – or rather lived · down on the south coast."

Registering that he had paused, Liv opened her eyes.

"Ah, did you have your eyes closed?" he asked.

She sometimes spent hour upon hour with her eyes closed. But, open or closed, dark glasses or no dark glasses, it was always an effort.

"I thought you might not be listening..." he explained.

"As it happens, I was," said Liv. "Please, go on."

"Right. One of our associate legal firms in Dorset, Winthrop and Hall, has asked us to brief you and get you to contact them about your mother's affairs."

"What about my father?" enquired Liv. "I'll bet he had some affairs too."

"Oh, Winthrop and Hall don't act for him," explained Tom.

"Lucky Winthrop and Hall," muttered Liv, suddenly overwhelmed by a craving for a stiff gin, or three.

Having opened her eyes, she was distracted by the undoubted quality of his shirt, above which his young face revealed several careless patches of stubble in between the spots. His hair was short to the point of extinction, as the current fashion seemed to dictate. For the next few minutes, she struggled to pay attention to his words. That was only partly because she was closely examining his countenance. It was mainly because it had only just registered that the fellow she'd bumped into outside her flat, had been wearing a flat cap – a black one.

How did she not notice that at the time? Perhaps her visual powers were in decline. Some hope... Unless his reappearance was a coincidence... but, no. No fucking way.

"Ms Fisher?" prompted Tom, eventually aware that he had actually, this time, lost her attention.

Blinking back at him, she murmured: "Er, sorry, can you repeat that?"

"Which part?" he enquired.

"Oh, all of it," she said, deciding that another run at the whole thing couldn't hurt.

As 'call me Tom' began to explain her situation again, she thrust 'black cap' to the back of her mind – though not all that far back. It wasn't easy trying to absorb what Tom Lawyer was saying whilst part of her brain was in overdrive processing the presence of 'black cap' outside her flat. The gist though, if she understood correctly, was that, though her parents had not yet officially been declared dead, there were still matters she needed to attend to – in particular, the house in Dorset which, in their absence, had apparently been declared unsafe by the local council.

"Unsafe," scoffed Liv.

It had felt pretty damned unsafe when she lived there, but she assumed the local council were worried about something other than the unremitting warfare of her childhood.

"Unsafe, how?" she enquired.

After checking his notes, Tom replied: "Er, yes, it's Sunrise Heights, isn't it?"

Liv always assumed that the name Sunrise Heights was an ironic term, since a band of tall trees blocked every sunrise from anyone who might attempt to witness it from the house.

"I believe it's falling into the sea," said Tom finally.

"Oh, good," remarked Liv, showing genuine enthusiasm for the first time.

"Good?" Tom, despite his general lack of interest, was momentarily outraged.

"But it's a major asset, Ms Fisher," he said, as if he was talking to someone who might actually care. "The house is in your mother's name so if, as seems likely, your parents are confirmed to be deceased, then I understand that she has left the house to you."

"Yeh? Great. Well, in that case, I'd definitely prefer it to be nearer the bottom of the cliff than the top," she said, with a tight smile.

"Er, right... But, anyway, Ms Fisher, you still need to go down there," persisted the trainee lawyer.

"To do what exactly?" she growled, because all this talk about her ancestral home was really beginning to depress her.

"Well, at the very least to liaise with the council and see how bad the danger to the house is. And there'll soon be your mother's will to deal with. I'll give you a contact number for her lawyers so that you can consult them about what to do while you're down there."

Removing her glasses, Liv looked Master Reynolds in the eye and declared: "I am not going back to that house, *Tom*. Not ever."

"Very well," conceded Tom, "but will you at least undertake to visit Winthrop and Hall?"

"You have my solemn promise," she vowed, "that, when I go to Christchurch, I'll pop in on Winthrop and Hall." Though of course, that assumed she had some intention of heading to Christchurch in the foreseeable future – which she certainly didn't.

Perhaps Tom was cleverer than he looked because he favoured her with such a disbelieving look, that she felt compelled to add: "Pinky promise?"

In response, Tom huffed, which Liv took as a cue to depart and return to her flat.

When she did so, she was heartily relieved not to find 'black cap' lurking nearby – and this time, she was certainly watching very closely. She remained resolute about her decision not to go down to Sunrise Heights in Dorset until she opened the door of the flat and trod on the envelope she'd abandoned earlier.

With a groan of submission, she retrieved it from the mat and tore it open to discover that the contents confirmed exactly what she feared: the dismissal tribunal had found against her. What really burned her to the core was the rank injustice of it all. A girl's life had been ruined – and hers too, for that matter – while the lying, privileged rapist responsible would no doubt sail on through life's untroubled waters for the rest of his days.

Having hurled the missive back down onto the mat, she was still reeling from that blow when an email pinged up cheerily on her phone. It turned out to be a not so cheery eviction notice which promised a letter of confirmation would follow imminently. The flat was terrible, but it was better than bedding down in the town cemetery, or sleeping on the streets. Liv knew, because she'd lived that life before and didn't particularly want to go back to it.

Within the space of a few minutes, she'd been made both homeless and jobless. Suddenly, the idea of returning to her childhood home – especially now that her parents were no longer there – didn't seem such a terrible idea after all. At least she would have somewhere to live while she decided what to do next. Sunrise Heights was, after all, just a building. And, if the two people she despised most in all the world weren't there, then what was the problem? Sure, it would bring back some pretty awful memories, but a woman who'd faced down the unruliest elements of Year 11 really shouldn't be phased by an empty house.

6

London, three weeks earlier

New York was five hours behind the UK, so Hal knew Brad would most likely still be working. His brother was always working and that wasn't going to change. But Hal simply couldn't wait any longer because this was something Brad had to know.

Picking up his cell, he navigated back to the newspaper account several months earlier, which bore the headline: "British business couple lost in plane crash..." and sent his brother a link to the story, which included a grainy monochrome image of the couple in question.

Though Hal had already decided what he was going to do, he still needed to tell his brother. More than that, he needed Brad to be on his side. So, he followed the link with a text: "Hey, bro', you know who this is, don't you?"

It was always the same when he texted Brad; he would have to wait some time for a reply because 'Brad was always working.' No doubt Brad would ignore the text until he was finished whatever he was doing. Ordinarily, Hal was OK with that because, Jeez, the guy needed to work every hour just to keep his business afloat. Since it was already half way down the can, Hal had to admire his brother's commitment in trying to salvage it. On this occasion, however, Hal was desperate for a quick response – any response.

He gave Brad less than five minutes before texting again: "Take a look - please."

Though it was a relief when Brad texted back, all his twin said was: "I'm working. I got deadlines."

After 'I got deadlines', his brother might as well have added: "which you don't."

Hal understood, but this was just too important to leave. At once, he despatched another missive: "Look closer." With it, he sent a different image but one that would be all too familiar to Brad because, in his early life, he had spent more than a little time brooding over it.

After that, Hal left Brad alone for a while and waited. Although he was impatient for a reply, he was all too aware that there was a limit to how far he could push his brother. The last thing he wanted was to piss Brad off so much that he didn't reply at all. Nonetheless, it took all Hal's considerable powers of restraint to leave the matter there. Sensitive to his brother's predicament, he decided to wait until Brad finished his work. It might, he hoped, lead to a more productive conversation. He had left the ball with Brad, who would either come back to him soon, or not.

It was in the early hours of the morning when Brad eventually responded.

"OK, bro'," Brad texted, "I agree it looks like him. But, so what? The guy's dead now anyway."

A fair response, conceded Hal, at after 9pm New York time. It was also the answer he kinda expected from his brother. Brad was focussed solely on his company. He was in permanent survival mode, which was something Hal, at least, knew all about…

Hoping to prompt a conversation, he texted back immediately: "Seems like he was rich when he was still alive though, bro'."

"It's a rabbit hole, Hal," texted Brad. "Ma's dead now too. Just leave it be. Get a job – or a wife – or both."

Wow. So that was a hard no… His brother's thoughts couldn't have been expressed more bluntly: get on with your life and stop pestering the shit out of me.

On one level, Hal was obliged to accept that his brother was right. Here he was, poking around in the ashes of an old fire, while Brad was fighting with all he had to reignite the flame of his business. Yet, Hal knew that Alice had never truly recovered from losing the father of her boys. It had defined the remainder of her existence. For the twins too, the feeling of abandonment had never quite disappeared. Faded yes, but still it lingered there.

"He owes us," texted Hal.

"You looking for a payout - or payback?" came the reply. No delay this time. Clearly, Brad wanted the conversation to be over fast.

"Both," replied Hal. "The bastard owes us."

A moment later, Brad enquired: "What you planning to do?"

So, there it was. Subject broached, it was time to come clean.

"Done planning bro'. I'm in London. Come on over. I'll tell you where."

"Shit, Hal. Wtf you doing there? I can't just drop everything. I got deadlines up to Xmas. And no spare cash," texted Brad.

Hal was about to send a text conceding defeat when Brad texted again: "I got some time off – after Xmas. If it gets real, call me."

Hal was almost in tears. Knowing his brother was at least with him in spirit, and might even join him in a few weeks, gave Hal all the encouragement he needed.

There was a tear in Hal's eye as he replied: "You bet, bro'."

More confidently, Hal began to plan how he would investigate the man he believed to be his father, secure in the knowledge that, when the time came, the two brothers could take on the Fisher family lawyers together.

Since the cost of the flight had used up Hal's most recent army pension check, he had arrived in London almost penniless. All he had was a UK telephone number that a fellow veteran had given him before he left Rochester. Without work, he knew he would be on the streets in days · which was hardly the place from which to launch the search for his late father's money.

All he could do was pray that his sole contact would lead to some sort of temporary employment – though he harboured a few doubts about the likely nature of that work. Before he even dialled the number, he was well aware that the person on the other end was not going to employ him as a shelf stacker or delivery driver. Fresh out of the US Army, Hal actually possessed one or two rather sought-after skills – well, if he was honest, just one. Once a shooter, he guessed, always a shooter. But private contracts would be a whole new deal for him. Despite that, he was no stranger to killing and, he reckoned, that it would be much the same wherever you happened to carry it out.

When he made the call, it was made abundantly clear to him that his comrade's recommendation would earn him only one chance. If he made a success of it, then that assignment might become the first of many. But, with a contract hit, there was only one way to make a favourable impression: take out your target with a swift, clean kill. Anything else was abject failure.

His first assignment was in London which suggested that he might well be observed or directly assessed. He was given detailed instructions about where to go which, despite his unfamiliarity with the city, proved easy enough to follow. As promised, a rifle in a sleek black case, was ready and waiting for him at the site. Before he even opened the case, he studied the immediate vicinity for some time and then focussed on his target area. Opening the case, he found the rifle inside another, softer bag, along with everything else he needed.

Assembling the weapon was easy enough for muscle memory seemed to take over. Yet, he felt a twinge of regret because he had hoped he would never pick up a rifle again. He was still unsure whether he should have ventured once more into the deadly line of work which had once defined him. But, for now, it was just a way to get some much-needed cash. Despite his misgivings, he held his nerve, took out his mark and tried not to dwell too long on the identity of the target.

That initial payday, though modest, would fund the first few tentative steps on his very personal quest.

His lousy father, the late Henry Fisher, had clearly been loaded and, if he was so wealthy, then Hal and Brad were owed their share of whatever the callous bastard had left behind. While he awaited another contract, Hal began his investigation. At an internet café, he accessed several national newspaper articles and explored their coverage of the Fishers' demise. It was frequently mentioned that the couple lived by the sea in Dorset, but there was no more detail than that.

Searching elsewhere online, he hoped to discover more but found even less information because the Fishers seemed digitally almost invisible. In the end, Hal decided he would learn nothing more unless he went to the Dorset coast himself. So, taking a train south from Waterloo station, he aimed for one of the more obvious south coast destinations: Bournemouth. In the old days, he suspected that, once in the area, he could have just searched the local phone books, but not now. Such printed volumes were slim and dominated by business entries. It was going to take a little longer than that, he reckoned, to track down the very private Henry Fisher.

After checking into a low-cost guesthouse on December 15th, he settled into his work at another internet cafe, but was frustrated to find no mention of Henry. All he discovered were fleeting references to a few other Fishers – usually fresh-faced young kids sharing embarrassing pictures of various private body parts. Were any related to his father? He rather hoped not.

However, he did discover in passing, one local newspaper reference that caught his attention because the reporter had clearly dug a little deeper than most of his colleagues. Henry Fisher and his wife were survived, the columnist said, by one child – an estranged daughter. How estranged, Hal wondered? Because, after all, anyone estranged from Henry Fisher might be a potential ally rather than a rival. In the meantime, since he had no idea where she was, or even her name, he started to search for traces of his late father the hard way.

For a few days, he arranged to meet local journalists in a nearby pub in the hope of plying them with sufficient alcohol to narrow down his search for Henry's address. It was a slow process that was mostly unproductive and consumed far too much of his recently-acquired income. When another contract came in just before his funds ran out, he had mixed feelings about it. Though it would certainly bring in welcome funds to refresh his war chest, it also required him to leave Bournemouth and return to London. But, since Henry Fisher wasn't going anywhere, he reckoned it couldn't hurt to delay a little longer.

A few days later, when he returned to the same guest house, he was much-chastened by his second assignment. As before, he had followed his instructions to the letter and located the weapon. But it was clear to him at once that this was a much harder shot than his first contract. Though successful, it was damned messy – which was his fault, because his mind had clearly been elsewhere. His mark was dead but there were several collateral deaths which were certain to draw unwanted attention.

In his guilty haste to leave the scene, he forgot to relinquish the weapon. The instructions had been most definite: he was to leave the rifle. He couldn't really explain why he took it but, having carried the light gun bag for a hundred yards or so, he decided he might just hold onto it a little longer. After all, it was a clean weapon so, when he returned to Bournemouth, he looked for somewhere to stash it. But there was no suitable storage at the station without paying with cash he just couldn't spare. He had no choice but to take it with him to the guest house and pray that he didn't arouse any suspicions.

Within minutes of arriving in Bournemouth, he received a curt text expressing 'disappointment' with the quality of his work - and, in truth, he could hardly argue. When they enquired where the 'package' was, he claimed to have thrown it into the Thames. There was no reply to that and he was both surprised and relieved when his payment came through.

He doubted, however, that another contract would be sent his way anytime soon. If that was the case then his resources for tracking down Henry Fisher were not only finite but likely to be very soon exhausted.

Since it was Christmas Eve, he was hoping to spend the evening in pubs pumping the local small-paper journalists for a little more about Henry Fisher. He was swiftly disappointed because it appeared that, with the seasonal spirit flowing freely, most either wanted to spend their time with their families or were intently focussed upon getting laid. Nonetheless, he picked up one more important scrap of information than he knew already: the Fishers used to live further east in a place called Highcrest. So, at least after Christmas, he could concentrate his efforts on a smaller area.

Buoyed by his success, he eagerly contacted Brad to tell him that he was getting closer and might need his help, hoping that his twin was still serious about coming over. Beyond that, the arrival of Christmas brought his enquiries to an abrupt close. Yet, while all around him at the guesthouse revelled in the festivities, he spent most of his time in his room. When, on Boxing Day, his resolve finally weakened and he visited the pub for something to eat, he discovered that they were only serving pre-booked meals. With a shrug, he decided he would just have to run on alcohol fuel alone.

He had consumed quite a lot while conducting an ongoing, if necessarily intermittent, chat with Lisa - one of the busy waitresses. Perhaps it was the Jack Daniels but, damn, she looked good and she had kind eyes. She was younger than him, he thought, though maybe not by too much. She looked maybe mid-twenties with short, glossy, blonde hair framing a small-featured, tanned face. Though not a beauty by any means, she was what Hal liked to call: 'smiley'. The briefest of red skirts, which seemed to be obligatory for all the servers, afforded Hal frequent opportunities to admire her long slim legs, which he drank in along with the whisky.

Their casual banter started with her expression of sympathy that he had nothing to eat and, intermittently, it carried on into the middle of the afternoon. When her shift ended, to Hal's astonishment, she took pity on him and quietly invited him back to her flat.

"But you don't know me at all," he said.

"You can tell a lot about a person from listening to him," she replied. "And, to be clear, it's just for a bite to eat ‑ and only 'cos it's Christmas…"

Though the invitation came out of the blue, it was very welcome. Since he could hardly pursue his quest over Christmas, an afternoon with Lisa would offer him a brief ‑ perhaps pleasant – distraction. For all he knew, she picked up guys all the time, though he'd seen her several times before during the holiday period and she came across as genuine enough. All of that apart, he was damned hungry and, as it happened, she was pretty so, well… who wouldn't?

7

Lisa's flat turned out to be close by the pub in an area that he had learned was mainly student accommodation. Though small, it was clean and tidy – qualities which Hal's mother had taught him to value highly. Also, though it was rented, she had certainly put her own stamp on the place with little ornaments and such like.

She was, he concluded, a nice young woman for, when he enquired politely about her family, she talked about them with affection in her eyes. Given his own family circumstances, he almost regretted asking but, he told himself, his troubles were hardly her fault. He was surprised how easy he found it to talk to her and, as he stood watching her cook them a cheese omelette, they chatted like old friends. Except, of course, most of his old friends were dead – and not just dead, but blown mercilessly apart into tiny pieces of charred meat...

"Are you alright?" asked Lisa, her face full of concern as she rested a gentle hand on his shoulder.

"Yeh, why?" he replied gruffly, causing her to snatch back the hand as if she had touched a flame – which, in a way he supposed, she had.

"Just that you look a bit pale," she explained, clearly a little embarrassed.

"Sorry," he muttered – and meant it.

She'd caught him off-guard and he knew his sharp reaction could not pass without some sort of explanation. With anyone else, he might not have bothered, but he saw the hurt in Lisa's expression – and, dammit, a trace of apprehension too.

"I'm sorry," he said again. "It's just...when I think of family... well, my mother died a few weeks ago. She was ill a long time... with all sorts of cancer. It was difficult. Also, I'm a vet..."

"A vet?" she said, looking doubtful.

Realising, that she was thinking of a very different sort of vet, he explained quickly: "Veteran. I served in Afghanistan and lost a lot of friends over there..."

When he saw the tear rolling down her cheek, he felt terrible for bringing his darkness to her door. But she just moved the omelette pan off the heat and folded her arms around him. There was nothing sexual about it. Just a hug, pure and simple. A sweet gesture of support.

As she held him, she murmured: "My big brother was killed in Afghanistan..." and he felt her tremble a little in his arms. Next moment, Hal felt hot tears on his own face, dripping down into her hair. For several moments they held each other, until Hal pulled away. Even then, she left her arms draped on his shoulders.

"I've upset you," he apologised. "I should go..."

"Look, we just shared a little moment of sadness, that's all," she told him, with a smile. "And that's OK - because Christmas time does that to us, doesn't it? Reminds us who we've lost. Anyway, I offered you food so, food is what you're going to have – even if the omelette's ruined..."

But it wasn't ruined so they sat together on her small, two-seater couch to eat it, washing it down with a bottle of red wine – which, she confessed, had been abandoned at the pub, almost full, on Christmas Day.

"It's good wine," he said, through a mouthful of omelette. Though Hal knew nothing about wine, he reckoned he owed her a compliment or two at the very least.

For hours they remained on the sofa with the empty plates lying at their feet. Their companionable conversation was interrupted only when he went to the can and she fetched another bottle of wine which, she confided, might not be as good as the first. Hal couldn't tell any difference – and he didn't care because, for the first time in years, he was spending time with a young woman he really liked.

Of course, however convivial their conversation was, he knew it was only a façade · perhaps not on her part, but certainly on his. Because, if she had known she was sitting next to a contract killer, she would have run away – damned fast.

"What was it like over there?" she asked softly.

It was a question he'd been asked many times before, but one he was always reluctant to answer.

"You really don't want to know about all that shit," he muttered.

"Probably not," she agreed, "but I do want to know what my brother went through in his last year of life."

"Trust me, it won't help him – or you."

"Maybe not, but I've never had the chance to ask anyone before and, who knows, it might help me understand a little..."

With a shake of the head, he replied: "It's war. So, it's impossible to understand."

She said nothing but simply looked him in the eye until he gave a nod of submission.

"At first, while we were training, it was kinda exciting, you know. And even when we got over there, we were nervous but still sort of pumped up. They told us we'd make a difference to the ordinary people who lived there, but that feeling didn't last long. Soon enough, even before the first body bags were flown out, we knew we were in the shit. I was terrified for the next few weeks and then, it became... I don't know, just the job. It was our daily work, like working a factory shift – only with the chance that every shift might be your last.

"Long before I went out there, I remember reading about how soldiers in World War One prayed for a wound bad enough to get them home but not kill them. I couldn't understand what the hell they were thinking – until near the end of my second tour, when the last of those I'd joined up with began, one by one, to fall all around me. Then I was right on the same page as those First World War guys. I can't speak for your brother, but that was my experience."

While he was talking, he hadn't dared to look at her. And, when he stopped, he could only brush away her tears.

"Thank you," she whispered, gripping his hand.

When he put an arm around her, she made no objection. Indeed, he felt her nestle against him in what he took as a gesture of trust. And she must have felt safe because she smiled up at him and kissed his cheek. Hal, turning his face, contrived to meet her lips with his. It was a long, sweet kiss but, when his hand crept onto her breast, she lifted it aside and entwined her fingers in his.

"Easy, tiger," she murmured, "because I'm not going to have sex with you."

"I'm sorry," he said, embarrassed that he had misunderstood the signals.

But her squeeze of his hand sent a thrill through him as she conceded: "I like you, Hal... but I don't really know you, do I? And well, I've been fucked before – and I don't mean sex. It seems, every time I've met someone I like, I've been... used. Then just chucked away like a condom."

"I get it," he said, forced to acknowledge, to himself at least, that he might well have treated her the same. Wasn't that exactly why he'd gone with her: for some food yes, but with the hope of a bit more than an omelette.

"You're disappointed," she murmured. "But... I don't think I led you on, did I?"

"No, you didn't," he agreed. "You promised no more than food and I've had a great evening here with you. You've let me into your home, fed me ˙ and wined me. I really like you, Lisa. But you're right: we don't know each other at all. I guess I've opened up to you more than anyone ˙ even my twin brother – but that's no sort of commitment. We only just met."

She grinned at him and breathed: "Good answer." Then, to his surprise, she kissed him again ˙ longer than before, tasting him with her tongue.

When their lips parted, she leant into him again and he held her close, revelling in the scent of her.

Finally, he murmured: "Hey, I'd better go... or..."

"Or?" she asked.

"Listen, Lisa, cards on the table: I'll be gone in a few days."

"OK."

"Maybe as soon as tomorrow."

"OK."

"So, I can't offer you something long term..."

"OK."

"I've got nothing to offer you."

"OK."

"OK?"

"Yeh, that's OK," she said. "But you could stay tonight..."

"But you said-"

"I said I didn't want to be used by some lying shit of a bloke and then tossed away," she told him. "I didn't say I wouldn't enjoy your company overnight."

"I seem to remember you said you weren't going to have sex with me," he reminded her.

"Oh yeh. Well, I might have changed my mind about that," she told him. "And I never said I didn't want to..."

"There's a lot I haven't told you about me," he confessed.

With a wry smile, she said: "No shit. But, if I never see you again, I don't need to know all your secrets, do I?"

However accomplished Hal was as a sniper, he was a clumsy lover – and he knew it. Lisa though, turned out to be as warm and giving under the sheets as she was fully clothed. It was, he realised, just who she was.

Waking in the night, he felt compelled to put a protective arm around this wonderful woman…perhaps in some vague attempt to keep her safe. Although, of course, she would have been a damned sight safer if she'd never met him.

In the morning, she wandered the flat in a loose T-shirt and knickers, making him breakfast while enquiring casually: "How soon do you have to go?"

"I should go back to the guest house this morning," he replied. "They must be wondering what happened to me."

"I suppose," she conceded. "But you could stay here, if you wanted…"

"I don't want to impose," he said.

Staring back at him, open-mouthed, she said: "Impose, Hal, seriously? You can't spend the night with a girl and then say you don't want to bloody impose. Look, if you have to leave right now, that's OK 'cos that's what you said last night. But, if you're staying in Bournemouth a bit longer, then you could stay here and save a bit of cash on your room."

"Oh, so, you're promoting sleeping with you as a cost cutting deal," he said slyly.

"You'd be sleeping on the sofa obviously," she replied solemnly, "because, you know, last night was a kind of 'special offer' deal for one night only."

Only when she saw his crestfallen face did Lisa relent and reach up to kiss him on the cheek and whisper: "Further offers might be available though, as they say, for suitable applicants…"

So, Hal checked out of the guest house and checked in with Lisa, because she was just… a revelation. If she noticed that one of his khaki bags was slightly longer than usual, she didn't comment upon it. Perhaps it was because the whole thing was so unexpected. His mom would say that it was meant to be – and maybe she was right. When Lisa left to do a lunchtime shift at the pub, he was still warm at the thought of her and, in the evening, though he went to the pub for a drink, it was only to escort her home. Jeez, this woman was definitely worth the long journey from Rochester. Except, of course, that the longer he stayed with her, the more appalling was the thought of leaving her. Let alone never seeing her again. But, he had to see his search through to the end · whatever the outcome.

When he left several days later, it was even more painful than he imagined it would be. It was such an unfamiliar feeling that he found it difficult to process. Schmucks like him simply didn't fall in love with good-looking, warm-hearted waitresses · except in films. Love? Really? They'd only known each other for a few days, but he found himself promising her that, once he had taken care of the business that brought him to the UK, he would come back to see her.

"You don't have to say that," she told him. "I'm a big girl. And truly, I'd rather you didn't say it · unless you actually do mean it."

"I do mean it," he insisted, because at that moment he genuinely did.

Studying his earnest expression, she murmured: "OK then. Put your number into my phone, 'cos then I'll know you really do mean it."

So he did, because, for the first time since he'd left the army, he actually felt happy. Happy enough to give up his embryonic career as a contract killer and go back to her? Well, maybe, because she made him feel so damned good about himself. And, with luck, he'd be a wealthy man by then and she wouldn't need to wait tables any more.

For now though, he steeled himself to leave her and set his eyes on the prize, because Henry Fisher's wealth was not simply going to drop into his lap. He purposely didn't give her any clue where he was going in case she ever tried to find him. If his grand plan turned to shit, he didn't want her caught up with it in any way. He had already killed to earn some cash and it was perfectly possible that, in the next few days, he might have to kill again. He didn't want to but, in his experience, people with money were usually damned reluctant to part with any of it.

The closest he had gotten to discovering his father's address was a suggestion from one of the reporters that he should take a look in Highcrest, so he caught a bus there to make a start. The journey took about an hour and, once he arrived, there was no option but to walk the streets asking questions in what he described, rather unconvincingly, as a search for a 'distant cousin'.

From the outset, he targeted postal delivery workers because they often knew more than most about who lived where. It turned out to be a lot easier than Hal feared, because the Fishers' deaths had made them something like local celebrities – at least for a time. And because they were dead, folk seemed all too eager to tell Hal what they knew. Even if it was precious little.

All the same, some polite interrogation gave him a road and even a house name: Sunrise Heights, which sounded about right for a wealthy family. After that, the rest was all too easy for, once he located the house, he could start talking to the neighbours. However, the property, perched on a clifftop, was quite large and set some distance away from the nearest houses which were another fifty metres or so from the cliff edge. If there ever had been houses next door. they no longer existed and the house was also shielded from prying eyes by a swathe of woodland.

The nearest neighbour proved to be an elderly widower, Charlie Burns, who lived a hundred metres further west along the road.

"A nice couple," Charlie told Hal, "kept to themselves a lot... not much else to say about them really – except they ought to have moved out of that house!"

"Thanks," said Hal, realising at once that he would learn nothing useful.

"Mind you," added Charlie, "their daughter... now she was a wrong 'un."

"The wrong one?" said Hal, confused.

"Wrong 'un - you know, she got up to all sorts. My Hilda used to say that, whenever there was ever any trouble round here, that girl would be right in the middle of it."

"What happened to her?" enquired Hal.

"Hilda? She died two years ago," lamented Charlie.

"No, the daughter - does she still live at the house?"

"That place?" scoffed Charlie. "No, Olivia left years ago – and good riddance too..."

Hal thanked Charlie, who he reckoned would have been happy to talk for several more hours, and returned to Sunrise Heights. So far, he was making excellent progress: he had the family home and he knew the daughter's name – along with confirmation that she was almost certainly still 'estranged'. The next task would be to explore the house itself because, as every good sniper knows, you need solid intel on the ground.

However, since the Fishers weren't coming back and it sounded as if the daughter was unlikely to show her face either, Hal was in no hurry. He had an opportunity to break into the house and, in his rucksack, he had a few tools to help him deal with that. He should have plenty of time to conduct a thorough search for anything of value.

As he stood outside the property, he was convinced that it was empty but, since the newspapers had informed anyone who might care that the Fishers had died, it was quite possible that the daughter or some other, as yet unknown, surviving relatives would be making some sort of claim on the Fisher legacy. In case any of them picked this particular time, in the holiday period at New Year, to visit Sunrise Heights, he decided it would be prudent to watch the house for a while. His hunch proved right far sooner than he expected when, within five minutes, a cab drew up on the street.

8

Reading, on New Year's Eve

Liv's fresh sense of purpose only lasted for a few hours because, though she'd resolved to go down to Dorset the following day, that plan was scuppered by another inebriated early morning return from the Orange Lobster. So, it wasn't until early on New Year's Eve that she managed to board a crowded train to Christchurch. Even that proved too much of a challenge because, having fallen asleep, she missed the Christchurch stop and ended up in Bournemouth. It was fortunate that the train terminated there, otherwise Liv might have slept on for many more miles. Even then, it was only the train manager's second arrival announcement which woke her up.

Stumbling out onto the platform into the pouring rain, she rummaged in her small holdall – she always travelled light – for the umbrella she remembered putting in. It was one of those push-button umbrellas that seem really cool at the point of purchase but then, when you actually try to use them, turn out to be completely fucking useless.

Unable to locate it quickly, she stooped to prop the bag on a narrow bench to search more carefully. The umbrella was not only right at the bottom but had, of course, had become entangled in her clothing. So that, when she wrenched it out with a certain amount of frustrated venom, one of her size 34D bras flew out with it. If she hadn't turned sharply to see where it had landed, she would never have noticed the last passenger alight from the train and stride past her. Even then, had he not trampled her errant underwear into the damp grime of the platform, she might not have shouted "Wanker!" after him.

The offender showed no sign of having even heard her and continued blithely on his way while Liv snatched up her pale blue bra now embellished with a grubby sole print. Staring after him, her anger swiftly turned to apprehension when she recognised him. The set of his shoulders and the overcoat might have been enough but the flat black cap welded to his scalp was the clincher. Shit...

Just for a moment, she considered calling after him again but, in the end, she simply watched him go and absent-mindedly stuffed her belongings back into her bag. So distracted was she that she put the umbrella back in and tossed the dirty bra on top as well. Then she sat down on the wet bench for a few moments, sucking in long, deep breaths.

OK, so he had followed her, but what did that mean? If he wanted to hurt her, he could already have done so on several occasions. But he hadn't. He was just there – again; and it was unnerving. She might have pondered on it a little longer but, with the rain still falling, she got up and left. As she walked through the station building, her eyes were the narrowest of slits. It was only when she walked out again into the pouring rain, that she remembered the umbrella was still in her bag.

"Shit," she muttered, as she waded across the road through six inches of filthy water in search of a taxi.

Of course, it was New Year's Eve, so taxis were, unsurprisingly, in high demand. Naturally, there were none waiting – it being sodding wet... In Reading, she might have hopped on a bus, but in Bournemouth she had no idea which number bus would take her anywhere near Sunrise Heights. Ten years earlier, she might have known, but not now. As she waited, soaked through to the skin, she was joined by a gaggle of other dripping, if hopeful, travellers. To her relief, 'black cap' was not among them – but then perhaps he knew which bus to catch.

Having waited half an hour for her taxi, she was then bombarded with pleas from several of those behind her in the queue to share the vehicle. At home, she would have done so willingly but here, in unknown territory and with the presence of 'black cap' still fresh in her mind, she did not dare. Since his sudden reappearance couldn't possibly be sheer chance, she was feeling vulnerable. A wholly unfamiliar sensation for a woman who thought nothing of wandering the streets deep into the night. So, despite the hostile responses of those in the queue, Liv refused all requests, including one that would have required an unlikely degree of physical flexibility.

Aside from the rain pattering against the windows, it was a quiet thirty-minute drive to Sunrise Heights. But, when the taxi came to a halt near the entrance to the drive, Liv's unease began to surface because everything she saw prompted a persistent trickle of grim memories.

"You can drive up to the house," she informed the driver.

"It's too narrow," argued the cabbie. "And you can't turn round at the other end."

"But it's pissing down," cried Liv, pointing to the water cascading over his vehicle.

"Sorry, Miss," said the not-at-all-sorry cab driver who was, no doubt, anxious to return to the ever-lengthening and lucrative queue of punters marooned at Bournemouth railway station. He was far too busy to be wasting valuable minutes going up driveways.

"Right, well thanks so much for your help," growled Liv, hurling a handful of cash at him which, rather like the seeds sown in the biblical parable, fell in a variety of awkward places. Snatching up her bag, she prised open the door and clambered out into the rain, snarling: "Have a very happy, fucking New Year, why don't you?"

Fervently hoping that she had massively underpaid the unhelpful little shite, she bullied the car door shut. Though the drive turned out to be a little narrower than she remembered, where trees and shrubs had encroached, she was pretty sure you could drive an HGV lorry along it – never mind a taxi. As she fumbled for her old door key, she was grateful for the porch which at least offered her a little shelter. She didn't recall there being a porch when she lived there before but, very soon, she became aware of a few other quite significant changes – such as the shiny new lock on the front door, which her key didn't fit.

Abandoning her wet holdall in the porch, she squelched around on the gravel to the side of the house. Yet another recent development was that access to the back of the house was now restricted by a gate and a short length of timber fencing. Facing the new barrier, with rivulets of water streaming off her hair, a seething Liv kicked the gate hard – and instantly regretted it. It proved remarkably robust so, moving along to the two metre high fence panel beside it, she lashed out a boot once again and, this time, heard the reassuring crack of several weather-worn timbers. Not only did a few more savage kicks allow Liv to clamber through but they almost demolished the fence.

A grim smile played across her lips because there was something particularly satisfying about destroying anything that her parents had erected. With any luck, she hoped, the rest of the festering old building would fall apart just as easily. Moving down the side of the house, she eyed the drainpipe at the rear corner which, when she was fifteen, she had regularly climbed to gain access to her old bedroom. Back then, of course, she conveniently left the window open but now each one seemed firmly shut.

The rear garden had once been large but Liv noted that the cliff was now a great deal nearer than in her day – dangerously nearer. In fact, only a sliver of bare earth remained with two scarecrow shrubs clinging stubbornly to the sandy soil. A single broken post was a mere suggestion that there had once been a rear fence, but there was nothing now to interrupt her view of the grey unruly sea below.

Grateful that the strong south-west wind was driving her back towards the house, she stepped up onto the raised veranda, which extended all around the side and rear walls of the house. As she did so, she felt the decking give a little under her and noticed that some parts were completely rotted through. So far, Sunrise Heights was not offering her a great sales pitch, but the double-glazed ranch slider doors – probably installed in the 1970s – still appeared pretty impregnable without the aid of specialist tools – like a sledgehammer.

Despite the buffeting rain, she cautiously crossed the rear decking until she reached the back door which had a small window beside it. For once, she was grateful that her miserly father had been too cheap to get the window double-glazed. In her rain-drenched fury, she prepared to thrust an angry fist through the glass but, at the last moment, lost her nerve. Envisaging torn flesh, with tendons and muscles sliced through, she decided that she could really do without being hospitalised just now.

Casting about for something a little more durable than flesh and bone, she eyed a folding wooden chair. It was light enough to wield with force, but would it be hard enough? When she tapped it lightly against the glass, her doubts were removed along with half the window pane. But it was only a qualified success because, though it enabled Liv to climb inside out of the rain, it also allowed substantial amounts of rainwater to fall into the room.

Carefully negotiating the broken glass, Liv made her way through the gloomy house and found that she could open the front door easily enough from the inside. It felt strange walking through that cold house again with every item in its proper place. Both her parents were obsessively tidy yet, at the same time, the house felt... abandoned · which actually suited her perfectly. Once she had retrieved her holdall from the porch, she stripped off her wet clothes and put on some clean, dry ones from the bag. Towelling her bedraggled hair a little drier, she took pleasure in scattering her sodden clothes at random to dry out over the furniture in the living room. Finally, she sank down into the sofa with an enormous sigh.

A glance at her phone told her it was almost one o'clock and a wicked thought struck her: it was surely not too late for a pre-lunch drink. Making for her parents' drinks cabinet, she was relieved to find that it was still remarkably well-stocked. A veritable Aladdin's cave of a walk-in bar. Small wonder that, from an early age, she had learned to seek solace in alcohol. Now she was older, though probably not, she had to concede, much wiser, she needed a few moments to contemplate the extensive range of possibilities before her. In the end she plumped for an old favourite and, though some might think it was still a little early for gin, that had never stopped her before. Helping herself to a generous measure, she quickly discovered that there was not a drop of tonic in sight. Quel dommage...

Having taken care of important matters, Liv wandered into the kitchen and attempted to start the boiler. But, even when she'd finished, she wasn't sure whether she'd been successful or not. Conducting a swift examination of the kitchen cupboards and fridge, she was disappointed, though not surprised, to find that her mother must have binned all the foodstuffs before she left. In the absence of anything in the house to eat, her pre-lunch drink lasted deep into the afternoon, while the rain clattered against the large living room window. The staccato and unrelenting hammering provided a fit accompaniment to Liv's spiralling gloom. After a time, she squatted on the floor, clinging onto her empty glass like it was her last friend – which, of course, for a woman who possessed no others, it was.

She had only been in the house for a matter of hours, but already she knew that coming home had been a serious mistake. Even from the grave, it seemed her parents had the power to punish her. Plummeting earthwards in a light plane whilst on holiday in Bermuda might have enabled Monica and Henry Fisher to escape, but not her. Death, as she already knew, had grim consequences for the living. She would have to sort through her parents' worldly goods or pay someone – with money she didn't have - to clear the house.

Ah, yes, the house... and there lay an irony of truly epic proportions. For many, inheriting a large, four-storey house by the sea might seem a windfall to be celebrated – unless, of course, it turned out that the residence in question was an ancient, decrepit house devoid of any redeeming features. Not only was there extensive rot - evident even to her utterly untrained eye – but, as the afternoon wore on, the heavy rain accentuated another of the house's faults. A small torrent of water was now trickling through a hole in the dining room ceiling. Before she arrived, she had considered the possibility, given her recent downturn in fortunes, of living in the house, or perhaps renting it out, or even selling it. But her short time at the family mausoleum had swiftly disabused her of all such possibilities.

It was true enough that its location near the sea with wondrous views all around, might once have made the house attractive to potential buyers. But in recent years that strength had clearly become its Achilles' heel because it was now far *too* close to the sea. The rear garden, where Liv had rambled as a child, had been worn away by the determined wind and rain. Now, hardly enough remained to prevent the crumbling edifice from dropping into the sea. Perched as it was on the edge of a rapidly degrading cliff, the building was, in a word, unsaleable.

It had a view to die for, as anyone rash enough to go within ten feet of the edge, would soon discover. Yes, very soon Sunrise Heights would undoubtedly follow its late owners into oblivion. Hence, presumably, the reason for the recent intervention by the local council - though Liv was shocked to find out that the council actually did anything at all. How her mother must be cackling in hell at the thought that she had saddled her errant daughter with an impossible legacy.

Even staying in the house overnight worried Liv because there was ample evidence that it was infested with rats. She had noticed several old traps outside the house and others inside too. She had read something recently about the increasing number and size of urban rats. Apparently some could grow to half a metre long and that grim thought sent a shudder running through her as she contemplated the possibility of death by giant rodent.

Well, fuck you, Monica Fisher.

9

After downing her third substantial gin, Liv began to wonder if the solution to her problems lay in taking the short walk to the cliff edge. But the notion passed swiftly · in part, because the memory of the railway suicide – if it truly *was* a suicide · was still too fresh in her mind. But her reluctance to hurl herself over the cliff might also have had something to do with the worrying possibility that she might join her parents in the afterlife. So, instead, she stood gazing out over the raging sea, as she had so often in her teens. And nothing much had changed, because still, there was rage within and rage without.

Startled by a sudden squall which rattled several of the more ancient window frames, Liv got up to check they were all firmly shut. Storm winds were forecast, which was more than a little disturbing, in a house where the windows were ill-fitting, the gutters overflowed and the roof boasted more holes than your average colander. Just bloody delightful...

Scanning the grey bank of cloud to the south-west, she noticed a small patch of white which seemed to offer a brief respite from the weather's onslaught. And how Liv needed to escape. Even ten minutes of fresh air, she reckoned, might help.

However, just as she was about to go out, the house's rather eccentric musical doorbell heralded the arrival of a visitor. Since she had only just arrived, it couldn't be anyone she knew. Quickly, she thrust aside the random thought that 'black cap' might have followed her there, because it seemed somehow unlikely that he would ring the doorbell. It would suit Liv if no-one rang the doorbell ever again because, even when she opened the door, the musical chimes continued to rattle through a whole assortment of tunes.

In a hand behind her back she gripped an empty gin bottle – just in case.... But she was relieved to find that her visitor appeared to be unarmed. The lanky, pale-faced and rather lugubrious looking fellow claimed to be a man from the council. Having thrust his credentials at her, he launched into a prepared speech. The occupiers - her parents – had, he alleged, failed to respond to the council's series of letters concerning the erosion of their back garden.

"That's because they're dead," explained Liv.

But, apparently, death was no excuse for wilful disregard of council communications.

"Do you realise that this house could fall into the sea at any moment?" he declared, brandishing a bright yellow laminated sheet of paper. "It's been condemned as unsafe and you shouldn't be living here."

"I'm sure you're right," she agreed. "Would you like to come in?"

"No," he retorted. "It's not safe."

"But, with every glass of this," she told him, brandishing the gin bottle, "it feels a little bit safer."

"You're drunk," he observed. "I'm not talking to a drunk."

"I think you are," Liv sparred playfully.

"Is there no responsible adult here?"

"Yeh, well, I used to be one," Liv confided, "till I lost my job... and my flat... and did you miss the bit about my parents being dead?"

"Yes, yes and I'm sorry for your loss," he muttered, as if lamenting a wayward ball lost over the nearby cliff.

"I'm sure," slurred Liv.

"Alright," he conceded, "but if you're still here after the bank holiday, there'll be trouble."

"I might not be here," said Liv.

"For now, I'll just fix this notice to the gate," he told her.

"Will it stop the erosion?" enquired Liv.

Regarding her as if she was an imbecile, he said merely: "I'm putting it up now."

"I'll look forward to reading it," lied Liv. "Oh, and Happy New Year."

Making no reply, he trudged back down the drive with a cloak of disappointment weighing heavily upon his drooping shoulders.

Shutting the door, Liv pressed her head against it. He was right: she should get out now – but to where? There was hardly any point in paying for a train journey back to Reading to a flat from which she was already being evicted. Still, if the rain held off, she might as well take a walk and clear her head a bit. Armed with her shades, she stepped outside, but regretted it at once because, though the rain had certainly eased, the wind had scarcely abated at all. She dimly recalled that Storm Barry, or Ayesha ⁃ or whatever other ridiculous name the weather professionals had come up with - was supposed to blow itself out that day. But apparently, neither Barry nor Ayesha had got the email...

The path that had once wound down from the garden to the sea — a hazy recollection from her childhood - was another victim of the grinding erosion. In its absence, Liv decided to take the long way down which entailed using a far from stable flight of steps twenty metres east of the house. They had been carved into the sandstone centuries before, by smugglers, it was said. Once, they had been sited twenty metres from the cliff face, but now they descended almost parallel to it. Since the steps were not only crumbling but slippery, it took her so long to descend that, by the time she reached the shore, it was spitting again.

Along much of the coastline, large landslips had deposited tons of earth and rock at the water's edge which, for a time, helped to protect the remainder of the cliff. But, directly below Sunrise Heights, the cliff remained sheer. The erosion there had been more gradual with no major slips so, as a result, the beach below the house was barely a metre wide. However, because of the high tide and strong onshore winds, it shelved steeply and every storm carved away a little more from the base of the cliff. It should have collapsed long ago which would have saved Liv a great deal of trouble.

As she watched each successive wave crash in, she soon became aware that she wasn't alone. Because, there he was again, walking slowly towards her along the narrow shore.

"Oh shit, not you again," she growled, directing a bleak stare at 'black cap'. "Everywhere I look, you're there," she cried. "What do you want with me?"

Spreading his hands wide, he grinned at her and replied: "Only to talk."

"Leave me alone."

"Just give me a moment," he said.

Liv's eye for detail observed the stress evident in his face. The beads of sweat, on such a cool day, belied his calm demeanour.

"One moment then," she conceded.

But he didn't get a moment because, as he closed upon her, he was spun around and tossed into the water. She hadn't heard the shot, but what else could have felled him in an instant? Torn between diving flat for cover and going to his aid, Liv did neither. Instead, she crouched down on the gritty sand and gazed about her. She could see no-one else on the beach, nor any boats offshore. What she did see was a trace of blood showing in the foaming spray where 'black cap' was floundering in the water. Shutting her eyes, she erased the wounded man struggling against the relentless waves.

Liv was a strong swimmer but did she really care enough about this man who was tracking her every move? Except, though still wary of him, she couldn't forget that he had saved her life at Slough.

"Grow up, you silly bitch," she muttered and, kicking off her trainers, splashed out into the surf.

"Shit, that's freezing!" she gasped.

Wading out a little further, she cursed as the chill crept up her legs and her recently-donned dry jeans were soon soaked through. Bracing herself against the next incoming wave, she reached out a hand to him. With a groan of effort, he clambered to his feet and took her hand, but the next wave knocked him off balance and he fell down again. When his fingers slipped through hers, Liv took a step further out and, thanks to the steep shelving, sank down at once up to her chest. Snarling as the freezing water lapped at her breasts, she was swamped by the next inrushing wave which tore off her sunglasses. Disorientated, she looked around for 'Black cap' but there was no sign of him.

"Oh, shit," she spluttered, assuming he had been swept away.

Even the briefest look at the darkening sky persuaded her that retreat was now the only pragmatic option. But, as she turned for the beach, a hand lunged abruptly out of the water and seized her arm. Liv reckoned that even her parents, in whatever particular hell they now found themselves, must surely have heard her scream. It sounded so shrill and manic that she was disgusted with herself. She'd never been a 'screamer' but, as she wrestled to raise up her submerged stalker, she might have screamed a second time had she not been swept under the water.

Just as she surfaced again and, choking, tried to haul him up, his face emerged from the boiling sea to stare straight at her. It was a face neither cruel nor sullen, but desperate - achingly desperate. Though he looked exhausted, with Liv's help, he managed to lift himself a little more out of the water, revealing a shirt that was bloodied and torn.

For what seemed an age, the two sodden individuals just clung to each other, while the sea toyed with them. So that when he spoke, it startled her.

"Leave Sunrise Heights," he croaked, staring up at the top of the cliff.

Ignoring the disturbing fact that he knew where she lived, she gritted her teeth and growled: "I'll help you to the beach."

But, when she tried to haul him in, he resisted, crying: "We're safer in the water."

"We're fucking not!" protested Liv, as yet another wave slammed into her.

"You need to get out of that house," he insisted.

"Just give me your hand," she cried, for the cold was permeating her entire body and she was growing ever more impatient with him.

Though, in the end, he complied, it was only to draw her closer and hiss: "Leave it, you understand? Get out of that house now · while you still can."

"Just let me help you," she argued, sorely tempted to beat some sense into the wounded moron.

"Liv!" he cried, squeezing her hand.

Since only her friends had ever called her 'Liv' and she didn't have any of those left, she tried to back away. Soon enough though, a rogue wave tossed her back to him.

"How do you know me?" she demanded.

"No time to explain," he said.

Perhaps sensing her fear, he released her at once, but warned: "They're coming for you, Liv..."

Fighting to stay upright in the water, she made no reply.

But he persisted, his voice breaking: "Just remember who you are and you'll be OK."

"Why are you hounding me?" she cried.

"I'm not hounding you," he pleaded. "I'm warning you."

Easing himself a little more out of the water, he gasped: "I helped you at the station. I can help you again."

But he couldn't, because his head chose that moment to explode in a crimson spray of blood, bone and flesh. Liv felt the bloody sheen upon her face and tasted it in the salt spray that washed against her lips. Eyes fixed upon the headless body, bobbing in the surf, she couldn't seem to move her legs. Then a brutal, truculent wave suddenly swept her back hard against the cliff. Winded, she lay against the sandstone, until a fragment of it burst out beside her head, cutting her cheek and stinging her eyes.

Years of denigrating women who screeched at the slightest provocation evaporated in an instant, as Liv screamed again. Because, she was actually being shot at...

Without thought, without stopping to consider consequences, she abandoned 'black cap's floating corpse. Scrambling out of the water, heedless of several more chunks of sandstone flying off the cliff in her wake, she fled along the shore. The man with no head and no name was wrong. They weren't *coming* for her; they had *come*.

Hurrying along the shore, she stumbled crazily up the steps until she could seek shelter among the tall trees beyond her house to the east. With every frantic step, she expected a bullet to crash mercilessly into her, rip a hole through her body and put an end to her. Though she glanced out to sea, the driving rain made it impossible to tell whether there was a boat out there. If there was, it could only be the poor visibility that was keeping her alive. Unless, of course, the shots were coming from closer to the house, on the beach itself.

10

Sunrise Heights, Highcrest

It was late afternoon when Liv, squatting on the living room floor, attempted to persuade herself that the ordeal was over. The police had come and gone, the body had been scooped up from the shoreline and now she was alone once more. Usually being alone was fine. Better than fine. Liv had a great deal of experience of it and thrived on the independence it gave her. Except now, being alone meant something rather different. Alone meant vulnerable because, if the late 'black cap' was to be believed, 'they' were coming for her. But, whoever was coming for her, she felt sure 'they' must have mistaken her for someone else.

Though, in her youth, there had been some scary times, she had never actually been shot at before. That was definitely a first. 'Black cap' had begged her to leave Sunrise Heights, but she was still there. True, her bag was still sitting, largely unpacked, in the hall. So, perhaps she should take his advice and leave now before 'they' could get to her. But, if she fled, would 'they' not just follow her? It wasn't just about her being in that house, because it seemed more than likely that someone had already tried to kill her at Slough. And where could she escape to anyway on New Year's Eve?

The police had done their best to reassure her. The dead man, they suggested, was very likely suffering from some serious mental health issues. That seemed a stretch to Liv because, as far as she knew, such issues rarely caused heads to spontaneously disintegrate. In fact, when she thought about it, the police had acted quite oddly. But then, perhaps everyone acted a little oddly on New Year's Eve.

Belatedly, it occurred to her that she had never asked for ID. She wasn't usually that careless but, in the immediate aftermath of the 'beach incident', it hadn't entered her head. From their arrival to their departure, they seemed very efficient. Hardly any time elapsed before a vehicle – unmarked, she noticed · arrived to collect the unfortunate corpse. The detective in charge, a man of indeterminate middle age, introduced himself as Inspector Brian Payne, but his interrogation was brief to the point of absurdity. Except, it was New Year's Eve so, who cared about the fate of an anonymous dead man? Liv, noticing the sand on Inspector Payne's shoes, wondered if he'd been called out from home.

After ten minutes, he was done, leaving his local colleague to, as he put it, 'tidy the loose ends' – one of which, Liv assumed, was the imminent threat to her life. The inspector sauntered out and, after lingering for a while on the gravel drive, presumably to admire the trees, he left. To her astonishment, Liv recognised the woman in plain clothes at once because, half a lifetime ago, she had attended the same prestigious local secondary school as Liv. Her name was Grace Walter. But shit, never had a girl been so inaccurately labelled.

Since Liv had spent almost every moment she could immersed in sport, she rarely ever glimpsed the ungainly Grace. Over the years though, they had one or two fiery run-ins on the hockey field. But, despite that, Grace greeted Liv like a bestie.

"Bloody hell, it is you: "'Crack' Fisher," she cried, reminding Liv of one of her more enduring school nicknames. The name Olivia 'Crackhead' Fisher, which most of her teachers assumed referred to careless use of drugs, actually arose from her reckless – some would have said murderous – use of a hockey stick. So she was known – not exactly affectionately – as 'Crack' Fisher.

"I'm touched you remembered," said Liv, noting that Grace's hair seemed redder than ever.

"Remembered?" said Grace. "I'm not likely to forget 'Fuck-it' Fisher, am I?"

Liv winced at the reminder of yet another sobriquet – this one born out of the largely inaccurate, but irritatingly pervasive, rumour that the teenage Liv was willing to engage in sexual intercourse with anyone at all. At the time, she supposed that she might have encouraged the whole myth because it enhanced her notoriety as an equal opportunities service provider. As an added bonus, it also seriously pissed off her parents when they learned of it.

Grace seemed far more interested in Liv's life since leaving school than the shooting on the beach. Liv, however, was keen to steer the conversation away from her sorry life story, towards the man with the large gap where his head had been. All the while, Grace glanced around, eyes exploring the room carefully. Perhaps she expected one of Liv's deceased parents to pop out of the woodwork at any moment. When Liv eventually managed to enquire about her own personal safety, Grace's advice was simple.

"If you're worried, the best place to be is in a crowd," she advised. "Make sure you're noticed."

But Liv hated crowds and particularly disliked being noticed.

"It is New Years Eve," Grace reminded her. "Go out and enjoy yourself – forget about all this, eh?"

Why not, thought Liv? Because, of course, it would be so easy to forget about a man's head exploding in her face. How could she bury his dire warning when it had been given so much more credibility by his brutal death. And, of course, there were the bullets directed at her – so easy to ignore those too.

"Even if I did go out," groaned Liv, "I'd still have to come back here, wouldn't I?"

"Fair point," acknowledged Grace, whose sympathy, it appeared, had limits.

Though Liv was tempted to ask about the possibility of round the clock protection, the prospect of enduring Grace's company for more than a few more minutes, persuaded her to keep her concerns to herself.

Finally, with only a fraction of her curiosity sated, Grace was persuaded to leave and Liv, in relief, opened a bottle of wine which she guzzled down in half an hour. The resulting euphoria proved to be short-lived because, though she was glad to see the back of Grace, she was also, unusually, apprehensive about being alone. At least, for now, she decided to take Grace's advice and find a crowd to hide in. Better sober up quick if she was going out on the town. Town? If

Highcrest counted as a town, then the bar was set pretty low.

11

Jeez, Hal was confused. From the moment he'd observed the dark-haired woman arrive, everything had gone to shit – real fast. Her initial exasperated 'Fuck!' - repeated quite a lot of times, would have been sufficient to convey her mood even before she began to kick the front door. For a fleeting moment, he considered introducing himself but, watching her casually break into the house, made him think twice. Naturally, he wondered if she was the daughter. But, if she was, the fact that she didn't have a key suggested she was still pretty estranged from her parents when they died. Not that it mattered much, he supposed, now that they were lying at the bottom of the Caribbean.

At the sound of shattering glass, Hal retreated up into the dripping trees to conceal himself there so that he could watch the house - or at least the front of it. He needed to find out who she was. If she was Fisher's daughter she didn't appear especially approachable. Perhaps she was just tired and fed up after her journey there. That happened to everyone once in a while. But did he really want to know someone who would happily smash into the family home? Thoughts of Lisa crept unbidden into his head, because he doubted that she would curse so much, or batter her way into a house.

All the same, this unknown woman wasn't his enemy – at least not yet. So, though Hal possessed the means to take her out, he had no good reason to do so. She might even turn out to be an ally. But, if she proved to be an obstacle to him getting his share of her father's legacy, that would be a whole different story. He gave a shiver, not because it was cold, but because his quest had just become real. Now he was dealing, not with old photos, but actual flesh and blood people.

Hal was also learning that being a sniper without a spotter was damned lonely work. Not that there was room for anyone else to perch on his sloping branch amid the fir tree's damp foliage. Though he had chosen his position to give him as much shelter from the elements as possible, somehow random squalls of wind still, every now and then, drove rain into his face. For several hours after the woman's splintering entry, Hal lay there watching. Since all had remained quiet in the house, he assumed that she had no plans to demolish the entire building.

Though he had been so driven to get where he was now, if he was honest, it was all a bit of a let-down. True, the Fishers had left a big old house but it looked as if it needed a whole lot of work doing to it – and it also seemed damned close to the cliff edge. He needed to focus on how he was going to get any of what the Fishers had left behind. Perhaps he had been wrong to go to the house at all and maybe instead he should have tried to discover who the Fishers' lawyers were. But then, he was hardly a trained investigator.

His fruitless pondering was interrupted by the scrunch of gravel along the driveway. The tall figure shambling up to the house could have been anyone, but he had an air of officialdom about him which suggested to Hal that he might well be a lawyer. Though the woman answered the door, Hal couldn't make out any of the conversation that ensued. His momentary interest was dispelled when the daughter appeared to send her visitor away with a flea in his ear. If he was a lawyer then clearly she disliked them. The stranger left quickly, pausing only to affix a brightly-coloured laminated sheet to the gatepost. It wasn't something Hal thought a lawyer might do. Another mystery then, he decided, making a mental note to go and read the notice when the opportunity arose.

Not long after the front door slammed shut, Hal heard movement in the trees nearby. Edging forward, he leaned out and caught a glimpse of her, braving the elements as she wandered dangerously close to the cliff, before passing out of sight. Praying she wasn't going to throw herself over the edge, he shifted his position, hoping for another sight of her. But, since he could not get eyes on the beach below the cliff, all he could do was scan to left and right along the shoreline. When he did, something seized his attention on the beach a few hundred yards to the east.

No-one but a sniper would even have spotted the dark figure lying on the sand behind a small outcrop of low rocks. But it was Hal's business to notice such things since, in the army, his life and those of many others would hang on picking up such details. Experience had taught him to recognise enemy snipers in all sorts of positions even from a considerable distance. But why was there one on the beach? He almost laughed out loud when he remembered that there was one in the trees too...

Since he couldn't see the woman at all, he focussed his attention upon the distant marksman, framing him in his telescopic sight. What was the guy – he could clearly see it was a guy · looking at? Had the woman ventured down on the beach below the cliffs? But why would anyone want to take her out? Swiftly, he abandoned any further conjecture because he just didn't know. So, in the absence of good intel, he relied on a trusted and a well-worn strategy: just wait and watch.

Moments later, the sniper fired and, though Hal heard nothing, he was unsurprised because he had already observed the suppressor on the man's weapon. What did concern him was who the guy was firing at. Hal might not have a high opinion of the woman but, if she was his half-sister, he certainly didn't want her dead – at least, not before he'd had an opportunity to talk to her.

When the sniper fired again, a desperate scream speared up from somewhere below the cliff. Perhaps she was already dead but, if she wasn't, he had better run some interference. One shot should be enough – and in any case, two would certainly give away his position to an experienced sniper. As he took aim, however, he hesitated as it occurred to him that the mystery shooter could, for all he knew, be on his side. He just didn't know enough to go randomly taking out anyone yet. So, a kill shot was just not appropriate.

He was lining up a warning shot when the guy fired again several more times and Hal swiftly loosed off a round at the rocks, before sliding half a metre back on his branch. When he risked another look, the sniper had disappeared and Hal could only pray that he wouldn't regret his intervention later. If the woman was already dead then he had revealed his existence to an unknown third party for no advantage. If she was still alive, well, maybe she could thank him later.

In the late afternoon, there was a brief flurry of activity at the house which told him four things. One, the woman had survived. Two, someone else hadn't. Three, the woman was almost certainly the new householder – the daughter. And four, she believed in the rule of law. When shit happened, her instinct had been to call the police, which was surely a promising sign if he hoped to persuade her to support his claim.

After the police left, carrying a body bag with them, Hal contemplated going to introduce himself to his newfound kin but lost his nerve. He was feeling suddenly very exposed, so he withdrew again to his position of concealment. There he continued to freeze his balls off while reflecting upon the surprising events of the afternoon.

12

Highcrest, on New Year's Eve

Outside the wine bar, Liv hesitated, wondering whether its clientele would constitute enough of a crowd. It hadn't always been a wine bar, of course. Back in her teens, when she lived every day on the edge, it was just a regular pub, the King George. How she hated that place with its 1970s paint peeling off the yellowed walls, its cracked, stained formica table tops and a floor that always felt sticky.

Yeh, she'd hated it, but staring at its new incarnation was enough to make her yearn for that traditional old pub. Rebranded 'Casa Georges', it was all plate glass and shiny surfaces. It could have been an airport lounge - a far cry from the visceral watering hole which, on New Year's Eve, used to be heaving with patrons. Most would be crushed inside, elbow to elbow, their pints slopping onto the floor as they shouted to make themselves heard. Others though, like Liv and her dodgy friends, would have spilled outside to continue their revelry on the pavement or even in the street.

Those were different times but, when she was feeling especially low, she did sometimes wonder how she'd been drawn into that world of excess and abandon. Whatever happened to the five-year-old who wanted to be a Spice Girl? True, she couldn't sing a note in key, but that hadn't stopped Posh Spice. At ten, she'd morphed into a football-obsessed tomboy who wanted to be David Beckham. And, at least she could play a bit. But that particular dream imploded when they told her football was a boys' game.

Looking back, she reckoned that was the beginning of the end and though, for a time, hockey became her new passion, that was really only because it was a sport where you could literally hack the living shit out of girls you didn't like. And Liv didn't like any of them. Only when she was banned from hockey did she truly go over to the 'dark side'.

The George was one of the places frequented by those with whom the teenage Liv had once run. Mainly because it proved to be a reliable source not only of alcohol, but also drugs. But, if she'd known then that, at 28, she'd be a sad, broke, failed PE teacher, she'd have hurled herself under a bus and saved herself a shitload of grief. So, yeh, regrets she had a few…

But right now her priority was just to stay alive another day. And to do that, she needed to seek sanctuary amid a crowd of strangers. Nostalgia notwithstanding, the wine bar seemed to be the best, indeed in Highcrest, probably the only, option. The music emanating from within was not especially encouraging. Whatever happened to Velvet Revolver anyway?

Deep breath, she told herself.

There was so much light inside that her poor eyes hurt already. With a groan, she half-lowered her eyelids and stepped over the glistening threshold into Casa

Georges, where someone had clearly been careless with a glitter spray. Though she intended a low-key, cool saunter to the bar, her entrance proved rather more spectacular. Perhaps the wine she had consumed during her troubled afternoon was still taking its toll, or the shimmering floor, like the rest of the place, was too highly polished. Either way, her initial relaxed gait morphed immediately into a barely-controlled skid. Sliding past several tables of startled patrons, she sped to the far end of the bar counter where, mercifully, a stub wall arrested her progress.

"Get a grip, you daft cow," she muttered, worried she might be ejected before she'd even managed to infiltrate the crowd.

Steadying herself, she beamed what she hoped was a charm-laden smile at the barman, who surely couldn't have been more than eleven.

"White wine," she said.

The child prodigy behind the bar studied her worn leather coat, short skirt and inviting cleavage and then glanced towards the door. When she showed no inclination to move on, he explained, as if to a child: "It's table service, madam... so, you have to order from a table-"

"I know what table service is," she snapped and, giving him a dismissive wave of the hand, turned away to select a table. If she sat in some dark corner, she would surely only be inviting a stealthy blade to her heart – always assuming the assassin could find it. But, since the bar was very busy, the choice was rather more limited than she expected.

In the end, she was obliged to choose the only vacant table which was vaguely in the middle of the room. Sitting centre stage went against all her well-honed survival instincts. But it was that, or walk back out again – and she certainly wasn't going to do that. At least, she consoled herself, she would be surrounded by exactly the sort of strangers she sought – ones that didn't intend to shorten her life.

After draping her coat over the stiff-backed chair, she angled it slightly to the side so that she could see both the main door and the bar. Instantly, she regretted it because it also meant that her eyes were bombarded with twice as many flashing lights. She was missing her dark glasses that were probably by now somewhere along the Solent. Sitting down, she shuttered her eyes even further so that she was peering as if through the narrow slot of a letter box. Only then did she set her small clutch bag down on the table and relax a little.

Keeping the bag within easy reach was essential since it contained the only two weapons she'd been able to locate before venturing out. Finding those familiar companions from her teen years in a dusty shoe-box in her old bedroom had actually given her a bit of a lift. Mind you, the self-defence spray was so old now she doubted it would have much effect. But the blade, now that was a different story.

She'd carried that knife everywhere but had thought it lost years ago. The slim, folding blade had been a present from an admirer. Well, he must have admired her at least a bit since he was in the habit of trying to fuck her senseless on a Saturday night. And, in her own way, Liv had to admit she was genuinely fond of him because, unlike most of the drunken tossers she knocked about with, he did at least seem to care whether she was there or not.

The waiter who sauntered to her table bore an uncanny resemblance to the eleven-year-old at the bar.

"What can I get you... madam?" he enquired with his gaze focussed upon her bosom.

Madam? Not even a Miss – or a Ms? But that's what 28 years of pissing people off got you.

"Dry white wine," she replied sweetly.

"Bottle?" he enquired, with a leering grin.

"No, a glass - but, before you ask - a large one."

Barely suppressing his disappointment that she had not opted for a bottle, he tore his attention away from her breasts and drifted lazily back to the bar. Liv began to do what she did habitually: study, through half-closed eyes, those around her. Make a game of it tonight, she told herself, since it's New Year's Eve. Since she was going to absorb every detail anyway, it might be marginally more interesting than her usual experience. 'Usual' meant binge drinking alone on the sofa in her flat, or at the Orange Lobster where she already knew most of the punters and didn't want to know them any better.

She started with the young pair at the very front in the left corner beside the window. A couple, she supposed, but probably not married because they were still holding hands across the table. She was fair-haired and fresh-faced with glowing cheeks, a stark contrast to his dark hair and olive-skin. They were younger than she was, maybe early twenties? But they looked so bloody happy. Bastards...

To the right of the door sat three middle-aged men who might have been clones since their faces all boasted the same rough, dark, stubble. What ever happened to men shaving? From time to time, one or another of the trio would glance in her direction because that's what a skirt up to your armpits did. It made men look – and not just men either. Anyway, this evening that was rather the point. She had set out to attract the full glare of people's attention and her stark dress code was clearly working. But, who was she trying to kid? She looked like a right slapper.

By the time she shifted her attention onto those sitting rather closer, her interest was already flagging. It was a relief to close her aching eyes, at least until the waiter returned with her wine. After his brief visit, however, she was left to stare mindlessly into her glass, before starting to numb her fears once more with alcohol. Perhaps Grace was right and there was no real threat to her life at all. But it hardly mattered now because the seed was so firmly planted in her head that, when the door swung open to admit a lone, sombre-faced man, all her apprehension - irrational or otherwise – flooded back. As his eyes swept across the room, Liv looked away to avoid eye contact because he looked as if he could easily be an assassin. Only when he passed her and went to the bar, did she breathe out.

After a short conversation with the boy behind the bar, however, the newcomer returned to stand over her. She gulped down half her wine in one mouthful but, by then, even the wine couldn't stop her trembling. Fearing that, despite the crowd of strangers, he was going to off her right there, she slammed her eyes shut and hid in the darkness.

"Is that seat taken?" the would-be assassin enquired politely.

"Yes," she snapped, without opening her eyes. "My boyfriend's sitting there."

"Not much to him, is there?" he remarked.

"Gone for a piss, hasn't he?" she blurted out. "He'll be back any minute."

"The barman said you're alone."

"Like it's got fuck-all to do with him," growled Liv, eyes flying open as genuine anger eclipsed her fear.

"He thought you might be happy to share," ventured the deadly killer.

For the first time, Liv risked a closer look at her nemesis. "That's because the little shit thinks I'm here on the pick-up," she said. "But, believe me, I'm not."

"Me neither," he said quickly. Perhaps, she thought, rather too quickly.

"You can piss off then, can't you?" she groaned.

"Come on, it's New Year's Eve," he pleaded, grinning down at her.

"I said: piss off."

"You know any other words?" he grumbled.

"Yeh. Fuck off."

"Why don't I join you?" he suggested, resting his hand near hers on the table.

Liv, reckoning that, if he got close, he could snap her neck in an instant, decided she couldn't afford to hesitate. Sliding a hand into her bag, she retrieved her blade, flicked it open and slammed the point into the table top barely an inch from his hand.

"Shit. I must be drunk," she muttered, as the blade quivered in the polished wood surface.

Trying to assess his reaction, she thought he looked a lot more shocked than any cold-blooded assassin ought to, although not quite as stunned as your average punter would be.

"It's alright," he said, with surprising calm. "No harm done."

"It's not alright," she snarled. "I was aiming for your hand."

At that point, surely any normal person would have backed off, but he lingered there which did nothing to allay her suspicions. This man was clearly not afraid of the occasional knife blade but, while she was still trying to decide what the average assassin might look like, he sat down opposite her.

Before she could protest, the waiter stormed over and glared at the blade embedded where she'd left it in the table.

"Who did that?" he demanded, his face a mask of outrage.

"I did," confessed Liv.

"You've ruined the table," he cried. "That's solid oak."

"Yeh, well, if it's hardwood, it'll just be a tiny scratch," Liv replied, extricating the blade with rather more difficulty than she would have liked.

"You've cut a great gash in it," protested the waiter.

"Scratch or gash - let's not argue over words," said Liv, attempting a placating smile.

"I want to know who's paying for the damage," insisted the waiter.

For the first time, Liv met her new companion's eyes and, as if in unison, both declared: "Piss off!"

Dumbfounded, the waiter retreated to the safety of the bar to confer with the other children. At once, Liv broke eye contact with the stranger and the pair sat in awkward silence. For her part, she reckoned that if she said nothing, he would soon go away and find someone more amiable. Unless, of course, he truly did intend to kill her.

"To be honest, I could do with some company," he confessed. "My girlfriend's just left me."

His revelation struck Liv like a lightning bolt from Aphrodite. And now she knew that her table companion was something far worse than a soulless executioner. He was that most miserable of specimens: a discarded man. And, all too soon, the nightmare began...

"Bloody Christmas Day," he moaned. "I mean, who leaves their bloke on Christmas Day?"

Though Liv made no reply, she reflected that it was certainly a hell of a present for the man who had everything. She'd have to store that one up... should there ever be a time when she wanted to end a relationship... should she ever actually be in a relationship to start with....

"A whole year we were together," he lamented. "A whole bloody wasted year of dinners, films, presents - not to mention a whole shedload of promises – clearly all empty ones on her part."

"I don't want to know," she told him, "because I don't care about you, or your girlfriend."

"Barbara."

Liv winced. Were women still called Barbara?

"And she did it by text," he complained.

Classy, thought Liv, wondering how she could extricate herself from the painful exposition that was certain to come.

"And her parting line," he continued, "was that I don't - what was her exact phrase - stir her blood. Stir her blood? What was I supposed to do, drink it?"

"You're supposed to go and whine to someone who might give a shit," grumbled Liv, sorely tempted to resort to the knife again.

"All the same... Christmas Day," he said. "She could have waited. You'd have done that, wouldn't you?"

Fashioning her most fiery glare, Liv replied: "No, I wouldn't. Because I wouldn't have put up with a self-pitying shit like you for a minute, never mind an entire sodding year."

At last, she had scored a hit because he looked straight at her and declared: "Christ, you're a real bitch, aren't you?"

"Oh, you've finally noticed," she gasped. "Yes, I'm a genuine full-on bitch. So, in future, you might want to choose your pickup with a bit more care."

"I suppose I should've known," he said, scowling at her.

"What does that mean: 'you should have known?'" she hissed. "You don't even know me." But then she fell silent, because there was one reason he might know her. If he was the one charged with her extinction.

Somehow her response must have wrongfooted him because his reply was all bluster. "No, I don't know you at all," he said.

But Liv knew bullshit when she heard it.

Perhaps to retaliate, he asked abruptly: "Why's your hair piled up in that sort of lopsided fountain on top of your head? Is that a style now?"

Stung by his sudden, brutal candour, she retorted: "Yes. It's an 'I had fuck-all time to do my hair' style."

"Right, well that would explain it then," he conceded. "You've got a lot of hair... and I suppose it looks... interesting."

"You should go now."

"Even though my girlfriend's just ditched me," he murmured.

"Yeh, smart girl, that Barbara," replied Liv, unable to resist another taunt.

Responding again in kind, her companion mused: "I wonder what you'd look like with all that makeup blowtorched off?"

"Piss off," she hissed, unwilling to look at him any longer. How in God's name had she been saddled with such a rude bastard? An assassin would have been a lot less stressful. The trouble was, she didn't want to leave and go out onto the street again. Streets had lots of dark places...

For a few moments neither spoke. Liv considered her predicament. If he was her assassin, why hadn't he already taken her out? She suspected that cold-blooded killers didn't usually stop to exchange insults with their victims. So, if he wasn't a threat then she had fuck-all to worry about other than spending an evening with a complete jerk. She'd hardly eaten all day, so she resolved to hold her nerve, stay in the open and address her hunger. Turning her attention to the tapas menu, she held it up to block out the annoying face opposite.

The wine bar offered a range of small dishes, any of which right now she could have swallowed in a single mouthful.

Lowering the menu a few centimetres, she made one last try: "Now would be a good time to stop harassing me and just leave."

"I'm not harassing you," he replied. "OK, I suppose my observations were a bit over the top. But I'm staying right here."

Staring back at him, Liv studied his face closely for the first time. Eyes first, naturally: light brown with tiny flecks of green. Sandy hair flopped forward over a round, open face – another stubble-strewn one. Alright, she had to admit he didn't have the eyes of a killer; just the eyes of a man who had been summarily dumped.

She might as well stay where there were plenty of people. Casa Georges was well-lit and she had to concede that she felt as safe there as anywhere. Perhaps she could at least tolerate him for a little longer and his presence might actually deter a real assassin. To her surprise, it suddenly occurred to her that, since he had sat down, she had paid no attention at all to what lay around her. So, his presence had at least distracted her from the endless stream of visual data her brain was in the habit of receiving. So, yeh, maybe she could stay with this loser for a while longer.

Decision made, she tossed the remaining half a glass of Pinot Grigio down her throat, and declared: "I need another drink."

"I'm sorry," he said, with what passed for an engaging smile, "if my attempt at banter got out of hand."

"That wasn't banter," she scolded.

"Believe me, Olivia, I've had a bad day," he told her.

"A bad day?" she scoffed. "You've no idea what a bad day even is."

Only as she was waving to the waiter, did she register exactly what he had said. And her stomach churned because, once again, he was no longer who she thought he was. Forcing herself to take several long breaths, she then enquired coolly: "How do you know my name?"

"It is you then, isn't it?" he said: "Olivia Fisher... from Sunrise Heights."

Liv swallowed hard, because he hadn't just moved the goalposts, he'd bulldozed away the entire pitch. In an instant, her bag was open again and her hand on the knife.

"It's Liv, actually," she breathed, heart pounding in her chest. "You seem to know me. So, who are you?"

Liv suddenly became aware that everyone within earshot was awaiting his response with rapt interest.

"You've got one sentence to explain yourself," she warned.

"How long a sentence?" he asked, with a grin.

When a woman at the nearest table tittered, Liv spat out: "Mind your own business, you nosy cow."

At once, heads turned sharply away and low conversations circled around the ill-matched pair's table.

Turning back to him, she said: "So, explain fast — and you can start with your name."

"Graham."

"Is that your real name?"

"Why wouldn't it be?"

"Alright, Graham, explain. And remember, you've got one sentence. After that, I'm gone."

But Graham didn't manage a syllable, let alone a sentence, before the plate glass windows of the wine bar shattered into a million pieces. In that instant, Liv picked out a spray of bullets scoring through the air with fragments of glass, both large and tiny, following in their wake. Scraps of blood, flesh and God knows what else flew at her. Mesmerised, she sat welded to her chair, until Graham hurled himself across the table and swept her to the floor onto a carpet of shards. As yet more debris scythed over them, she lay beneath him, with glass fragments gouging into her bare legs and thought: I guess he's not the assassin after all...

13

Casa Georges, on New Year's Eve.

In the smoky haze where Liv lay beneath Graham, an eerie silence prevailed for several heartbeats. Though many of the lights were out, sparking electrical outlets provided some stark flashes of illumination. Liv had a feeling that she didn't want to see too much because, beyond the flickering gloom, she could now hear voices. Some cried out, several others closer by just groaned or whimpered. In the near darkness, misery befriended panic and, every few seconds there was a scream as some new horror was discovered.

"You alright?" whispered Graham, resting a gentle hand on her shoulder.

Though her whole body was trembling, she replied: "Yeh, I think so. Wait, is my leg bleeding?"

"Which one?"

"Either of them," she growled.

"Hang on," he said, running his hands lightly over her legs.

"Shit," she gasped. "I think you've found it…"

"Yeh, you've got a sliver of glass in your left leg. Hold still a minute."

She obeyed whilst he attempted to remove the offending sharp object.

"A bit of window?" she murmured.

"Er, no, Chardonnay, I fancy... I think it'll just bleed a bit, that's all," he told her.

"You think? Are you a medical man?"

"No, but it doesn't look like anything vital's been cut," he replied. "I'll wrap a napkin round it."

"OK," she acknowledged and, when he'd finished, she started to get up.

"Stay down," he hissed, hauling her back to the floor.

Hitting out at the arm which held her down, she said: "I need to get my coat."

"Sod your coat."

"I think those shots were for me," she said.

"Yeh, probably," he agreed.

"So I need to get out of here – and I'm not leaving without that coat. And what do you mean, probably?"

"It'll take a lot more than a sentence to explain that," he replied, "but, you just need to know that I'm not your enemy."

Letting that thought sink in for a moment, she asked: "Will they have gone yet?"

"Doubt it."

"So what do I do?" she groaned. "I thought I'd be safe in here."

"Just now Liv, I'm not sure there's anywhere you're going to be safe."

"Wait. I didn't actually hear any gunshots," she said, "but I'm sure I saw bullets..."

"It was a sniper using suppressed, subsonic rounds," he murmured absently.

"Would a couple of bullets shatter that glass window though?"

"No, but a whole magazine would."

"Shit."

"Someone really doesn't like you..."

"Shit."

Raising herself up a few inches, she peered towards the front of the wine bar where traces of light blinked in from the street. Though she couldn't see much, she saw enough – in fact, more than enough. Stark, jagged remnants of glass adorned the broad window frame. Of the young couple, there was no trace. If the lovers hadn't been shot, they must have been shredded by flying glass · and that, she really didn't want to see. Nearer to her, diners littered the floor, some moving, but others worryingly still. Could all this... all this carnage, really be because of her?

"Stay down!" Graham called out, as several of the customers began to move. "Please, for God's sake, keep down!"

But, before he'd even finished his warning, they were plucked down, one after another, as if by some unseen hand.

"If I told you to wait here," he whispered. "Would you?"

"Not very likely," she retorted.

"Yes, that's what I thought you'd say," he muttered. "Well, you're right: we do need to get out."

"You think?"

"I'm trying to help you," he said.

"Yeh, but I don't know you," she argued. "Maybe you're leading me out into a trap. Maybe I'm wrong and, if we just wait... I mean, the police will be here in a few minutes, won't they? Anti-terrorist squad, or whatever..."

"I guarantee you, Liv that, even if someone does eventually come, they'll be too late to save you," declared Graham. "So, unless you want to die here, you need to trust me."

"I have some trust issues," said Liv. By which, she meant she mistrusted all men as a matter of course. Mind you, she didn't trust women much either.

"Great. Can we talk about your issues later?" suggested Graham.

Liv gave a truculent nod because, though she didn't trust him at all, he appeared to be offering her a lifeline – and it was the only one going.

"We need to crawl to the rear exit," he told her. "There'll be a fire door there."

"Shouldn't we try to help some of these people first," she breathed.

Reaching a hand up to pull down her leather coat, he draped it over her shoulders and replied: "Best thing we can do for them is to get you the hell away from them. Now, watch where you put your hands if you don't want to end up cut to ribbons."

He set off on his hands and knees and, a few seconds later, Liv followed. It took several long minutes to reach the bar counter, during which Liv was obliged to slither past the dead, the dying and the just plain terrified. Though several times she pressed her palms down onto glass shrapnel, she contrived to escape any serious cuts. On the floor beside the counter, they discovered the waiter who must have been standing beside the bar when his head and shoulders were flayed by bullets, or glass or both... His best friend wouldn't know the poor bastard now.

For self-preservation, Liv needed her eyes wide open, except that her facility for close observation left nothing to her imagination. Embedded in the waiter's jugular was a fatal shard, his cheek was also sliced open to the bone and blood welled up from a vacant eye-socket. Even when she closed her eyes, the grisly image lingered.

"Don't look," he hissed.

"If only," she groaned.

"Just stay down," he ordered, "while I take a gander."

But, as he moved to do so, a large splinter of the 'solid oak' counter flew past his head forcing him to drop back down again. So, someone was still out there – and Liv guessed it wasn't the emergency services. Graham crawled on across the floor away from the counter and towards the door that led to the toilets. Liv, desperate to escape the horror show, scurried after him.

At the door, he turned back to her and hissed: "As soon as I open it, they'll know where we are. So, we'll have to move fast."

"How will they know it's us?"

"They won't – not for certain. They'll come in and check."

Passing through the doorway, they entered a darker space, lit now only by several dim safety lights. As she rose to a crouch, he said: "Shooters could come in front or back, or both. And, if you're truly their target, they won't hesitate for a second. You understand me?"

Liv did understand. She understood that she was as good as dead. Opening her bag, she reached inside and took out the knife.

"What are you going to do with that?" he enquired.

"Probably nothing," she told him. "But I'll feel better with it in my hand. Come on, let's go, if we're going."

"You sound very calm," he said.

Calm? The one thing Liv wasn't was calm. Angry and resentful, yes. And horrified at what her presence alone appeared to have unleashed upon the unsuspecting clients of the wine bar. But once, half a lifetime ago, she'd known how to use a blade. So, if she was going down now, she'd go down like the street rat she used to be.

"Keep quiet now," he warned, as he set off along the corridor. "Stay behind me and try not to stick me with that damned knife."

Though sorely tempted, Liv restrained herself and followed him. At the end of the passage was a fire exit with a crash bar but, before they reached it, Liv could hear that someone was already attempting to force it open from the outside.

"Oh shit," she whispered, earning a glare from her companion who, bracing himself behind the door, motioned her back.

The wrenching open of the door seemed impossibly loud in the confined space. By the time it was half open, Liv caught a glimpse of a black-clad shadow. As a gloved hand gripped the edge of the door, Graham slammed his shoulder into it. Somehow, though the intruder managed to loose off two rounds into the passage, he missed them both and his shots ricocheted around the walls.

Anticipating a third, Liv dropped to her knees but by then Graham was grappling for the gunman's weapon. When it clattered to the floor, Liv gave a gasp of relief but the assassin was far from finished. Bursting through the door, he slashed a blade at Graham. Fearing the worst, Liv raised her knife. But, just for a breath, she hesitated because the two dark shapes were wrestling close together. She wasn't sure where to strike until her laser-focussed eyes found what she was looking for. Darting forward, she plunged her knife hard through the assailant's neck. Once, twice and once again... because apparently the flesh of a man's neck could put up some stiff resistance.

She only stopped stabbing when Graham tried to wrest the blade away from her.

"What!" she snarled at him.

"He's dead," cried Graham. "Stabbing him again won't make him any more dead."

Liv squinted down at the crumpled body of the stranger which was now wedged in the doorway.

"Are you sure he's dead?" she enquired.

"Yes, I think the three stab wounds were enough," he replied wryly, as he hauled the body inside. "You could easily have cut me though."

"Tempting," she snapped. "But you're still alive, aren't you? I was just trying to help. Sorry I bothered."

"Well, thank you," he said. Though she wasn't sure that he meant it.

"Who do you think he is?" she breathed.

"No idea," said Graham briskly. "And I don't care. Let's just see if he's got a friend out there."

"The sniper?"

"No," said Graham. "He's probably still at the front – unless, of course, he's moved..."

From inside the wrecked wine bar came the sound of people moving and Liv prayed it was the survivors. Somewhere, a siren sounded and relief flooded through her for, at last, the authorities were coming. Just as she was about to say as much, Graham set off out of the fire door, moving low and fast along the rear of the block.

"Wait," she cried, realising from the trickle of warm blood on her bare knee that her leg wound had opened up again. But Graham didn't stop so, rather than stay there alone beside the fresh corpse, she slipped on her coat and limped after him. Gritting her teeth, she put up with the pain because pain, she told herself, was infinitely better than death.

After only a few metres, her shoulders were hunched against a chill drizzle and she no longer felt the leg wound because all her limbs were numb with cold. When they had covered about fifty metres to the street corner at the end of the block, Graham slipped into a telephone kiosk and pulled her inside after him. Since the internal light was broken, it was dark enough to conceal them. It also reeked of piss... and worse.

"Stay perfectly still," he instructed, as he studied the darkened buildings all around them.

Liv, eyes wide, scanned the surrounding space for shadowy figures and saw none.

But next moment, Graham grabbed her and hissed: "Get down!"

Before she could protest, he pulled her down and did not release his hold until she thrust a knee hard into his groin.

"Men don't touch me unless they're invited," she stormed.

Both were on their knees: he, for the obvious reason, and she because, having struck him with her cut left knee, she was also in agony. As they fell forward, they cracked foreheads and collapsed so that they ended up sitting at the base of the booth facing each other.

"What were you thinking?" she groaned.

"I was trying to protect you," he protested. "I thought someone was coming."

"Trust me," she said, "no·one was coming. I'd have seen them."

"Well, you can't know that."

"I can," she declared, nursing her knee. "Because I can see an ant move at five metres. And you can think yourself lucky I'd put my blade away."

For several moments longer, they sat facing each other frostily in the gloom.

"You're a very difficult person to help, you know," he said.

"Yeh, well maybe because I don't need to be helped – or protected," she muttered.

But Graham wasn't the first to make the point and he was just another in the long line of would·be helpers.

"Would you rather be dead?" he asked.

Not really, she thought, though she didn't say so.

With a shake of the head, he levered himself up off the floor and then, sheepishly, offered her his hand · a hand covered in blood and whatever filth the floor of the phone booth had to offer. Liv accepted it anyway and, as he pulled her up, both, this time, made sure to avoid clashing heads.

"I'd better see to that leg," he said, and, tearing a strip from the bottom of his shirt, he bent down to bind up the wound.

"Thank you," she said stiffly.

"And I should see you home," he said, "just in case..."

"Yeh, just in case they're waiting there for me," she murmured.

"If they are, we'll deal with them," he assured her.

"I still don't know who you are," she said.

"I'm Graham..."

"So you said, but how do you know me?" she insisted.

"Later," he replied, "because that explanation might take a while."

"Not if you stick to one sentence," she growled.

14

Sunrise Heights, late on New Year's Eve

As they entered, Liv reached instinctively for the light switch, but then hesitated. Did she want to announce her return so obviously? She thought not.

Graham appeared to agree: "Yeh, let's not tell everyone we're here."

"You think they'll be watching?"

"I've no idea."

"Whatever," moaned Liv. "I need a drink."

The walk back to the house had not improved her leg so she limped into the living room and made straight for the drinks cabinet she'd raided several times earlier in the day. On the way, she cracked her left shin on the coffee table and felt like screaming. She didn't. There were plenty of others who had good reason to scream that night, she reflected, but not her. While Graham wandered through inspecting the downstairs, she opened the bar. Not an occasion for a gin and tonic, she decided. Something rather stronger was required so she selected a bottle of very fine brandy.

When Graham returned, she was half-filling two glasses.

"What we both need," she said, offering him one, "is some bloody strong liquid fortitude. It is New Year's Eve after all."

"No," he told her.

Liv still had more than a few doubts about him and needed to know who he was. She was hoping the brandy would help but, when she offered it to him again, he protested: "I need to stay sharp."

To Liv, however, it appeared that Graham's refusal carried little genuine conviction and, sure enough, a few moments later, he reached out for the brandy. Only then did she notice that his hand was trembling. A warm-hearted woman might have wrapped her arms around him and given him a hug. Sadly for Graham, Liv was not that woman. Instead, she simply stared at him, bewildered, which only made him shake even more until he was obliged to put down the glass and subside into one of the several large, lavishly-upholstered armchairs.

"What's wrong?" she enquired brusquely. "Oh, shit, you're an alcoholic and I've persuaded you to have a drink."

"No, I'm not an alcoholic," he assured her. "I've just got a few issues, that's all."

"Issues? What sort of... 'issues'?"

"That's none of your concern."

"I think it is," she replied, "as you're in my house..."

For a moment, he stared back at her – a stare so bleak that she was about to relent when he murmured: "Mental health stuff, alright... it's not something I tend to share much with others."

"'Mental health' issues?" she scoffed. "I reckon we've all got those. These days it's like a fashion accessory."

It was a typically insensitive response from Liv – and she was intelligent enough to know it. But discovering that her saviour had 'issues' of any sort did not fill her with confidence for what might lie ahead. Added to that, the phrase 'mental health issues' always unsettled her a bit because she was never quite sure what it meant. And, of course, she had plenty of her own 'issues' which she would rather not be reminded about.

"It's like a panic attack," he explained abruptly.

"But you've just fought off a gunman – and you didn't panic."

"Yes, but … afterwards… that's when it gets me."

"But it was me that killed him," retorted Liv.

"Yes, and you'll see, it matters, taking a life," he said. "It'll hit you when you least expect it."

But Liv knew it wouldn't.

"It's a cliché, but taking a life changes you," he added, swigging down a generous gulp of the brandy.

That was true enough, thought Liv. It did change you. But, in her case it already had, because this was not the first life she'd taken. Not that Graham needed to know that.

"So, are you always like this," she asked, "with the shakes?"

"Usually, it's worse."

Encouraging, she thought. "So, what do you do to… sort of… get over these… panic attacks?"

"Stop going on about it," he chided. "I wish I'd never mentioned it."

"So do I."

After a lengthy silence, he said: "You don't get over it, Liv. You just wait and cope with it - or not..."

In the absence of being able to offer anything approaching empathy, Liv poured them both another brandy.

"I think it's time you told me what all this is about," she said. "Did it all start with the man shot on the beach."

"What man?" Graham murmured absently.

"Some random guy who's been following me and turned up down here on the beach. For Christ's sake, I assumed you must already know about him."

"No. Was he a seaman, do you think?" asked Graham, suddenly more alert. "What did he look like?"

"Hardly matters much what he looked like," she retorted, "since he pretty soon had a fucking hole where his head was."

Graham was glaring at her now and, seizing her hand roughly, he demanded again: "Just tell me what he was like."

"Get off," she protested, pulling away to retreat across the room. "Just calm down."

"I'm sorry," he said at once, slumping back into the armchair. "But I need to know these things..."

Perhaps he did, thought Liv, but she was still struggling to erase the last forensically-detailed image she had of the poor guy on the beach.

"I can't actually remember his face now," she said. "But he was sort of thin, but strong and wiry, I suppose you'd call him."

Graham nodded glumly. "Hair colour?"

"I don't know, greying, I guess. But he always wore a black cap."

"What?" gasped Graham, jumping up again.

"Yeh, every time I saw him, he was wearing it – except the last time…and then he was in the sea and there was a lot of spray and it was raining…"

"Bloody hell," muttered Graham. "It sounds like Mark…"

"You think you knew him?"

"Bloody hell, if it was Mark, then this is much worse than I realised," he muttered, before downning the second brandy in a couple of gulps.

Liv couldn't see how it could be much worse but when his shaking hand raised the empty glass and shaped to hurl it across the room, she darted forward to snatch it from his grasp.

"Listen," she said, "haven't we had enough broken glass for one night?"

But Graham stormed across the room, ranting almost incoherently as he kicked aside any small items of furniture that happened across his path.

"Stop kicking my stuff all over the place," she cried.

Grasping a narrow, glass-fronted bookcase, he would have pulled it down upon himself, had she not seized his arms and dragged him away. In his sudden rage, he swung a fist at her, but years of evading wayward discus throws enabled her to sway to avoid it. Out of practice though she was, Liv was still quick and strong. Wrapping her arms tightly around him, she wrestled him to the floor and pinned him down on his back.

Eventually, his anger subsided and he just lay beneath her, sobbing and trembling.

Exhausted, she flopped down by his side and murmured: "Mental health issues, eh?"

Turning his head aside to avoid meeting her eyes, he confided: "Mark was my friend - a very good friend. Probably my only friend, I suppose. Not that I saw him often. But when we did catch up, it was as if we'd seen each other every day."

Unable to recall ever having even one friend, she muttered: "I'm sorry."

It was about as caring as Liv Fisher ever got because, in her experience, showing sympathy was just another way of ensuring you got screwed over. Struggling wearily to her feet, she thought about offering him a hand, but decided against it. In Liv's world there were threats and non-threats, and she still wasn't entirely sure in which category Graham belonged. Safer then, to leave him on the floor.

"It's a bit of a stretch that he was your friend," she said.

"Not really," confessed Graham, "because he was supposed to be keeping an eye on you."

"What? Why?" she cried. "Will you just tell me what's going on?"

But then, because even she registered the depth of hurt he appeared to be experiencing, she softened her tone: "Look, you have to give me something here."

"Alright, I'll try to explain," he murmured, before enquiring sheepishly: "Any chance of another drink?"

"As long as you're not going to try and smash the glass," she warned.

"I promise," he agreed solemnly.

So she refilled his glass and handed it to him. Fortified by more alcohol, they sat on the floor together as Graham began to talk.

"Mark and I were loosely working together-"

"Yeh, I've worked that out, but working on what?" she asked impatiently.

"If you listen long enough, I'll tell you," he grumbled. "Look, we're both, in our own separate ways, investigators-"

"Police?"

"Christ, woman," he groaned, "do you want answers or not?"

"Don't call me 'woman'", she snarled. "At least, not if you plan surviving the night."

Then, acknowledging that she still needed answers, she spread her hands in submission, leaned back against the sofa and said: "OK, I'm listening."

"I checked you out-"

"Yeh, I saw you checking me out at the wine bar."

"Not that sort of checking out," said Graham. "I mean your background, job and so on."

"What, like a stalker, you mean?" growled Liv.

"Jesus! No. I'm an investigator, remember. We were interested in what your parents were doing and, once they'd... gone, I started to investigate you because you were all we had left. I talked to some of your colleagues at the school-"

"That must have been entertaining," scoffed Liv.

"Oh, it was, because your fellow teachers had very straightforward views about you. My favourite, which has rather stuck in my mind, was: 'she's a wholly self-absorbed, thoroughly unlikeable and permanently angry bitch.' Imagine my surprise at the wine bar when you appeared to match that description perfectly."

"You're supposed to be explaining what you're doing," grumbled Liv, "not insulting me. Who do you work for, Mr Investigator?"

"Mark and I do - did - contract work and sometimes we worked for Regional Crime units – in this case, the SWROCU-"

"The what?"

"It's the unit that deals with organised crime in the south-west region," explained Graham. "Anyway, we were working on the inside – under cover, if you like. Mark was supposed to keep tabs on you while my job was more in the forensic accounting area, shall we say."

"Really?" said Liv, who was tempted to enquire whether his forensic work involved corpses, but managed to suppress her curiosity long enough to allow him to continue.

"I was supposed to find out about you and gather financial evidence about you."

"That wouldn't have taken you long," said Liv, "since I haven't got anything in my bank account."

"Well, to be honest," he conceded, "both lines of enquiry sort of came to a halt. That's why, in the end, I approached you directly."

"You know that I've not the slightest idea what you're talking about, don't you?" she told him. "What financial evidence were you looking for? Because, God knows, I haven't got any money."

"I know that now," he said. "But your parents had a great deal of it and I was trying to find out whether they'd given some of it to you."

"They were quite well off, I suppose," she said, "but I never wanted a penny from them."

He frowned. "They weren't just well off, Liv.... Surely you must know that."

"Know what?" she growled. "Stop talking in riddles."

"Are you seriously telling me you don't know what your parents did for a living?"

"Well, they retired a few years ago but, before that, as far as I took any interest in anything they did, I thought they were both in banking."

"Hah. Banking," scoffed Graham, unable to suppress a laugh. "Yes, Liv, they were bankers, in a way. They were bankers for one of the largest crime syndicates on the south coast. And they certainly hadn't retired – because it's not a job from which anyone usually retires."

Liv gave an involuntary shiver. It was the shock, she supposed. It wasn't so much the criminality of it that surprised her, but rather that her parents might be capable of carrying out anything quite so dangerous – and well, just a little impressive...

"But they're dead now anyway," she pointed out.

"They are indeed," agreed Graham, "but the bank accounts they serviced aren't. And, as far as anyone outside the cartel can see, something has gone wrong with those accounts."

"I don't even know what that means," she grumbled.

"The problem is: nor do I," admitted Graham. "But something's definitely off."

Banking, indeed money matters generally, usually gave Liv a headache because, in her experience, whatever income she had, it seemed to disappear all too swiftly.

"So, what you're telling me," she said, "is that, not only did my amazingly awful parents die and leave me a house that's fast disappearing off a cliff, but they also dropped me right up to my neck in the shit with a gang of criminals."

"Er, yes, that's about it, I suppose."

So, it was all about money, thought Liv: the grubby profits of crime. Thanks parents. Thanks again for your oh-so-generous legacy. It took another brandy for Liv to even attempt to process that and, while she did so, Graham kept quiet.

"Alright," she conceded finally, "so I get that my parents might have left behind some very pissed-off criminals, but why is everyone shooting at me?"

"To be honest, Liv, I don't really know," confided Graham. "But your parents' deaths have provided an opportunity for law enforcement to get into their accounts."

"But aren't they the cartel's accounts?" asked Liv, though she really didn't want to know.

"Well, that's where it gets interesting," said Graham.

Liv, still not finding the accounts particularly interesting, asked: "How so?"

"Because it appears that no-one can access those accounts."

"But don't crime syndicates have accountants for that?"

"Your parents *were* their accountants," said Graham. "Don't you know anything about them?"

"No, because all I've ever wanted to do was forget I knew them," she snarled. "Don't you understand?"

"I think I'm beginning to. But the trouble is that you're the only one still standing who might actually know where anyone could look for security passwords and that sort of thing. It's also likely that your parents left a large stack of cash behind. So, I don't suppose you...."

"No!" she cried. "How would I know where anything is? I've not lived here for ten years. I didn't even have a key to get into the house. I wouldn't know where to start looking for anything."

"The thing is, Liv, nor does anyone else," he explained. "So you see, everyone thinks that you, as your parents' sole surviving relative, simply must know where everything is. And, since you're not a child, they'll assume you knew what was going on all the time."

"But I didn't," she insisted. "What about the police? Do they know about this? Because they interviewed me about... about the one you think was Mark..."

"How long were they here for?" enquired Graham.

"Not long, I suppose. They just asked a few questions and took the body away."

"Right. Then either they've been warned off," replied Graham thoughtfully, "or they weren't the police at all."

"Of course they were the police. One of them wore a uniform…"

"You can get hold of those easily enough," said Graham. "Did you call them out yourself?"

Liv's silence confirmed that she hadn't. But, at the time, she'd just assumed that someone else had seen and reported the incident on the beach.

"But I thought you and Mark were working with SWROCU – so you're police anyway, aren't you?"

"If you recall, I said it was contract work. So, we sometimes do work for SWROCU. They sort of buy in our expertise…"

"That sounds very vague," said Liv, who was beginning to have more doubts about Graham because what he was telling her didn't somehow seem to ring true. Police who weren't police? That just didn't seem very likely.

"It's not vague," he insisted. "But who I work for just… varies, you know."

Liv didn't know. But just then it was only one of a hundred things she didn't know and Graham's rather cryptic responses were not helping much.

"But why do you think the police who came here weren't really the police?" she said, desperately trying to get her head around that particular deception.

"I'm only saying it's quite possible," asserted Graham.

Liv nodded as if she understood though, of course, she didn't. She did, however, feel strangely more comfortable with the idea that her old school alumna, Grace, was some sort of criminal. Posh grammar school girl turns to crime - or was that a little unfair?

"Let's look at this another way," suggested Graham. "How did you find out that your parents were dead?"

Liv pulled a face. "Would you believe online news?"

"The worst way," sympathised Graham.

And Liv supposed that it would have been, if she actually gave a shit about Monica and Henry Fisher. As a rule, she wasn't a great seeker after news on the grounds that it always depressed her. So she had just stumbled across the article about a missing plane. Even then, the tagline: 'British business couple missing after tragic accident' hadn't piqued her interest until she spotted the name Fisher. It wasn't an unusual name but still, it caught her eye.

She tried to recall what she had felt at the moment she realised who the ill-fated 'business couple' were. Not grief certainly, nor even regret. In fact, the first, rather grim, thought she remembered was thinking that perhaps she should go down to Sunrise Heights to check they weren't still alive. But, preoccupied by the dismissal proceedings against her, she hadn't done so. With all she had going on, it certainly wasn't hard to thrust it to the back of her mind. Even when she received the letter from Travis, Travis and Humboldt confirming that her parents were feared dead, it didn't somehow seem that important. If there was ever a time when she felt any love for her parents, she had no clear memory of it.

Misreading her silence, Graham said: "I'm sorry if I've brought back your grief."

"Don't be," she said, "because there is – and never has been – the slightest grief."

Clearly uncertain how to respond, Graham savoured the last of his brandy, while Liv attempted to fashion some clarity from all that had happened in the past week. It was crystal clear now that 'black cap' must have been looking out for her from the start at Slough. So, all the time she was worried about his presence, he was very likely trying to keep her safe. Since he'd been shot, they – whoever they were - had shot at her on the beach and then they had done so again at the wine bar. But why?

"I still don't understand why anyone's trying to kill me," she groaned.

"Perhaps, at the beach, they were just trying to scare you a bit," suggested Graham.

"Well, that worked," she muttered. "But going back to Mark, you say he was working with you?"

"Mark? Yes," he agreed, "But I had little actual contact with him since we were both supposed to be under cover on this job."

Though aggrieved to be referred to as a 'job', Liv let it slide and said: "He came to warn me on the beach, you know."

"Who, Mark?" he said, clearly surprised. "I wonder why he broke cover to do that."

"Well, that's what he said, but I think he'd been keeping an eye on me for the past week or maybe more."

"Yes, but neither of us was supposed to be actually protecting you," replied Graham.

Scowling, Liv said: "Good to know... but, he did protect me. And you, if you weren't supposed to be protecting me, why did you come straight over to me in the wine bar? When I think about it, the shooting there only started when you joined me. Could it be they were trying to kill you, not me?"

"It could be, but I doubt it," he replied. "In fact, the way they were spraying bullets around was crazy... amateurish even. It didn't feel like a proper hit at all."

"Well, it felt like one to me," grumbled Liv. "But, alright, let's say they don't actually want to kill me – just scare me. Couldn't I just tell them the truth: that I don't know anything about my parents' business?"

"Yes, you could," he said, "but I think they might take a lot of convincing about-"

He broke off as a low groan vibrated up through the floorboards and seemed to ripple through the house.

"Shit," grumbled Liv.

"That was like... an earthquake," muttered Graham.

"That," announced Liv confidently, "is the cliff slowly giving way under us. Maybe my parents should have listened to the man from the council."

"Is it going to collapse?" he asked.

"They've been saying it will for years," scorned Liv. "But I bet this house will be here after we've gone."

"Yes but, after this evening, that might not be too long," he replied.

"So, what then?" she cried. "What am I supposed to do?"

"You need to start looking for what they want," advised Graham. "And the sooner you find it, the better. Then you'd have something to bargain with. I can help you."

"We're not going to find anything at this hour," she groaned. "I'm too knackered and my leg still aches."

"Listen, Liv, they could come at any time," he told her. "So, sticking your head in the sand isn't going to keep you alive."

Greeting his advice with a stony glare, Liv nonetheless joined him in searching the house for a laptop, hard drives, a stash of notes, or just... anything at all that seemed to shout out criminal financial activity. It occurred to her, as she rummaged through cupboards in the living room, that her parents were probably 'old school'. Perhaps there was a safe somewhere that she didn't know about.

When the clock on the mantlepiece told Liv it was close to 2am, she decided she really didn't want to look any longer.

"I've had enough," she declared. "I'm dog-tired - even if you're not - and I'm going to get some sleep."

Even Graham's enthusiasm for the search seemed to have waned for he nodded in agreement.

"We can start upstairs tomorrow," he suggested.

Sunrise Heights boasted plenty of bedrooms, ranging from musty at best to positively grim at worst. Some of the old bedrooms had clearly been re-purposed since her departure years ago for they were now crammed with items of furniture that her parents probably intended to throw out but never got around to it. For two people so organised, the chaotic jumble in the bedrooms was surprising. Just looking at it depressed Liv.

"I'll use my parents' room," she told him. "You can sleep wherever you like - as long as it's not with me."

"The sofa will do," murmured Graham, flopping down on it without another word.

Somewhere, very deep inside, Liv felt at least a tiny bit aggrieved that he hadn't tried it on with her. But most likely, the episode in the phone box had put him off. Or perhaps he was gay. But, far more likely, his initial assessment of her had been enough to discourage him. He thought she was a colossal bitch - and, of course, she was....

15

It was still dark. On the bedside table, Liv's phone glared 4.23am. She'd hardly slept much more than an hour and the one thing Liv usually found easy was sleeping. Having spent her youth passed out on benches and pavements or, at her very lowest ebb, in doorways and gutters, she'd learned to fall asleep just about anywhere. So, something had woken her.

Somewhere outside the house, a large object fell heavily, or was knocked over. Earlier in the day, that had been happening all the time, thanks to the howling gale. But, when they returned from the wine bar, she'd noticed how much the wind had dropped. And now, of course, every sound out of place had to be treated with suspicion.

In the darkness, she wasted a few moments feeling around for her clothes until she realised that she was still wearing most of them. Apparently, all she had managed before collapsing onto the bed, was hauling off her boots. Sleeping in her clothes wasn't such a bad idea since it was freezing cold in the house. It seemed that Sunrise Heights's ancient boiler was up to the same mechanical standard as her parents' chartered aeroplane.

With a groan, she slid, stiff-legged, off the edge of the bed and smoothed down the skirt which had rucked up above her waist. To be fair, it didn't have very far to travel. Picking up her phone, she fumbled to switch on its light only to recoil from the sudden glare.

Stretching her limbs, she winced at the discomfort in her left leg, still adorned by a bloodied scrap of Graham's shirt. A brief examination confirmed that it was still wrapped securely around the cut so she left it alone. Instead, rolling down from the neck, she attempted – and failed · to touch her toes. Shit, she was miles off... but another sound from the back of the house reminded her why she had gotten up in the first place. With a shrug of her aching shoulders, she began to tread a path from the bedroom to the stairs but, at the top of the first floor landing, she stopped abruptly.

"Shit," she muttered. Why was it that when you got up in the middle of the night, the first thing you wanted to do was piss? Of course, the urgent need to relieve herself was entirely explicable and it crossed her mind that perhaps it was that alone which had awoken her. However, another clattering on the veranda below argued otherwise.

Nonetheless, the urge to relieve herself was too great to ignore, so she slipped into the bathroom. Though she reached up for the light pull, she lowered her hand at once because from outside, there was a definite creak of movement on the veranda. Nonetheless, Liv sat down on the toilet, because taking on an intruder with a full bladder seemed risky on several levels.

In the silence of the night, Liv thought the trickle of water sounded like a gushing torrent that whoever was creeping about outside surely couldn't fail to have heard. Whether they had or not, they must certainly have heard the toilet flush and Liv cursed her stupidity. Not for the first time in her life, she decided she was not cut out for stealth. Still, the damage was done now so she groped her way back to the stairs, wondering whether Graham was awake too. Unless he was a light sleeper, she suspected he might not be, as he'd consumed at least as much brandy as she had.

Just for a moment, she was tempted to go back to bed and hide under the duvet. But that was not exactly her style because, as a general rule, Liv's preferred modus operandi was to go for the jugular and fuck the consequences.

Since Graham was sleeping downstairs, they would find him first. She was appalled when the thought crossed her mind that his presence might distract the intruder long enough for her to sneak out of the front door. Swiftly, she thrust that shameful idea aside. She could hardly just leave the poor bastard because, despite his 'issues', he had saved her at the wine bar.

Slowly descending the stairs, she gave her eyes a chance to get used to the absence of light. Since she couldn't yet hear anyone inside, she hoped there might still be time to wake Graham. At the foot of the stair, she listened for the slightest sound but heard nothing. Whoever was outside must know that she was in the house, but did they know that Graham was there with her? For several moments she stood in the hallway, pondering what to do. If she stayed where she was, she had options: upstairs, into the kitchen, down to the cellar, or out of the front door. But once she ventured into the living room, she risked being trapped there.

In the movies, the 'woman trapped alone in the house' always went to the kitchen and found a knife to defend herself – though it usually ended badly. At least Liv was extremely familiar with sharp objects, but what had she done with her own knife? Shit! It was still in her clutch bag which she'd left upstairs in the bedroom. Still, she needed a weapon – so, movie time it would have to be...

Darting along the hall to the kitchen, she went to the worktop and located the knife block. Years ago, as she recalled, it held six blades, but she could feel only five hilts. Choosing a mid-size one with a narrow blade that tapered to a sharp point, she crept out of the kitchen and back through the hall. When she reached the lounge doorway, she paused there and scanned the room for Graham. Her sharp eyes pierced the darkness with ease and she saw at once that he wasn't any longer on the sofa. So, it was safe to assume that he had woken up. But where had he gone?

Long minutes passed, punctuated only by the occasional scrape of a foot on carpet. What was the intruder playing at? He must be new to the game because he seemed to be taking forever to get inside. If he was trying to unnerve her, it was certainly working. The purgatory of waiting came to an end with the sound of a door creaking open at the rear of the house. Oh, shit. She'd totally forgotten to lock the back door after they had returned from the wine bar.

Impatient to do something, she considered going to meet her visitor head-on. 'Go for the jugular and fuck the consequences'... The only worry was that she might, in the darkened room, find Graham's jugular instead.

But, hey, better to seize the moment while the intruder was still finding his way about. Stepping across the threshold into the living room, she was poised to enter the dining room when, from the far side of the room, a voice whispered her name.

She wasn't sure whether Graham's intervention was going to be a help or a hindrance because she was used to fighting her own battles. She won or lost on her own – until the wine bar, of course.... While she hesitated, Graham flitted across to join her.

"I need to get you out," he breathed, taking her arm.

"Don't do that," she hissed, shrugging off his hand. "I don't want to be pawed – and certainly not led away like some bloody lamb."

"But I think there are three of them," he argued. "That's too many for us to fight off."

Baring her teeth, Liv snarled: "Who says?"

"But-"

Scarcely registering Graham's whispered protest, Liv darted across the living room, kitchen knife gripped firmly in her hand. In her head, she was a brave, determined woman who refused to be forced out of her own house by scum. Scum being a generic term she applied to anyone who appeared to be an opponent. These particular scum would soon learn what it meant to tangle with Liv Fisher. But her bravado was blunted somewhat when she slammed her knee against a dining chair – the damned left knee again! - and fell headlong. Yelping, more from shock than pain, she rolled to a standstill against a pair of trousered legs.

"Oh, shit," she muttered.

Unsurprisingly, the intruder · no doubt rather bemused · couldn't suppress a contemptuous laugh. It was a rookie error though, for anyone who intended to subdue a fuming Ms Fisher. In her fury, she plunged her knife up fast at his thigh – once, twice, three times. There would have been a fourth if he hadn't managed to kick her aside with his other leg. But by then he was already falling with, Liv prayed, bright arterial blood pumping out onto the deep pile beige carpet. Having abandoned her blade in her victim's leg, she scrambled backwards across the floor.

She was still crawling across the room when, to her astonishment, Graham swept past her to crash into a second assailant who had abandoned his bleeding comrade to pursue her. With difficulty, she staggered to her feet to help Graham, though her ribs felt bruised at the very least by the wild kick. Fuelled by a rush of adrenalin, she drove up from the floor only to be knocked back down again with Graham sprawled on top of her. When a sudden torch beam sliced through the darkness, both tried to scuttle out of its glare.

Liv dived behind the sofa but didn't see where Graham went. All she heard were several short popping noises and, only when a vase shattered a few inches away from her, did she realise that shots had been fired.

"Watch out!" warned a low voice. "Don't kill the girl yet."

Liv, elated to be referred to as a girl, was also pleased they wanted to keep her alive, though that didn't mean she was going to reciprocate. Just then, darkness was her friend but she needed to find a viable weapon before someone decided to flick the light switch on. She might be strong but, in a wrestle with the two remaining intruders, she would not prevail.

Swiftly, she called to mind every detail of the room as it had looked the previous day. She was next to the long sideboard where the now-broken vase had stood. But what else had been on there? What could she use as a weapon? In an instant, she remembered the bowl of artificial fruit and grinned.

The intruders, flashing their torches around the room, would locate her in a matter of seconds. Unsure whether Graham was alive or dead, she opted to go on the offensive. Some basic reconnaissance seemed prudent so, taking out her phone, she switched on the light and pointed it towards the door to the dining room where she had last glimpsed the two men. It was only the briefest of moments and the soft beam illuminated only one man there. With genuine regret, she saw no trace of Graham.

Finding only one of her enemies meant that she needed one more look, so she cried out: "Don't shoot. I'm coming out."

In fact though, she didn't move a muscle. Instead, leaning against the sideboard, she scanned the light around the room. Gotcha, she thought: one was still by the entrance to the dining room while the other was standing in the doorway to the hall. Blocking the exits, she assumed, was probably standard procedure. That was all well and good if your quarry was intending to escape. But Liv wasn't.

Though she had excelled in many sports at school, her true love had been athletics - though not exactly the running or jumping kind. With the positions of the two men fixed in her head, she switched off the phone light and laid it on the sideboard beside her.

"Are you coming, or not?" growled the man in the hall door way.

"Oh, I'm definitely coming," replied Liv.

Picking up an apple in each hand, she felt their weight and then hurled one at each man. At least one of her targets emitted a startled grunt, so she took a pace to the left and found the foot-operated button for the standard lamp. By the time she pressed down on it with her bare foot, she was clutching another apple in one hand and a smooth, shiny pear in the other. As soon as the room was lit up, she let fly with both left hand and right. It helped, of course, that she was ambidextrous...

The second apple caught one assailant smack in the forehead and he collapsed in a silent heap. His companion was already raising his pistol when the pear struck him just below the eye. Rooted to the spot, Liv was relieved to find that the acute pain in his eye had affected his aim rather a lot as his bullets struck the wall to her right. So, apparently, there were circumstances in which they *would* try to shoot her.

Having exhausted her supply of fruit, she was relieved to see Graham rise up from the floor holding a gun. That prompted the surviving injured man to hurry back out the way he had come – out of the rear dining room door and around the veranda. The thing about the veranda was that much of it was untouched by rot but, here and there, it paid to be a little careful...

Pursuing him through the dining room, Liv directed her phone light outside and picked out the fleeing criminal as his leading foot went right through the timber boards. His cry of anguish certainly seemed genuine as he desperately yanked out his leg and tumbled off the veranda away from the house.

"Oh, no," muttered Liv, "not that way..."

As he plummeted off the cliff, his scream split the silence of the night. Liv almost felt sorry for the fellow – almost. By the time she returned to the living room, Graham had switched on the main light to inspect more closely the remaining two interlopers. Both were dead. One had bled out copiously after Liv's frenzied knife assault and the other... well, who said fruit was good for your health? It turned out that if an apple hit you hard enough on the head, it could kill you – particularly if the apple was made of marble. But even Liv was surprised, and rather satisfied, because her true skill really lay with the javelin.

"Jesus Christ," muttered Graham, "you're more lethal than I thought. How did you even do that?"

"Hand eye co-ordination," said Liv.

"Nobody's that accurate," he argued.

"Yeh, well... my eyes are better than most."

Perhaps Graham might have pursued the point but, when he slowly lurched down onto the sofa, Liv noticed that there was a patch of blood on his shirt. The intruders' bullets had not, apparently, missed everything. And she'd been so pumped up by her own triumph that she hadn't given a thought about Graham.

16

The Pavilion Pub in Highcrest, evening on New Year's Eve

When the woman at Sunrise Heights left the house in the early evening, Hal took his chance to do the same. He was cold and hungry for his flask of hot chocolate had been emptied hours earlier. So, he headed to Highcrest hoping to find a suitable place to eat and stumbled across the Pavilion pub. Though it wasn't very large, it had a certain atmosphere on New Year's Eve and Hal was reminded just how far he had come from Rochester, Minnesota.

At the Pavilion he texted Brad to keep him up to date and also called Lisa, because he knew that just hearing her voice would be enough to lift his flagging spirits. When she didn't pick up, he couldn't help feeling a pang of disappointment though he imagined that, on New Year's Eve, she would be fully occupied serving drinks. For Hal, it was proving to be a chill, damp and lonely New Year. But that didn't stop him fantasising about how life might be if he stayed in England with Lisa.

Hal liked the Pavilion which was both homely and welcoming, though he was lucky to find a table because being New Year's Eve meant it was very busy. After his uncomfortable hours in the trees, it was pleasantly warm and the Americano he ordered was hot and very much to his liking. Indeed, after some fresh-cooked food and another two coffees. Hal was feeling rather good. Being able to relax for the first time since he had left Lisa, gave him some valuable time to reflect.

Sure, things had not gone to plan at the Fisher house, but once the young woman returned, he would introduce himself properly and see if they could reach some agreement. Since she was apparently not very close to her parents, he thought that some sort of a deal might be possible. He would wait until daybreak and then go for broke.

After paying the check and finishing up his last mouthful of cold coffee, he began the walk back to the house. It had been dark for several hours by then so he took his time. Expecting that the Fisher woman might return to the house late, he was in no hurry. If she did happen to have returned earlier, there would be a light on – and there wasn't.

By the time he had settled himself once again in his little eyrie, his attention was caught by the all too familiar sound of sirens. They were some distance away - most likely, he suspected, at the other end of the town. So, thankfully, that was one thing that was not his problem.

After about an hour or so, he decided that this might be a good opportunity – maybe his only one - to explore the house while she was out. He could do a quick search and familiarise himself with the layout. However, just as he dropped to the ground, voices alerted him to the approach of others. Quickly, he realised that it was the woman who he had come to think of as Fisher's daughter, returning with some random stranger in tow. Jeez, she didn't waste much time, he thought – until a gentle flutter of guilt reminded him how fast his connection with Lisa had formed and developed... and deepened.

With a sigh, he retreated once more into the shelter of some conifers to observe the body language of the pair. It took him only a moment to decide that they were not together – for there was little show of affection between them. So, who or what was he? If he was just a guy she'd picked up then she didn't seem into him at all. Maybe he was the family lawyer who she'd arranged to meet in the town. But that didn't seem very likely at such a late hour.

Of course, on New Year's Eve all kinds of shit could happen between complete strangers. It only served to remind him how little he knew about the Fisher family. He even began to wonder whether Brad might have been right in his initial reaction that they should just let their dead father go. Except that, if Hal had followed that course, he would never have met Lisa.

Only when the pair clambered past the broken side gate, did Hal realise that the daughter had still not located a front door key. Lights soon came on and, for an hour or so after they disappeared into the house, he heard occasional sounds from within and, at one point he fancied he could hear raised voices. Again, he contemplated going in, but very soon calm returned so, he deduced, either they had killed each other or settled down to sleep – unless, of course, they had embarked upon a less restful activity.

For a trained sniper patience was a way of life, but no shooter wanted to linger for too long in an exposed position. Get in quick, make the hit and get out again. That was the mantra. Also, well-hidden though Hal was, several of the other trees were winter leafless. There were only so many evergreens like the one he had chosen. Being so close to the target area – in this case the house · was another big change from what he was used to in the army. Often he was hundreds of metres away rather than a lousy fifty. But any further away and his lines of sight would be severely compromised by the other trees. Right now, in the night shadows, there was little danger but, when daylight came once more, he knew he would again feel too close and too exposed.

Since Paris, there had been no more contract offers which was a slight worry in one way but also something of a relief. Nevertheless, it meant that it was even more important for him to squeeze something out of the Fisher estate. But at least he had a clear plan: talk to the daughter, see the lie of the land there and then wait for Brad. Together they would go to a lawyer's office and declare that they were Henry Fisher's heirs, which a DNA test would surely confirm.

Before all that though, he would have to endure the remainder of the chill night outside and he was sure it was going to seem an exceptionally long one. But Hal was not left undisturbed for very long. It must have been around 3am, just as, for the umpteenth time, he was giving his calves and ankles a rub to ease the stiffness. Below him on the gravel driveway, he heard the crunch of movement. Taking care to ensure that he was still hidden from view, he watched as three dark figures ghosted towards the house.

Visitors at 3am were unlikely to be making a social call, he reckoned, and sure enough, after a brief examination of the heavy front door, they made for the side of the property where, no doubt, they were only too pleased to discover that the gate had already been forced open. Inside the now-darkened house, all remained quiet but, since Hal knew there were two people in there, he didn't expect the silence to prevail for very long. The question was: were the newcomers intent on searching the property, or did they intend grievous harm to those inside – or both?

Jeez.. now what was he supposed to do?

While he didn't wish any harm upon the Fisher daughter, he couldn't take on everyone in the house. Nor did he owe anyone there a thing and he had to concede that he was increasingly bewildered by the sheer number of rather shady people who appeared to be taking an interest in the Fisher family. By contrast, he was feeling particularly isolated. This was lonely work and, at least in the army, you were a member of a team.

When noises began to drift up to him from the house, he hunched down even lower. It went against the grain but he just couldn't get involved. If the woman made it through to morning, he'd talk to her. If not, so be it. All the same, he hated not knowing what was going on and, only when he heard the sound of breaking glass, followed by a scream from a fleeing insurgent, did he suspect that perhaps the house might have been successfully defended. The thought brought a grim smile to his face – albeit briefly.

When dawn was close, Hal sensed the tiny, incremental changes in the light. However, since he was facing west with trees all around him and low cloud hugged the coastline, it was difficult to be certain about the first rays of daybreak. It had been a long, tedious night and, while Hal the sniper was absolutely ready for whatever happened next, Hal the lover would right then rather have been snugly tucked up in bed with Lisa.

17

Sunrise Heights, on New Year's Day

It was close to dawn when Graham woke up and at once Liv told him: "Grace gave me a number to ring, so I've called the police."

Graham, propped up on the sofa, gasped: "Why on Earth would you do that?"

In response, Liv eyed the two corpses on her living room floor and retorted: "Why wouldn't I?".

"Yeh, well, calling the fake police isn't going to help those two much, is it?" he scoffed.

"You're paranoid," accused Liv. "We don't know they're fake and we can't deal with this on our own. At least they can take the sodding bodies away."

"You shouldn't trust this Grace person," he warned.

"I didn't say I trusted her," replied Liv, "but I think she maybe can help us."

Graham looked doubtful.

"I knew her at school," said Liv.

"Did you get on with her?" asked Graham.

"I didn't 'get on' with anyone," said Liv.

Except Ellen, of course. But Liv had no intention of mentioning her. Nor did she tell him that she had taken great pleasure in persecuting Grace over a period of years. Grace had never struck her as the forgive and forget type, though perhaps that was all water under the bridge now.

"And that was what... twenty years ago?" hazarded Graham.

"Thirteen or fourteen, maybe," retorted Liv. "I'm not that old."

"Anyway, it's best she doesn't see me," said Graham.

"Why? If she's one of yours-"

"I really don't believe that she's police," he insisted. "And anyway, I'm undercover, remember? Christ, I need to get out of this house before she comes."

Liv, wondering how stressful being undercover might be, imagined trying to infiltrate Year 11 and frowned. Shit, no wonder he had issues. She studied his pale, bruised face until her eyes were inevitably drawn back to his torso which she had rather inexpertly bandaged. For a PE teacher who'd attended a shedload of first aid courses, she knew she'd done a crap job. Although, to be fair, since they were devised for teachers, none of the courses had dealt specifically with bullet wounds. He was a lucky sod because, though there'd been a bit of blood at first, the bullet appeared only to have nicked his side without damaging anything vital. It had been a long time since she'd seen that much blood close-up – well, apart from the wine bar. Even so, it scared the shit out of her. What was she getting into – or rather what had her parents gotten her into?

"You shouldn't leave," she told him, trying to sound matter of fact about it. "You'll only make that wound open up."

"We haven't got that sort of time," he insisted. "And I can't be seen by Grace – whoever she is. It'll heal fast."

"Alright," agreed Liv gruffly. "Just piss off then. It's not as if I need you anyway."

Though, of course, she probably did.

Levering himself up out of the sofa, Graham attempted a fragile grin which morphed into a wince of pain. Before he even reached the living room door, he was leaning against the wall, cursing.

"Come on," she said briskly, taking his weight on her shoulder. "You can hide out on one of the upper floors – if you can climb up there."

With a nod of resignation, he accepted her help but, even with it, mounting several flights of stairs up to the second floor was hard going. By the time they reached the uppermost landing, Graham's pallor was worse and even Liv was exhausted. The door to the neglected attic bedroom seemed reluctant to open until persuaded by a savage kick from Liv. Belatedly, she reflected that persistently kicking things with her left leg when the right was unharmed was probably a mistake. Inside the room, there was a sea of dust and she feared that the spiders up there would be both plentiful and enormous.

While Graham leant against the wall, she carefully lifted off the bedspread and folded it in on itself to trap the months of dust inside. Underneath it, the bed was not made up, so the bare, terminally-stained mattress would have to suffice for now. With her support, Graham staggered over to the bed though, as he collapsed onto it, there was an alarming crack and Liv ended up pinned to the mattress under him.

Struggling to extricate herself, she complained: "Trying it on again, eh?"

"It must be your irresistible charm," he groaned, allowing her to squeeze out from under him.

With a shiver, Liv realised that the attic room was even colder than the rest of the house, probably because the heating struggled to work above the ground floor but also because, she observed, the window was stuck open by several centimetres. Without something over him, Graham would soon be freezing, so she hurried down to the floor below to retrieve the duvet she had slept under. By the time she returned she was breathless and lamenting – not for the first time - how far she had let her fitness levels slide.

"Maybe I should take another look at that wound," she told him.

"Nurse, are you now?"

"A PE teacher is a mistress of all skills," she replied simply.

But before she could examine him, the manic doorbell started to chime... and chime... and sodding carried on chiming as it went through its extensive repertoire.

"I suppose that'll be the police," she murmured. "I'd better go down."

"Can't believe they'd roll up so soon," he remarked. "Anyway, don't tell them about me - please."

"They're not gonna believe I fought off three armed men on my own, are they?" she argued.

"Yeh, fair point, I suppose," he conceded. "Alright, tell them we met by chance at the wine bar and I saw you safely home. After the attack, I lost my nerve and ran off."

"Sounds like you, but for Christ's sake stay quiet up here," she warned, before thrusting the duvet over him and hurrying back downstairs.

The merciless doorbell showed no sign of relenting until, finally, she reached the front door and flung it open. Grace, she observed, had not come alone.

"God, Liv, we were just about to break the door down in case your intruders had come back."

Liv, aware that her parents had installed a heavily-reinforced door – though she only now understood why – suspected that even the police might have had their work cut out to break it down. There was no detective this time with Grace but there were two others in plain clothes. The moment she ushered them in, the pair sprang into action and went in search of the bodies.

"Have you got a forensic team coming?" enquired Liv.

Grace took her aside and said: "It's a bit awkward, Liv, with you admitting to killing two of them. So I thought, for old times' sake, I'd keep this under wraps for now - till we find out who these clowns are, eh?"

"Thanks," murmured Liv, wondering just how accurately Grace recalled the 'old times'.

"You poor thing," commiserated Grace, "you've had so much to cope with in the last twenty-four hours and now you've got us traipsing all over the house asking questions, eh? We'll take these guys off to ID them then have a quick look round to make sure no-one else is lurking about, eh?"

As she watched one of the bodies being carried out, she remarked: "There's not a mark on that one – how in God's name did you kill him, eh?"

"Apple to the head," replied Liv.

"Oh, yeh, well, you always were good at throwing stuff, weren't you?" remarked Grace, with a thin smile. "I remember when you threw that hockey ball at me – you know, the one that broke my arm..."

"Yeh, I'm so sorry about that," said Liv at once.

"Yeh, well that's all whatsit under the bridge now, eh?" declared Grace, unsmiling. "I'm a professional, Liv. Even if I hated you for it – which obviously I don't · I wouldn't let that affect my work."

Liv winced.

"Is there somewhere we can talk?" enquired Grace. "You can tell me exactly what happened, eh?"

"The kitchen," suggested Liv, reckoning that if Grace continued to add 'eh?' on the end of every sentence, there were still several knives to hand.

"Perfect," agreed Grace. "Did they come in here?"

"No."

"Right, this'll do then, eh?"

As they sat down at the large kitchen table, Liv tried to compose herself so that she gave an account that minimised Graham's role in what had happened.

"You're starting to rack up a rather substantial body count," remarked Grace. "Even at New Year, that's bound to attract some attention."

"Well, I'm sorry if the threat to my life causes you any inconvenience," growled Liv. "But I didn't exactly ask for all this to happen."

"Are you sure about that?" replied Grace, her black eyes fixed upon her. Liv had completely forgotten those crafty, beady little black eyes.

"So, what's your version of events, eh?" enquired Grace.

"It's not my 'version'," growled Liv. Though, of course, that was exactly what it was.

"Alright, help me to understand what happened," invited Grace, with a reassuring smile.

But, as Liv began to do so, she couldn't help thinking that even the parts that were true sounded very unlikely. When she had finished, Grace looked thoughtful and enquired: "Tell me more about this guy that helped you get out of the wine bar. Because fleeing a crime scene is, of course, a serious matter–"

"We were running for our lives!" cried Liv.

"So you said... Then you came back here and what... he stayed the night? To comfort you, was that?"

Feeling her hackles rise, Liv fought to remain calm and decided that perhaps it had been a mistake to allow Grace to interview her where there were so many pointy objects.

"I slept upstairs and he fell asleep down here on the sofa," explained Liv. But was she cross at the insinuation, or peeved because there was no truth to it?

"OK," said Grace, "so then someone broke in."

"Yes, and both of us were woken up. I came in here looking for a weapon and found a knife."

"Which, I believe, you used to quite deadly effect on one of the intruders," said Grace.

"Yes, I did – in self-defence..."

"It might have just been a burglar, Liv. But you stabbed him three times – fatally, as it turned out."

Liv glowered at her. "Yeh, but he wasn't a burglar, was he? He was trying to kill me."

"But you didn't know that when you assaulted him with a kitchen knife, did you? Eh?"

Liv shrugged. "After what happened at the beach and the wine bar, I'd say I was within my rights to assume the worst, wouldn't you?"

"What I'd say, Liv, is that, in the few hours you've been here, you've brought multiple deaths to our peaceful little village."

"I didn't bring them," protested Liv. "They were already here."

"And your mysterious partner in this frenzy of blood-letting just... disappeared, eh?"

"I think he was wounded in the fight and he just ran out," she said. "I can understand that."

"Can you?" asked Grace. "I mean, I can't... not really, I can't. It was before dawn, so still dark out. You'd just been, as you put it, 'fighting for your lives' and you'd overcome your attackers. Then he just buggers off - what a little shit, eh?"

"Well, I don't blame him," said Liv. "I think he'd just had more than enough."

"Of what? You?"

Liv, concerned that Grace's tone suggested she understood that feeling very well, replied only: "I don't know. I really don't."

After Liv had finished, Grace sat there for a few minutes before getting up to leave.

"I'll soon have to report all this to my superiors," she told Liv. "So, I suggest you stay put for now."

"You've not taken any notes," said Liv.

Grace smiled. "S'alright, I've got a great memory, haven't I? Never forget anything – even from years ago... Anyway, I'd better be on my way – it is New Year's Day after all, eh?"

"But I'm still not safe," protested Liv.

"I'll be surprised if there's anyone left to threaten you," joked Grace. "But I'll arrange for an officer to come by every hour or so – manpower permitting, of course..."

Manpower permitting, thought Liv, already starting to worry.

"But I'm here for you, Liv," Grace assured her. "You've got my number so, just call me, if you're worried – or if you just want to talk about something · anything, eh?"

"Talk about what?" asked Liv.

"Oh, just anything you might be worried about."

"Yeh, alright," said Liv, who had been worried about almost everything since the moment she set foot in Sunrise Heights.

"And don't trust that chap who brought you home," advised Grace. "If he comes back, I'd send him packing. He could be anyone."

Yeh, anyone, thought Liv, in that astronomically tiny set of people who were prepared to take a bullet for Liv Fisher. All the same, she had to concede that Grace might be right: she knew even less about Graham than she did about Grace. And she only had his word that he was an undercover investigator. What if he had his own agenda? Because she suspected that, when money was involved, loyalty was the first thing to go out the window.

Once Grace left, and Liv was on her own again, she decided she had to trust Graham at least a little, because he had stood by her twice. It felt like they were in it together – which was, in itself, a wholly new experience for her. However, when she went up to the attic to check on him, she found Graham so much recovered that she assumed his wound was pretty superficial after all. Only then did she realise how much Grace had undermined her faith in him. She'd seen the wound for herself and reckoned it was probably quite sore. She was looking for a betrayal that just wasn't there.

Then, to her surprise, the moment she appeared, Graham announced that he intended to leave.

"Trust me, Liv, I'll be back as soon as I can," he told her. "But there are just some things I need to do. I mean, we're more or less defenceless here."

"But you must have colleagues you can call on," she said.

"Not until I can close the case," he replied. "When I'm undercover, only a couple of people even know what I'm doing."

"Yeh, and I'm not one of them," muttered Liv crossly. "You must surely report to someone."

"Yes, of course I do."

"So call them from here."

"It isn't the sort of person you just call up at will," he explained.

"But... you will come back," she said, irritated at just how pathetic she was starting to sound.

"I promise I'll be back before nightfall," he assured her.

But he wasn't.

18

Liv had to concede that once she was alone again in the house she felt a little more exposed. But then, what was Graham to her? She'd only known him a few hours so, if he never came back, did she care? Anyway, relying on some bloke was not her way and, with or without him, there were still issues to resolve in the house. If her enemies wanted some information that was hidden there then she'd better start looking for it with a bit more urgency. If her parents had a safe, she couldn't recall ever having seen it. So, she began by removing anything hanging on the walls – mainly paintings because, of course, there were no family photos in the Fisher household.

Finding no trace of a hidden wall safe downstairs, she repeated the process upstairs, floor by floor and room by room. Still, she found nothing, which made no sense to her at all. She found it hard to believe that, if her parents were up to their armpits in shady money, they didn't have a safe. Where else would they hide the profits from their nefarious activities? So next, she turned her attention to the assortment of desks, cabinets and cupboards around the house – of which there were very many.

Careless of any damage she inflicted, Liv ransacked them all. Every drawer was investigated – broken into if it was locked – and the contents emptied out. If there was anything hidden there, she was going to find it and be done with the whole grubby little story. However, by around midday, Liv found herself sitting on the floor of the living room surrounded by small piles of debris – none of which appeared to refer to anything remotely financial.

Despite managing to create chaos out of her parents' ordered home, she had found nothing that seemed to match what she sought. No digital devices were squirreled away. No folders or files of paperwork such as bank statements, invoices, and so on. Nothing.

In her disappointment, she revisited the bar and opened a bottle of red wine, noticing vaguely that the stock of alcohol was dwindling. But the wine only seemed to make her even more despondent. How much, she wondered idly, did you need to drink to be classed as an alcoholic. However much it was, she reckoned she must be hurtling towards that particular destination at light speed. When she had been working, she only ever drank at weekends but, in the past few months, she had resorted to the bottle more and more. Recognising the slippery slope was one thing, but doing something to arrest her accelerating descent was quite another.

Her life had begun to unravel and it was all because of a self-absorbed, privileged, sixth form rapist. But, however grim her current state was, it was a whole lot worse for the youth's real victim. Even after Liv was suspended she'd kept in touch with the girl – right up until she overdosed, at which point the parents had denied her any further access. Now, all she could do was hope the poor kid was alright. Hope? Hope was just a piss-poor substitute for help.

Filled with a sudden dark self-loathing, Liv emptied the bottle and hurled it at the wall. She intended it to shatter into a million pieces but clearly, bottles were now made much more impact resistant, because it simply bounced off after chipping out a lump of plaster. Shit. She was a mess and it wasn't because her search had yielded nothing. It was... just... everything all rolled into one great fat turd.

She needed to pull herself together but it probably didn't help that she hadn't eaten so far that day. Rummaging amid the debris for her phone, she ordered a pizza before returning reluctantly to her search. It occurred to her that all the bedrooms had walk-in wardrobes – one or two quite large – so, she decided to tackle those next. Though each one was unceremoniously emptied of its contents, all she discovered, aside from an avalanche of dust, was a charity shop load of old-fashioned clothing, shoes and linen. Most folk would at least have a box of mementoes stashed away. Even Liv had one somewhere – albeit a small one. But not her parents because, clearly, there was no-one at all that they cared about enough to remember.

Tired and covered in dust, she prayed that the pizza would arrive sooner than later. Standing on the first floor landing, she grimaced at the plethora of doorways. After a time, her focus sharpened on the bedroom belonging to her parents, because there seemed to be something off about it. Some aspect of its symmetry looked wrong because, though it was the largest upstairs room, she realised that it had by far the smallest wardrobe.

Where was her pizza? The one time she actually wanted to hear the inane chimes of the doorbell, it remained stubbornly silent. Wandering back into the master bedroom again, she picked her way through the untidy heaps of clothing now scattered over the floor. Studying the interior walls, she decided that they didn't all appear to align exactly. Examining them more carefully, she wondered if there could be a space behind the rear wall of the wardrobe.

It was a foolish notion and she knew it, but it would give her something to do until the pizza arrived. And it would show Graham that she had tried - where had that thought come from, she wondered? Because she didn't need to try to impress a man who hadn't even deigned to come back. Yes, he'd helped her out, but he certainly wasn't her type - her type generally being half-wasted tossers who sought nothing more than uncomplicated fornication.

After ten minutes of hopeful investigation, she found nothing. No secret levers, pressure pads or buttons were discovered so, she gave up. Furious at the amount of time she had foolishly squandered, she smashed her fist at the wall facing her. All she got was very sore knuckles. Yet, there was some give in that wall because she'd bashed in the plasterboard. So, maybe there was a hidden compartment after all...

Thinking it was worth a bit more of her time and, since she had nothing better to do, she trudged downstairs in search of a blunt object to wield. Halfway down, the musical doorbell began to spew out another rendering of its death by music playlist. Though Liv had almost forgotten about the pizza, she hadn't forgotten the multiple attempts on her life. So, she didn't open the front door at once. Instead, praying that her visitor was only a pizza delivery man, she interrogated the poor guy through the locked door, until he dropped the pizza on the door step and bolted. Swiftly, Liv retrieved her lunch and slammed the door shut. Since no bullets were fired, she took that as a small win....

19

By the time Liv retrieved the pizza, she didn't really feel much like eating it. In any case, as she soon discovered, it was stone cold. After nuking it in the microwave, she noticed the text on the box which warned her not to do so. Nonetheless, some basic survival instinct persuaded her to start consuming it, chewy and flavourless though it was. The truth was she felt exhausted and being sleep-deprived probably didn't help much either. Abandoning her half-hearted assault on the wardrobe, she dozed off on the sofa downstairs with the half-eaten pizza, still in its box, discarded at her feet.

To cap her perfect day, in the late afternoon, the doorbell sounded once more. It turned out to be Grace, making a surprise visit and greeting Liv like a long-lost friend.

"I didn't expect you to call in," said Liv, diffidently, though there was at least a small part of her that was a little pleased to see anyone – even Grace.

"Well, I'm not supposed to be here," confided Grace, "with it being New Years Day - manpower shortages and all that. But I'm at the end of my shift and I wanted to talk to you again about that chap who came home with you last night."

"What about him?" asked Liv warily.

"Well, I've done some checking and all I can get out of those who should know is that there's no-one working undercover · on any case · in this area. So, whatever he is, he's definitely not the police."

In some ways, Grace was only confirming what Liv had been contemplating all morning. Because, though she wanted to believe in Graham, the longer he stayed away, the more she began to doubt him.

"Really, Crack," advised Grace, "he could be working for anyone – and all we want is to keep you safe, eh?"

"But why would he make it all up?" groaned Liv.

"To get you to trust him, of course," replied Grace. "Like us – the real police, that is · he knows something about your parents and what they were up to. But he's just trying to take advantage of you. He thinks you're on your own and vulnerable – but you're not. You've got us behind you."

Liv didn't know what to think because the idea of Grace having her back was hardly more attractive than trusting Graham. But what if she was right?

"He said he worked for SWROCU," muttered Liv. "But he said he was contracted... not permanent."

"What?" said Grace, her face suddenly clouded by doubt. "He actually said that, did he?"

"Yes, he did – but you think he's been lying to me all along, don't you?"

"I suppose he could be some kind of private investigator hired by SWROCU · short term," mused Grace, "for certain skills he might have."

"But you just said he wasn't legit," argued Liv.

"Well, I can't be certain he's not working for another branch, can I?" conceded Grace.

"You seemed pretty certain just now," grumbled Liv.

"Let's just agree you need to be careful," suggested Grace brightly. "If he comes back, text me – just to be safe."

Glancing around the living room, she clearly noticed the items piled up on the floor and remarked: "Having a clear-out, eh?"

Liv gave a shake of the head. "Yeh, my parents stuff – you know."

"Hmm. Well, if you remember anything else – however small, let me know," said Grace, putting a hand on Liv's shoulder. "It could help us with our enquiries, eh?"

But Liv, acutely aware that she had not truly sobered up since she first set foot in the house, had stopped listening. She knew she needed to forget Grace, forget Graham and just... dry out so that she could think things through.

Grace, however, was still talking. "If he comes back, just be on your guard," she warned. "And text me, eh? Text me and I promise you, whatever I'm doing, I'll call in a couple of our lads to come round and talk to him."

"What?" murmured Liv.

"Think about it," insisted Grace, perhaps realising she had lost Liv's attention. "A man you don't know at all walks into your life when the bullets start flying? There aren't many around like that, are there, eh?"

"No, there aren't," agreed Liv blankly.

"Unless he was trying to get into your knickers... Did he, er...?"

"No, he didn't," said Liv flatly. And she couldn't help wondering about that · not that she fancied him even slightly. But it would have been nice if he'd at least shown some interest. Perhaps the whole phone booth incident had put him off.

Having attempted to demolish what remained of Liv's confidence, Grace departed. Much of what she'd said made complete sense because, if Graham wasn't under cover for the police, then he didn't have a shred of credibility. Although, as soon as Liv mentioned SWROCU, Grace seemed a lot cagier about Graham. So, what was all that about? For Liv, both Graham and Grace were just two more strands of uncertainty in the whole web of lies spun by her parents. And, she suspected that even drying out wasn't going to make those go away. More wine, on the other hand, might be worth a try...

After selecting a rather fine and, she hoped quite expensive, red wine, she went in search of the remains of her lunchtime pizza. It turned out to be a less than suitable accompaniment to high quality wine. In the end, she just nibbled through one curling segment while downing half the bottle. No sign of Graham still. But did she want him to come back now, or not? He'd had ample time to be conspiring against her – especially if he was part of the criminal cartel he'd told her about.

By three o'clock, she'd resorted to supping her wine beside the kitchen window overlooking the driveway, like a wife in fear of imminent abandonment. By four, a second bottle of wine had been opened and consumed with only the merest trace of pizza. By five, when it was dark outside, she felt sick and, though she blamed the pizza, she had to concede that the two bottles of wine might also have something to do with it.

Whether Grace was right about Graham or not, Liv was convinced now that he was never coming back. In her heart, she knew that, if he'd intended to return, he would have done so, as he promised, before darkness fell. The next attempt on her life was likely to come during the night and it was looking as if she'd have to defend herself alone. So, by six o'clock, she was eyeing the broken window in the dining room with an empty wine bottle near her left hand and two of the remaining kitchen knives resting on her lap. Her mood was so dark that she decided to requisition another bottle - only for martial use, of course. But it would have to be emptied somehow...

A little later, as Liv raised the newly-opened bottle to her lips, a sudden tap on the patio doors surprised her enough to let some of the wine cascade down the front of her tracksuit top.

"Shit," she groaned and, relinquishing the wine, snatched up both knives.

Even without peering into the darkness outside, she knew it had to be Graham because her assailants were not, so far, in the habit of knocking before they burst in.

"Liv," cried a voice. "It's me."

So, yes, it was him – whoever and whatever he was.

"Let me in," he urged, banging a frustrated fist on the glass.

Fortunately, since the patio door was toughened glass, he would need more than a fist to break it. Though, if he was really keen, she reckoned he could gain entry through the broken window that he had boarded up himself after the previous night's incursion.

She moved across to stand at the glass door, until her face was level with his.

"What's wrong, Liv?" he cried. "Just let me in."

The story of the three little pigs sprang bizarrely into her head as she snatched up her phone and found the number for Grace's cell.

"I'm calling the police," she yelled at him.

"What? But it's me... Graham," he replied, looking utterly bewildered.

"I don't trust you," she cried, before retreating from the dining room into the living room to avoid hearing his continuing pleas. Setting down the knives beside her on the sofa, she considered following through with her threat. But surely Grace was no more trustworthy than he was.

A moment later, he had moved around to the living room window.

"What's changed?" he shouted. "What's changed? Because you trusted me enough last night when I fielded a bloody bullet for you."

Despite her uncertainty, she went to the window. "You lied to me," she accused. "You're not with the police · Grace told me."

"Grace?" he protested. "You don't even like Grace · and you certainly shouldn't believe anything she tells you."

"She checked up on you," retorted Liv. "And you're not undercover police, are you?"

"What? Do you think there's some kind of register where anyone can just look up undercover police?" he scoffed. "Don't be daft – she's lying to you."

"But why would she lie?" wailed Liv, scratching away the tears that were starting to roll down her cheeks. And she hated him for that because Liv Fisher never, ever cried. She'd weathered the despair of the beach, the terror of the wine bar and the house break-in, only for his lies to eat away at her last shred of hope.

"I trusted you," she snarled, putting her face against the glass only a few millimetres away from him. Her eyes bored into his as she demanded: "So, just tell me: did you lie to me, or not?"

The slight hesitation before his response told her more than enough. Thus the answer, when it came, was no surprise.

"It was just a small lie, Liv," he replied. "But it doesn't change anything between us. We trust each other."

"Well, I definitely don't trust you," she declared.

Before he could say any more, she swept the long, dust-encrusted drapes across the window.

"You need to listen to me, Liv," he entreated.

But Liv had heard enough and she just needed to think. Grace might not be a friend but she appeared to be right about Graham. He had lied to her – and she'd had more than enough of that. She'd hoped he was different, but apparently not. But then, Grace... How had Grace come back into her life?

After the beach, she would have phoned the police – except they had arrived almost at once. How? Had some neighbour summoned them? But neither the beach nor the house was overlooked by even the nearest neighbouring properties. So, how did Grace, etc get there so fast? Right now, Grace was no more trustworthy than Graham. Liv could, of course, just dial 999. Then whoever turned up would be the genuine article – the real police. Except, Liv's previous encounters with the real police had never ended especially well…

20

When the world's most irritating doorbell sounded, Liv assumed it was Graham trying a more conventional approach. It wasn't. It was Grace, who was either clairvoyant, or had someone watching the house. And Grace hadn't come alone.

The instant Liv opened the door, two men she remembered from earlier pushed past her carrying an unconscious Graham. There was a cut and darkening bruise on his temple.

"What have you done to him?" gasped Liv.

"Nothing much - yet," said Grace brightly. "We're just going to ask him a few more questions."

But the moment she slammed the door shut, Grace's cheery grin vanished and she started barking orders.

"Take him into the kitchen and wake him up," she told her companions.

While Liv looked on, a little shocked, Graham was swiftly tied to a straight-backed kitchen chair and doused with a bucket of water. Suddenly wide awake, he took in the room at a glance, but his gaze focussed upon Grace.

"Oh shit," he murmured. "You're *that* Grace..."

"Hello, Graham," said Grace, with what sounded like genuine pleasure.

Staring, at Liv, Graham cried: "Get out, Liv, get out now."

To Liv's dismay, one of Graham's captors delivered a sharp slap across his face.

"You know her?" said Liv, puzzled. "You know Grace?"

"Just get out, Liv," he pleaded, before a punch to the body struck him.

Though he opened his mouth to protest, a fist to the stomach swiftly silenced him. After that, he just groaned, as another blow followed and then one to the face, which opened up a narrow cut under his right eye.

"Grace? What are you doing?" cried Liv.

"We're questioning him."

"But not like that!" protested Liv. "You haven't even asked him anything yet."

"Just warming him up," grinned Grace.

Unsure how to react, Liv glared at Grace and demanded: "Who are you?"

"Save the questions, 'Crack', because you're not in charge here," warned Grace.

Even as Liv was eyeing the wooden block containing the remaining kitchen knives, Grace muttered: "Better tie that bitch up too."

Shocked by the sudden change in her circumstances, Liv scarcely moved a muscle as her hands were hauled roughly behind her back and secured with some sort of plastic tie. All she could do was glower impotently at Grace and bitterly regret not trusting her first instinct about her. But it was poor Graham, who had already taken a bullet in her cause, that was paying for her mistake.

Soon he was stripped to the waist to endure more punishment and she was forced to watch. When she squeezed her eyes shut, Grace growled: "Keep watching, 'Crack', or they'll hit him harder."

Opening her eyes, Liv winced to see that the bullet wound on his torso had split open as a result of the pounding. And her eyes recorded every savage cut and trickle of blood, every dark red welt and bruise... every shuddering blow. Hot, infuriating tears dribbled down her cheeks. But how could she not weep at the savage punishment being inflicted? A glance at Grace's smug expression told her all she needed to know.

"Time for the questions now, I think," remarked Grace.

Though Graham had set a brave face against the withering onslaught, Liv reckoned that he wouldn't hold out for long. He was not a hard man, who could take a beating and then fight his way out of a tight corner. Whoever he was truly working for, it was crystal clear to her now that he was simply an investigator who had been employed to unravel a mystery. Thus, after half an hour or so, he had told his captors all he knew. Not that it helped anyone much since he didn't actually possess the information they wanted.

When he passed out, by Liv's count, for the fourth time, they simply untied him and tossed him down the steps into the old cellar whose door led off the kitchen. That cellar was one place Liv hadn't yet explored. On the initial inspection after her arrival, she had been discouraged by the stench of damp and decay, not to mention the scrabbling of small creatures. At that point she had beaten a hasty retreat and closed the door on it.

Once Grace had finished with Graham, she turned her attention to Liv.

"So, dear Olivia," she said brightly, "it seems like it's down to you now."

But, if Grace imagined that the brutal assault on Graham would have weakened Liv's resolve, then she had clearly forgotten more about 'Crack' Fisher than she remembered.

"I've already told you I don't know anything," said Liv, even though there were a few things which she wasn't willing to share with Grace.

"You've seen what Danny and Ralph did to your friend," said Grace, employing a wheedling tone which grated with Liv at once. "Perhaps there's something you know from the past but haven't yet remembered. So, think about it, 'Crack', because this is your last chance."

"There's nothing," declared Liv. "I barely ever talked to my parents. You must know that. They disowned me. How could I possibly know what all this is about?"

"How could you not know?" countered Grace. "Living in this house all those years, only a fool wouldn't have picked up on what they were doing."

"Yeh, a fool, or someone who didn't give a shit what they were doing."

"We'll soon find out," threatened Grace. "I could say that I regret what's going to happen now, but we both know there was no love lost between us back in the day. You were such a bitch to me. Did you think I'd forgotten that?"

Glaring back at her, Liv said: "Oh, I really hoped you hadn't."

"There were so many times I wanted to give you a smack in the mouth for all your taunts..."

"Except... you were just too shit-scared of me, weren't you?" snarled Liv.

"Not now, though," said Grace.

"Alright then, go for it," challenged Liv.

So, Grace did and started by tearing off Liv's blouse and jeans.

"I bet you wanted to do that when you were fifteen," taunted Liv, while Grace's two helpers, Danny and Ralph, secured her to the chair in her bra and knickers. Both grinned at the tantalising glimpse of her breasts and Grace too looked on with evident anticipation. There was no doubt that her desire to hurt her captive came straight from the heart. When Liv ignored Grace's first question, she received a blow to the face from her fellow alumna. From then on, Liv's intransigent silence produced an escalating level of persuasion from Danny and Ralph.

Even when their initial assault yielded no results, Grace must have believed that it was only a matter of time. Since Graham had buckled after half an hour, she must have believed that even Liv wouldn't last much longer than that. Grace's assumption, though perfectly reasonable, was utterly flawed, however, because Liv, unlike Graham, was a warrior. Physical pain meant nothing to a woman who'd endured plenty in her life.

Living on the streets for two years meant being prepared to use a blade and be cut by one. It meant dishing out elbows to the ribs, neck or face and learning to take them too. No outcry, no fuss and definitely no tears. Just stern-faced resolve. True, the first couple of blows hurt Liv because she had gone a little soft in the weeks since she lost her job. But the muscle was still there and the sinews, ever-willing to strain until they tore. And, if it came to it, she had plenty of blood to spare.

After the interrogation earned them nothing, in their rage they hurled her bruised and bleeding body down the steps into the cellar and locked the door. Liv, relieved to reach the bottom of the stone steps with no bones broken, turned her attention to what might be sharing the cellar with her – and she didn't mean Graham. When a snuffling sounded close to her head, she lashed out with a fist but only succeeded in smashing her knuckles into the brick wall.

"Shit," she muttered, because it had just occurred to her that rats could probably see in the dark as well as she could.

21

During the day, Hal had observed several comings and goings at the house but, by the evening, it had suddenly gone very quiet and Hal didn't know whether that was good news or bad. It was sure getting busy in there though... The man who'd stayed the previous night had finally returned, only to get involved in an argument with the Fisher woman.

Though Hal heard only a few snatches of their conversation, the tone and volume of their exchanges told him that these two people were not enemies.

However, before their differences could be thrashed out, a car drove up and parked on the road. Two men and a woman made their way to the house and quickly overpowered the guy who'd been having the argument. Though he protested, they hauled him roughly with them to the front door and rang the bell. It was an incongruous scene, Hal thought, as they waited for the door to open. Hard to tell exactly what the hell was going on, he reflected, when you were outside and halfway up a tree. Nonetheless, the rapid turn of events gave him plenty to think about.

Over the years, bitter combat experience had taught him to pay close attention to how people moved as well as what they actually did. So, it was crystal clear to him that the three figures who disappeared into the house, hauling Liv's friend with them, were not there for a social visit. Their body language dripped with antagonism. They were there to persuade, to bully and, if necessary, to hurt... Hal had witnessed such demeanour many times before, though he'd hoped never to see it again.

The awkward question was: what should he do about it? And the answer was far from straightforward. However, since it seemed that they were now all shut up for the night, whatever he was thinking of doing, it would have to wait until morning. As he settled down in the chill darkness, he remembered that Brad would be there very soon and that thought gave him fresh hope. Because right now he was alone and, despite his service years as a sniper, he had rarely felt so isolated.

With his brother watching his back, the whole surveillance op. would be much easier. Surveillance op? Jeez, how easily he was slipping into work mode... because this was never supposed to be surveillance – or any sort of op. The plan, in so far as he had a plan, was to try to talk to the Fisher's estranged daughter and see whether he could reach some agreement with her. But there were so many other people getting involved now that Hal was beginning to wonder how he could ever get the woman alone.

With any luck, the newly-arrived vultures would only stay the night and then piss off in the morning. I mean, Jeez, how many other relatives could there be? Maybe he should abandon the house and daughter completely in favour of a visit to the Fisher lawyers – though he'd yet to find out who they were. He'd discuss it with Brad, when he arrived, but he guessed that it was always going to be a waiting game. He wished he'd stayed with Lisa. Lovely, warm Lisa...

173

22

"Are you alright?" hissed Graham, from the far side of the dark cellar.

Making no immediate response to his croaked enquiry, Liv closed her eyes to shut out the regret. Somehow, her mistrust of Graham caused her far more distress than her own damaged ribs, lacerated arms, half-closed eyes and bruised face. In her own defence, she never believed she could count on any man. Moreover, in the past two years, she struggled to trust anyone · of any gender. But even so, if she had just let Graham in, perhaps all this could have been avoided.

Her prolonged silence drew Graham to her. Of course it did, because he was a solid guy and probably cared how badly she was hurt. The sound of him crawling towards her filled her with dread. What could she possibly say to him? In the end, grateful for the darkness to hide her shame, she said nothing. By the time he inched over, her eyes had adjusted to the gloom and, though she tried to shrink away from his outstretched hand, the cellar wall stopped her.

When he rested a comforting hand on her shoulder, Liv instinctively swatted it away. If he expected an apology, he was going to be disappointed. Because Liv Fisher didn't apologise – ever · just like she never wept... except, in the past two days, she seemed to have cried a hell of a lot.

"You look awful," he said.

"Not helping," growled Liv. "Anyway, you can't even see me."

"I can imagine what I can't see – and I heard what they did to you."

"I'm good," she said.

"That's good then," he said. "That's... good."

"You alright?" she enquired grudgingly.

"Fine."

But the tremor in his voice suggested that he was far from 'fine' and, since she'd witnessed every blow of his interrogation, she knew exactly how not very fine he was.

"It's no disgrace to give in to such a beating," he consoled her.

"I didn't tell them a damn thing," she replied bluntly.

"No, of course you didn't," he murmured, and she could hear the rueful smile in his tone.

"She'd have had to kill me," added Liv. "And she knew it."

"Yes."

"So, she clearly wasn't ready to do that yet."

"No."

Liv feared that if his monosyllabic responses continued, they might earn him a second beating. So, lowering her voice, she enquired: "Any ideas about getting out of here?"

"I don't think you need to whisper," he said, "'cos these walls are pretty thick."

"What about the rats?" she muttered.

"I don't think they're listening," he replied, grinning back at her.

"I meant I didn't want to attract them," she grumbled and, without thinking, punched him on the shoulder.

"Christ, Liv!" he protested. "What's the matter with you?"

But that was a question Liv reckoned would require a very, very long answer which he was never going to get. However, in lieu of an apology, she explained: "I don't like rats... or spiders, for that matter."

"What? You're fine with having the shit kicked out of you, but you're scared of rats?" he croaked, as he attempted to laugh.

"I'm not scared," insisted Liv. "Did I say I was scared?"

But Graham's long sigh spared her any further embarrassment.

"How far did you get today with your search?" he asked.

Ironic, she thought, that his focus shifted swiftly to the very same thing that Grace sought by rather more brutal methods.

"Why aren't you angry with me?" she asked abruptly.

"Because I'm not angry," he told her, "just disappointed."

"That's got to be a line from a film," she groaned.

"Look, I understand," he said. "You didn't trust me. I get it. And that's more my fault than yours, because I wasn't straight with you. But do you see now that we need to work together?"

"I suppose," she conceded.

"So, did you discover anything useful today?" he said.

"Aside from the fact that I'm a piss-poor judge of character?"

"Yeh, aside from that."

"Well, I searched the first floor rooms but found nothing," she reported.

"I don't suppose it occurred to you to try tapping at any of the walls," mused Graham.

She gave a grunt of frustration at the memory. "I tapped, I banged and I fucking hammered my fist against them," she told him. "I found nothing. No safe. No magic door. No hidden compartment. Nothing."

"Your parents must have kept all the account information somewhere," he told her. "And I'd expect there to be a fair bit of cash as well. So, where's everything gone?"

Though she'd lived in the house half her life, Liv had no idea where anything important might be hidden. At the time, she supposed, she simply didn't care.

"We've got nothing," she murmured.

"True," he agreed, "but then, neither have they."

The bald truth of his observation offered Liv little consolation but, after a period of silence punctuated only by the rats, she said: "One thing I still don't understand."

"Just one?" he replied. "There's a whole shedload of things puzzling me."

"Who's Grace working for?" she asked, "because even I don't believe it's the police."

When Graham made no reply, she stared at him as a random thought struck her.

"Wait, you recognised her – in the kitchen – when you first came round, you looked at her and said: "You?""

"Did I?" he muttered.

"Oh, shit..." moaned Liv. "If you're going to keep lying to me, you might as well kill me now."

"I'm trying to keep you alive," he protested. "Knowing too much might kill you."

"Why don't you let me worry about that?" she declared. "All I want from you, Graham, is the truth. Exactly how are you involved in all this? Because, if you don't tell me, I swear I'll never trust you again."

With a sigh, he said: "Liv, I've already told you: I was hired to do some forensic accounting to investigate the cartel's accounts which your parents have been managing."

"So what were you supposed to do with the account information if you found it?"

"I report what I've found to my SWROCU contact. He'll pass it on to his superiors, SWROCU will close the accounts and confiscate the proceeds. And that'll be that."

"Alright, so, who is Grace working for?"

"I don't know."

"But you know her."

"I've... come across her before," he conceded,

"But she's not working for the cartel?"

"I assume not," he replied, "because they must surely already know their own account numbers."

"And Mark was working with you?"

"I just don't understand how Mark happened to find you on the beach," he said. "He was supposed to be..."

"Supposed to be what?" said Liv. "I said no more lies."

"Well, at the time, he was supposed to be looking out for me," revealed Graham sheepishly.

"Oh."

"Yeh, 'Oh'."

"But, whoever was behind all the attacks clearly wasn't fussed about any information I might have. They can't need me at all – and, if it's not you and it's not Grace, who the hell is it?"

"Truly, Liv, I don't know."

"But that's three separate attempts to kill me," concluded Liv, shivering at the implication of that. Then she remembered Slough station. "No, make that four. So, Graham, this is someone who really wants me dead."

"Given what little I know, I just can't imagine who that could be," he said, "unless there's someone else that you've pissed off in a big way."

"There's hundreds of bastards I've pissed off," said Liv. "But in recent years they're mostly spotty, sex-obsessed teens. A few parents too, I suppose, and definitely some other staff. In case you hadn't noticed, Graham, pissing people off is what I do best. I'd have thought a canny investigator like you would've picked that up by now."

"Alright, but can you think of anyone you've pissed off who might actually want you dead?" he asked. "What about someone with a grudge from your younger days · apart from dear old Grace, of course. And maybe just those at the top of the list to start with..."

"I don't know. I can't imagine that anyone from my past would hate me enough to go to the trouble of killing me years later. Most of them were off their heads anyway, so I'd be surprised if they even remembered me at all. Anyway, you said it was likely hired assassins. Most guys I rolled with struggled to organise their next fix, never mind hire an assassin. This seems so... personal."

"So, what are you thinking then?" asked Graham.

Thinking? Liv wasn't entirely sure she was thinking of much at all. And, as she worked through it in her head, she was left with no even remotely plausible explanation.

When she said nothing, Graham tried to fill the silence. "Let's put aside your unknown enemy for a moment, shall we?" he suggested.

"Yeh, why not?" she sighed.

"The immediate threat is coming from Grace who has, so far, stopped short of trying to kill you. But, if she thinks you're no longer any use to her employers, she could decide to finish you herself – given how she already feels about you."

"I've always been popular," said Liv, with a dark grin. But when he showed no sign of being amused, she added: "Alright, Grace is the immediate threat. So, what can we do about that?"

"I've been working on a way out," he said simply.

"What do you mean: a way out?"

"Come on," he said and began to crawl away across the filthy cellar floor.

Liv thought he must be deranged for, as far as she could recall, he was heading for a brick wall. But faced with the prospect of staring down a horde of hungry rats on her own, she scrambled hastily after him, though she felt every cut and bruise as she did so. Sure enough, when he came to a halt, he was facing the outer wall of the house.

"That, Graham, is a solid brick wall," she told him. "We're not getting through that – and, even if we did, it's just the cliff out there and a very long drop to the sea. I know. I've been down there... in case you've forgotten."

"Ah, but there's a drainage channel through the wall," he explained.

"Yeh, a pipe, but it's hardly big enough for a rat to crawl through, let alone us," she retorted. "Don't forget, I lived here and there were plenty of times I needed a fast way out. So, trust me, that pipe's far too narrow."

But it turned out that Graham, despite his injuries, had not been idle during his brief sojourn in the cellar.

"Who said anything about a pipe?" he chuckled. "Have you been down here recently?"

"Of course, I pop down here all the time," she replied gruffly. "You know, to chat to the rats and spiders."

"Yes, alright, so you haven't. But you know about the erosion."

"You think?" scorned Liv.

When he clasped her hand, she tensed, but managed to resist her first instinct, which was to lash out with a fist. Next moment, he held her palm up to the wall where she felt a cool, gentle breeze caress her skin. In the gloom, she moved her face closer to the wall and gasped when she saw how it was riven with deep cracks. The drain pipe she remembered from her childhood was no longer there at all. Indeed, it appeared as if the whole pipe, and several bricks attached to it, were missing. She hadn't noticed because it was pitch black outside, but now it occurred to her that she could clearly hear the waves washing against the cliff below.

Hope sparked for an instant, until hard reality struck.

"Alright, there's a big hole," she agreed. "But it doesn't matter because we can't just dive down into the water from here."

Even in the darkness, her eyes registered his smug grin.

"We don't have to," he explained. "Because there's an old inspection ladder that goes part way down."

"You're kidding. Surely that'll have rusted away."

"I kid you not, Olivia Fisher. It's rusty, but I've pulled at it hard and it still seems OK."

"Seriously? You're suggesting that we climb down into the sea at night on some rusty ladder that's probably over a hundred years old."

"Or we could just stay here with the rats and spiders," he said. "And Grace..."

"You're mad," she told him. "And I must be too, even to listen to you..."

"But?"

"But nothing. If you're so keen, you can go first."

"I was going to suggest ladies first," said Graham.

"We both know I'm no lady. So, go for it."

"OK. I'll go first," he agreed.

"Are you sure about this?" she enquired. "We're going to get very wet and very, very cold."

"But we'll be out of here," he argued. "As soon as I'm most of the way down, I'll give you a shout and you can follow."

The ladder, he explained, as he put his head and shoulders through the hole, was offset slightly to the left but was within easy reach. Wasting no more time, he grasped the ladder and hauled himself out, swinging a leg around in search of one of the iron rungs. After a wayward first attempt, he managed to locate one with the toe of his shoe and, a couple of moments later, he had clambered out onto the ladder.

With a posse of interested rats gathering behind her, Liv had to admit the ladder looked secure enough. Glancing back at the rodents, sniffing the salty air, she felt mightily relieved to be leaving their territory. When she turned back to Graham, he gave her a thumbs-up and began his descent.

"Be careful," she hissed at him – wholly unnecessarily since Graham was careful by nature. Not that any of that mattered because, surprisingly quietly, the ladder abruptly parted company with the cliff face and took Graham with it.

23

Dawn on New Year's Day

All night, Liv had squatted on the cellar floor, heedless of spiders and grimly swatting aside any rat who ventured within biting range. Graham was gone and there was no point in lamenting it. Except, what else was there to do - dive out into the sea and join him?

And she couldn't help dwelling on the fact that it was partly her fault for not trusting him in the first place. What sort of fucked-up person would spurn a man who, despite his lies and his 'mental health issues', had saved her life at least twice. She could have given him the benefit of the doubt. Instead, she was at the mercy of the grotesque Grace Walter - whom she'd disliked with a vengeance at school and cared a great deal less for now.

At the time, she'd been wallowing so deep in self-pity that she hadn't realised how foolish she was being. She could see it clearly enough now though – when it was far too late. But then, this cock-up was right up there with all those other critical moments in her life when she had unerringly chosen the wrong path.

Bad decisions had gotten her sacked, because, even if that sixth form rapist *was* most definitely a wanker, she shouldn't have told him so. And she certainly shouldn't have applied the same term – forcefully and repeatedly - to his parents. Even after all that, she might have salvaged her fragile career if she hadn't called the Chair of Governors the 'biggest fucking wanker of them all'. And, of course, typically, once she was suspended, she wasn't even able to support the girl at the centre of it all.

So, she had come to regret her whole giant sequence of misjudgements. And now she regretted the loss of Graham but there was nothing she could do about that either. Eventually, his loyal corpse, grey and bloated, would wash up somewhere further along the coast. His body would still bear the scars of the beating he'd endured. Shit, what a mess...

It must have been light for hours by the time Liv received a visit from Grace's cheerless confederates. If they looked suitably astonished by the gaping hole in the wall, they were even more surprised by Graham's absence · which was all too obvious in a cellar illuminated by the bright sunshine. One of them – Danny, she thought – even peered, bemused, out of the hole, as if Graham might be clinging to the cliff face below. He wasn't. She'd already looked.

In dismay, they hauled Liv back up to the kitchen, where Grace seemed less than pleased by the news that she had lost half of her human assets. Nonetheless, it appeared to Liv that her captor might finally have accepted that she knew nothing useful. Whilst that might mean an end to any further brutal interrogation, it also meant, as Graham had pointed out, that she might now be expendable as far as Grace was concerned. Well, Grace could join the queue with all the other lunatic sods that had already tried · and failed · to take her life...

Her worst fears were confirmed when Grace told Danny: "You might as well take her back down there and drop her out of that hole - a tragic accident for the bereaved daughter." She gave a dark chuckle. "Very appropriate that, following her parents into the sea."

Though Liv tried to struggle free from Danny's grasp, he was a strong bastard and she was only given a stay of execution by the jaunty intervention of the musical doorbell. For the first time since her arrival, Liv actually welcomed the annoying sound. This time, however, Grace appeared willing to wait it out.

"Whoever it is will give up and go away," she said.

But, as a precaution, she pressed the muzzle of her pistol to Liv's forehead and growled: "I swear, 'Crack', if you make a sound, all you'll do is get your visitor killed as well as you."

Eventually, the trill of the doorbell came to a reluctant end and Grace nodded with satisfaction. But her grin vanished when the bell started up again with a different, though equally irritating, tune.

"What do we do?" hissed Danny.

"We wait," snapped Grace. "No-one's going to hang about for a third ring."

When the second melody finally faded away, the four of them in the kitchen held their breath in tense silence. Clearly Grace didn't want to tempt fate by speaking too soon, but even Liv had to agree that it was unlikely that anyone would be so eager to talk to her that they would ring again. After a few more silent minutes, even Grace sighed with relief.

"Right," she told Danny, "get on with – oh, fuck no!"

Another cheerful ditty had launched from the persistent doorbell so, thought Liv, whoever was at the door was really pushing their luck.

"Right," Grace told her comrades, "I'll go to the door with her and you two keep out of sight."

The moment Danny released his iron grip on her arms, Liv tried to slip past Grace but only managed half a metre before she felt the gun barrel jammed against the back of her neck.

"Easy now, 'Crack'. You're going to get rid of whoever it is," Grace told her. "And you're going to be very convincing because, remember what I said: you get it wrong and they'll suffer the same fate as you. Clear?"

Glaring back at her, Liv reflected that she could have prevented all this unpleasantness if only she'd just bludgeoned Grace to death years ago with her hockey stick. Though, in truth, it wasn't for lack of trying. But instead of that happy outcome, she was now obliged to follow Grace's instructions and answer the front door. Her mind though, was a blank because what was she going to say? She was still in her bra and knickers...

"I've got hardly anything on," she complained.

"Yeh, well that'll give the persistent sod a quick thrill, won't it?" growled Grace. "Now, open the damned door."

With the gun pressed into the small of her back, Liv's intimate knowledge of the body's structure afforded her an informed insight into the catastrophic damage a bullet to the spine at point blank range would cause. Hence, she opted to open the front door and, in any case, a tiny part of her was just slightly curious to know who would bother ringing the wretched doorbell so many times – and on New Year's Day. It turned out, however, that both she and Grace had underestimated the commitment of the man from the council.

"You're still here," observed the inspector incredulously, before Liv could even say a word. "I told you I'd be back. And why are you answering the door in your underwear?"

Liv couldn't think of an appropriate response but Grace, with a vain attempt at a smile, explained: "I'm with the police and we're investigating this woman. You'll have to call back later."

But a man who rang the doorbell three times was not to be so easily discouraged.

"This is a matter of health and safety," he insisted, "and that trumps everything else. Do you think I'd bother coming round here on my day off if it wasn't? When no-one was living here, I wasn't so worried. But now, I want you all out of there."

A frown flitted across Grace's face before she replied cordially: "Why don't you come in and talk us through it then."

"I'm not crossing that threshold," he declared. "That house is a death trap."

"That's so much truer than you know," muttered Liv, prompting Grace to dig the gun harder into her back.

"Exactly who are you anyway?" he demanded of Grace. "Don't you know this building's unsafe?"

"And you are?" enquired Grace.

"I asked first," asserted the council official.

"I told you, I'm with the police," replied Grace.

Liv winced at her tone suspecting that the inspector, for all his experience of health and safety, had no idea on what thin ice he was dancing.

"You're not in uniform," observed the official.

"Heard of plain clothes?" suggested Grace, her impatience building.

"Well, here's my authority," he said, whipping out his credentials like a gunfighter of the old wild west. "Where's yours?"

"Oh, shit," muttered Liv, as she felt the pressure of the gun barrel ease.

Grace, as Liv already knew to her cost, was not a patient woman. Nor, it appeared, was she one to refuse a challenge. A moment later, she levelled her pistol at the council official and told him: "Either you die out there on the door step, little man, or you come inside. Which is it to be?"

Whether the council man would have called Grace's bluff or not, they never discovered because fragments of brick and splinters from the door were suddenly flying in all directions. Perhaps it was the shock that prompted Grace to fire her pistol but, sadly for the hapless local government official, he was the one who was directly in her line of fire.

Even as he fell, open-mouthed and clutching his chest, a bullet grazed Liv's shoulder and she dived back inside – as did Grace. Several more bullets struck the door as Grace slammed it shut.

"What was all that about?" shouted Danny.

The three of them stood in the hallway. Well four, if you counted Ralph, who had somehow contrived to field a stray bullet and was leaning against the wall, shivering, with a bloodied hand pressed just above his groin.

"You alright?" asked Grace, in a voice that suggested she didn't much care either way.

"Course I'm not," gasped Ralph, staring down at the wound from which blood was steadily dribbling.

"Are you good to go, or not?" she demanded bluntly.

Ralph glared back at her and snarled: "I dunno, do I? Are you gonna to help me, or what?"

With a shrug, Grace said: "OK." and shot him between the eyes - because Grace was helpful like that... But no, definitely not a patient woman. Watching her late colleague slide to the floor, she grumbled: "Careless sod..."

"Who was that shooting at us?" asked Danny.

"They weren't shooting at *us*," retorted Grace. "They were shooting at 'Crackhead' here. It's probably those wankers from the wine bar fiasco but, luckily for me, they're a lousy shot."

Ralph though, Liv thought, had not been quite so lucky.

Darting a cursory glance at Liv's cut shoulder, Grace added: "They all want what we want but it looks like some of them aren't much bothered about talking to you."

"As I recall, you were just about to execute me," remarked Liv.

"Yeh, trust you to come out of it with just a scratch," complained Grace. "Just like at school, eh? The rest of us would end up with broken bones, but you'd just have a few cuts and bruises. Sooner or later your luck had to run out though, eh?"

Yeh, thought Liv, because just now she was on a really hot streak of good luck.

"Still," mused Grace, "maybe, if our rivals want you dead, your value's gone up a bit. I reckon I'd better keep you alive a bit longer."

"Marvellous," sighed Liv. "So, what happens now?"

"We've got all we need," declared Grace. "We've got the house and we've got you. So, we carry on looking – and you can help."

"And if I don't want to help?" said Liv.

"You should be grateful you're not lying outside the front door full of holes," snarled Grace. "But, if you don't want to help then Danny can take you back down to the cellar."

"But there's still that big hole in the wall," he muttered.

Staring at Liv, Grace scoffed: "She won't jump out of it, 'cos she knows her friend, Graham, is most likely floating somewhere along the English Channel by now."

Biting her lip, Liv decided she'd had more than enough of Grace and replied: "The cellar it is then."

"Whatever," said Grace.

So, Danny led Liv through the kitchen and back down to the cellar with its rats, spiders and very large hole. Tossing her torn clothing down the steps after her, he slammed the door. To Liv, the sound of the key turning in the lock was as good as a death sentence. She could have feigned co-operation, but then co-operation was hardly her middle name.

Feeling suddenly rather cold, she retrieved her clothes and wrapped the remains of her blouse around her, before wriggling into her jeans. Inevitably, she was drawn to the light and stumbled over to the hole in the wall. There, she supposed, the daylight would at least enable her to see the rats and spiders coming. Inevitably though, her restless eyes explored the shadows and discovered a stunning array of webs caught by the sun's rays. Some could have been fine-spun gauze, but others were highly-crafted networks and somewhere, close by, their hungry creators waited.

Sitting there, on the thick layer of dust and debris, she dropped her head into her hands because, much though she hated herself for it, she actually missed Graham. Locked in the cellar again, but this time without his reassuring support, she was utterly bereft of ideas. She was also ravenous, because she hadn't eaten since finishing some of the pizza the previous afternoon. Moreover, although the hole in the wall let in plenty of light, it also allowed the damp wind to scour through the cellar. Liv felt the chill on her battered body as she sat contemplating her rather limited options.

How long she continued to sit there, Liv couldn't tell, but she reckoned it must have been more than an hour. Eventually, punching her thigh in frustration, she muttered: "Snap out of it, you useless bitch. Nobody else can help you. You're on your own, so just make something happen..."

When the random thought flitted into her head, she was inclined to dismiss it at once. But it lingered there, like a smelly old sock which you can only ignore for so long. After a while, she thought: why not? Because it could hardly make her situation any worse – well, unless they killed her. So, easing herself up onto her feet, she rubbed her stiff limbs and cast around for a suitable tool.

Moments later, with a half brick in her hand, she stumbled across to the foot of the steps, aiming a savage kick at a pair of rats on the way. After several deep breaths, she began to climb the steps and, once at the top, smashed the brick hard against the door. Though it scarcely made a mark, she hoped that at least the noise would attract some attention.

It didn't.

In fact nothing suggested that Grace or Danny had even noticed. So, gripping the brick more tightly, she pounded it against the door again, harder – and again, as hard as she could. After a pause of a few minutes, she started again. She found it helped a lot to imagine that the door post was Grace's head. Finally, though her fingers were sore and bleeding, her efforts elicited a response. From the other side of the door, Danny barked: "Shut the fuck up, or I'll come in and shut you up."

Elated that she had at least got their attention, Liv cried: "Hey! I've remembered something. Something Grace will want to know."

Hearing Danny's footsteps retreat across the kitchen floor, she sank down onto the top step, exhausted. After a worryingly long silence, she heard his boots cross the tiled floor once again and the sound of the key turning in the lock rekindled her hopes.

Swinging the door open, Danny stood over her and demanded: "What? What've you remembered?"

"I know where the cash might be," Liv told him, "But I'm not saying anymore till I've had some food – because I'm starving."

"Tell me first," said Danny. "Then you'll get something to eat."

"Not a chance," insisted Liv. "I want feeding first, or I might as well stay down here."

"Get her something from the fridge," ordered Grace, materialising in the kitchen doorway.

"There's nothing in that fridge," muttered Liv. "You should order a pizza."

"Not happening," snapped Grace. "Check the freezer, Danny."

After only a few minutes, he retrieved a frozen loaf of bread and, taking out a knife, sliced open the bag. When he slammed it down on the kitchen worktop, it smashed into several chunks of sliced bread.

"Defrost some of that," he told Liv, pointing to the microwave.

"That's not proper food," she argued.

In response, Grace snarled: "It's that, or you can go back downstairs, because I'm not playing games with you."

Resisting the temptation to observe that Grace had only ever been pretty average at games, Liv selected a frozen lump containing three slices of bread fused together. Tossing it into the microwave to defrost, she waited until a sequence of beeps announced that it had finished. Reluctantly, she extracted the misshapen, half-defrosted object from the microwave and stared at it in disgust.

"That's all you get," said Grace. "Take it, or piss off back to the cellar."

With a grunt of resignation, Liv picked up the soggy bread and, though the centre was still half-frozen, she reckoned she was probably hungry enough to eat anything, Eating around the icy centre bit, she then tossed the remnant into the sink.

"Happy?" enquired Grace.

"Positively bloody ecstatic," replied Liv.

"So what is it you've just 'remembered'?" asked Grace. "And it'd better be good, Crack..."

"When I was searching upstairs for anything that my parents... you know..."

"We know," growled Grace. "Get on with it."

"In their bedroom I think there might be a hidden compartment behind the wardrobe."

"Bollocks," commented Grace. "You must've got that straight out of some film. Secret compartment, my arse."

"I didn't get round to searching it," said Liv, "but it looked like a hiding place so, I'm sure there must be something there. Otherwise, why would it even exist?"

"If it does exist," argued Grace. But, after a pause, she added: "Right then, show us it now."

Liv led the way upstairs, closely followed by Grace and Danny, and took them into her parents' bedroom. In the bare wardrobe, Liv could still see the impression left by her fist.

"Danny..." invited Grace.

Having brought up a rolling pin from the kitchen, he proceeded to batter the wall with it and, to Liv's surprise, he soon made swift inroads into the plasterboard wall. Dusty chunks of the stuff flew off in all directions because, clearly, Danny was the man for demolition duty. And who knew what damage such a simple culinary implement could do?

Grace stared at the widening hole in disbelief while Liv was grinning, because she had actually been right. Chuckling as she recalled a host of TV programmes and films where some hapless protagonist – often female - discovered a hidden body behind a false wall, she sniffed at the musty air and was relieved that she couldn't detect any unpleasant odours emanating from the space behind the wardrobe.

But Danny was only half way down the wall when his progress was interrupted by a fresh outburst from the doorbell. Grace scowled and looked up at the ceiling and, for once, Liv had some sympathy. That door chime would try the patience of the proverbial saint – and Grace was certainly not one of those.

With a furious shake of the head, Grace snarled: "Who stands and rings the doorbell when there's a fucking corpse in the porch?"

"Well, I doubt it's another man from the council," remarked Liv.

"Right. Downstairs," ordered Grace. "Danny, you keep her in the kitchen this time."

Turning to Liv, she warned: "You keep quiet and stay with Danny, eh?"

While Grace went to the front door, weapon in hand, Liv waited in the kitchen. Danny lurked by the kitchen door keeping one eye on Grace, who was less than twenty metres away from him.

Liv was considering liberating a few more slices of the slowly-thawing bread scattered across the worktop, when Danny suddenly tumbled into the room and lay still. His forehead, she observed, was now sporting a newly-acquired hole and, before she could shutter her eyes, she couldn't help but notice the way the skin around the hole splayed out like a little red star.

Instinct persuaded her to duck down below the kitchen counter and wait. But no-one came in. As she remained hidden, Liv weighed up whether an enemy of Danny might possibly be her friend. But not necessarily, she concluded, particularly if it was the moron who had opened fire at the front porch. But then, how had someone gained entry to the house past Grace?

Her ruminating was soon interrupted by Grace calling to Danny from the hall,

"Bring the Fisher bitch through here right now," ordered Grace.

When the deathly-still form of Danny showed no sign of getting up to answer Grace's summons, Liv assumed the woman would come looking for him, none too pleased.

But Grace didn't do that. Instead, she yelled: "Danny, get out here!"

A few moments later, she exclaimed: "Oh, shit."

Straining to hear what was going on, Liv heard no more until there came a sudden splintering of wood and glass reminiscent of a window being well and truly shattered.

"Shit. What now?" she breathed.

Hearing footsteps approach from the hall, she kept her head down and flattened herself against the kitchen cabinets. If it was Grace, she would come looking. But, after only a few seconds, the owner of the footsteps retreated once more and Liv heard the creak of the stairs. Sometimes, she decided, you just had to take your chance. So she crept out of the kitchen and, with only a quick glance to check the stairwell, she made for the front door.

She had this one chance to get out. But what if the shooter was still outside? Unless it was he who had breached the house and shot Danny. But then, where was Grace? As quietly as she could, she eased the front door open a crack. A while back someone rang the doorbell, but now the porch was empty – apart from the resident body of the council man. Opening the door a little wider, she peered at the trees and bushes along the driveway whence she suspected the earlier shots had come. Though she couldn't see anyone, that meant nothing.

Hearing movement on the first floor landing and then the stairs, she decided she would have to make a run for it. Slipping through the doorway, she was greeted by three bullets in quick succession. She would have died there and then but for the council man who, unwittingly saved her when, in her haste to escape, she tripped over him and fell headlong.

Bruising her chin on the stone step, she ended up lying at one side of the porch. She was a rabbit in the headlights – two sets of headlights. If she continued on out, she was probably dead, but then Danny's killer must have heard the gunfire and would surely be hurtling downstairs to investigate. So, make a decision, Liv... devil, or deep blue sea?

Scrambling awkwardly back into the hall, she shut the door once more, fully expecting to find herself face to face with the new intruder. But there was no·one in the hall, or on the stair so, she fled back into the kitchen in search of a weapon – which was becoming a depressingly frequent occurrence. Since there had been a bit of a run on kitchen knives, she rummaged in the drawers for some other sharp implement but found nothing. On the floor she noticed the rolling pin in Danny's lifeless hand and commandeered that. Then, for good measure, she retrieved her half·brick from the cellar doorway. Two blunt instruments would have to suffice.

Just as she was about to leave the kitchen, she heard footfalls on the stairs, but was it Danny's killer, or Grace? Again, she waited behind the door with rolling pin raised. But, whoever descended the stairs didn't come back into the kitchen and, though Liv lingered in silence for a little longer, she heard nothing more. She could hardly stay in the kitchen for the rest of her life – though that, of course, might only be measured in minutes.

Damn it, she told herself: you're a strong, independent woman · though, admittedly, a rolling pin wasn't exactly the best look for a modern woman. But she also had a brick – or at least half a brick... What she wouldn't give just now to have a sleek, shiny javelin in her hand. Still, she'd just have to make do with a brick and a rolling pin. Switching the brick to her right hand, her slightly stronger throwing arm, she stepped out into the hall.

Both hall and stairs were empty but, when she peered into the living room, she discovered that another window was broken – well, more demolished than broken. But who had exited through it: Grace, or someone else? At the familiar sound of a glass chinking against a bottle, Liv swivelled around to face the drinks cabinet with her right arm poised to hurl the brick.

Beside the bar cabinet, in the large armchair, sat a smiling figure. In one hand was a glass half-filled with brandy and, in the other, was a handgun. But neither of those things really interested Liv at that moment because her attention was entirely focussed on the face of someone who should be dead.

24

The coast near Highcrest, early morning on 2nd January

When Graham hit the water, he was still clinging to a section of ladder, one end of which struck the seabed hard. By the time he released his grip, the impact had almost wrenched his shoulders out of their sockets. After that, he floundered around in the dark for several moments and sank under the chill waves. Though he was probably only in about ten feet of water, that was plenty to suck him down without trace. In his immediate panic, he thrashed his aching arms about and gulped down several mouthfuls of gritty seawater, until he remembered that he could swim.

When his feet reached the stony bottom, he thrust up to the surface, but his relief was soon swallowed whole by a brutal wave that swept out of the darkness to slam him against the base of the cliff. Head ringing, he blinked the stinging salt from his eyes and laboured to kick further out to sea on his back. For a time he trod the icy water, barely keeping himself afloat, while he sought in vain for a glimpse of some shoreline lights. But, with every moment, the cold was draining what little strength he possessed, while the waves kept buffeting him back inexorably towards the cliff face.

Again, he frog-kicked out to sea, managing a few more metres as he tried once again to orientate himself. At last, he was rewarded by the sight of Sunrise Heights above, where several lights still showed. Feeling that a westerly current was pushing him ever eastwards, he went with it and headed along the coast. Good luck, Liv, he thought, as he rolled over and changed to breaststroke. He was acutely aware that he would only be able to swim in his sodden clothes for perhaps another five minutes · ten at most. So, in that time, he needed to put as much distance between him and Sunrise Heights as possible.

As he recalled, the high cliff sloped down as it stretched eastwards and led to a long stretch of shingle beach. So, that was what he needed to aim for. But the chill water weakened him much faster than he anticipated and he was flagging before he could even make out the beach. His legs were sluggish and his arms flailed at the water. If he missed the beach, he'd be drawn further along the Solent until he would simply slip, exhausted, under the waves. But moments later, a knee scraped the gravel bottom and he staggered to his feet in waist-deep water. Knowing the shoreline must be close, he followed the sound of the breaking waves and saw an outcrop of sea-smoothed rocks only ten metres away.

Trudging ashore he flopped down onto the shingle, shuddering with cold. But, as he lay there exhausted and shivering in the dark, he knew he was safe at last. After a while – he had no idea how long – he found that a gentle but persistent alarm was nagging at him. A voice in his head suggested politely that exhaustion was not his friend because, if he lay there getting steadily colder for much longer, he'd never get up again. Forcing himself to get up onto his knees, he realised that the cold alone now was sapping his strength.

He needed to get off the beach lest he was spotted by someone at Sunrise Heights. But where to? Hiding would require some significant movement and he wasn't sure he was up to that. On the other hand, the voice of reason suggested, do you really want to die here on this bloody beach? A small, broken, part of him was sorely tempted because it would be far less effort just to stay there and let it all go. After all, it wouldn't be his fault; his nerves were shot through. Except, the irritating voice reminded him that he still had a job to finish...

"Sod the job," he groaned aloud. And then looked around sheepishly in case anyone had heard him. But no-one had heard, so it didn't count, did it?

"Come, you idle bastard," he muttered. "Get moving. Work those aching limbs and get yourself off this damned beach. Because you're Liv's only hope."

Ah yes, Liv · the poor sod who he dimly recalled was supposed to be escaping with him. Christ knew how he was going to get her out now. He'd scarcely escaped himself. Not that Liv would expect much from him because she knew he had issues · and he'd left her before... Slowly he scrambled towards some scrub and low trees just up from the beach. If he found a quiet hiding place, he could rest there for a few hours.

He must have been well-hidden because no-one found him – not even one of the dogs and there were plenty of those nosing about. Mind you, he probably smelled to them more like seaweed than an actual person. He slept for hours which, he supposed, was hardly surprising after the pounding he'd taken from both Grace and the sea. What time was it, he wondered? Habit made him glance at his left wrist but, of course, his interrogators had taken his Fitbit watch earlier on – along with his wallet. So, he had no money either. The gods were surely against him.

From where the sun was, he estimated it must be late afternoon and many hours since he had left Liv. In his current state though, he'd be of little help to her. She would be safe with her captors as long as Grace believed that she might know something. He desperately needed some hot food to warm him up. Then he would slip back into the house under cover of darkness and hopefully free Liv. Except, to get food he would have to move again and move a lot further. Walking into Highcrest would surely require more energy than he possessed.

"Bloody Grace Walter," he complained to the bushes gathered around him. But, even as he berated her, and merciless fate, for his hopeless situation, some long-buried piece of information was prodding at his dulled wits, demanding his attention.

"Damn it," he cursed, because surely an undercover operative should have been prepared for such a setback. In the field, a little cash could make all the difference. Only then did the insistent fragment of memory break the surface like a leaping dolphin. He *was* prepared because, sewn into the lining of his right trouser leg, there was a bank card to be used only in an emergency. He'd clean forgotten it because he'd never needed to use it before. But he decided that his present situation must definitely count as an emergency.

Despite the weariness in his legs, he contrived to sit upright so that he was perched on a pile of stony earth. That was so uncomfortable that he soon opted to get to his feet - albeit unsteadily. His legs felt like two great blocks of ice so, if he didn't move, he would just fall back down again. Taking a few moments to massage his limbs seemed to help a little. But, in the end, he concluded there was probably no substitute for putting one leg in front of another. So, it seemed that, without consciously doing so, he had made his decision.

Plodding away from the shore, he glanced back along the cliff, shrouded at its eastern end by tall trees – which was probably the only reason it hadn't collapsed into the sea years ago. The trees would, however, also shield him from anyone else nearby who might be watching – and he suspected there would be someone there, close by the house with their binoculars out. Because, apparently, half the criminal gangs in southern England had an interest in the financial affairs of the Fisher family.

As he stumbled along the uphill track, he considered going straight back to Sunrise Heights. But who was he kidding? He was as weak as a kitten. What he needed was to eat and get warm. Until he did, he'd be no help to anyone. So, for now, Liv was on her own - again - and he prayed that she could hold out for a little longer. But she was tough, he reasoned, a lot tougher than he was anyway...

Fuelled by that vain hope, he found a footpath which took him up to a road at the top of the cliff. Since it seemed to point inland towards the fleshpots of Highcrest, he headed along it. Half-dressed, with his only clothing damp and filthy, he reached a parade of shops in the town. He knew he must look a fright, decorated by cuts, bruises and bullet scars, That alone might prompt some law-abiding citizen to call the police...

Keep focussed, he told himself, because no-one called the police these days and, even if they did, they didn't expect anyone to actually respond. First, he had to find some cash, then food. So, look for a bank. Why was there never – oh shit, he was standing next to one. At last, a break · thank Christ for that. As he rummaged around inside his trousers, however, he became aware that he was providing yet another reason for the local constabulary to be alerted. It might have occasioned a little less suspicion, he decided, if he'd retrieved the card before he reached the damned cash machine. Though he attracted a few dubious glances, to his relief, he finally pulled out the card. A sudden gasp from a woman close by suggested that she feared he might be yanking out something else.

But, all was well and, five minutes later, he was on the move again, comforted by a small wad of notes in his pocket. Only a short walk away, he found a pub, the Pavilion, that offered the hot food he craved. He was surprised, given the state of him, that they didn't just throw him out on the street. As it was, he just fielded a lot of suspicious looks and it wasn't long before he was tucking gratefully into a plate of fish and chips. Hot and fatty, it was heavenly and he wallowed in its calorific wickedness.

As he wolfed down another forkful, he could almost feel his strength returning and it occurred to him that perhaps, finally, the gods were no longer working against him. After all, the fall from the cliff-face ladder alone should have killed him. Having savoured for as long as possible the last scrap of food from his plate, he felt ready to take on the world. Fuelled up with fresh determination, he resolved to go back now to that wretched house and get Liv out. He was feeling a pang of guilt that he hadn't told her the truth. But the truth, of course, made him look like a petty criminal and he didn't want her to see him like that.

He had just gotten to his feet, when a man sat down opposite him – a clean shaven, affable-looking, grey-haired fellow.

"Who are you?" enquired Graham, eyeing the route to the door.

"Sit down," ordered the newcomer.

"Why should I?" retorted Graham.

"Because, if you don't, you won't make it as far as that door."

25

Sunrise Heights

"Why aren't you dead?" accused Liv, pointing the rolling pin. "You're supposed to be dead."

"Are you planning to take up baking or bricklaying, Olivia?" enquired her mother. "And I see your language hasn't improved."

Liv, recognising Monica Fisher's disappointed sigh as affectation, snarled: "I've had a rather bad few days... mother. So, unless you give me some really good answers, I will cheerfully crack your head open with this brick."

"Oh, Olivia," groaned Monica, "I'd forgotten what a little drama queen you can be."

"Yeh, well, whatever I am, you made me that way," argued Liv. "So, stop prevaricating."

"And long words too," observed Monica. "Surprising for a girl who ended her schooldays under rather a large cloud."

"It wasn't a cloud," snapped Liv. "It was a fucking thunderstorm. But I didn't leave school – or home – just to get wasted in some gutter. I left to get my life together. I went to college and trained to teach PE. And that's what I did, well, at least, until recently."

"Well, you never stuck at anything for long, dear," lamented Monica.

Ignoring the jibe, Liv suddenly remembered Grace and spun around to inspect the room, half-expecting to see the squat redhead lurking behind her.

"You seem a little anxious," remarked Monica.

"Yes. Because there's an armed woman around here somewhere. Another one, I mean."

"Would that be the woman who took one look at me and hurled herself out of that window?" enquired Monica.

"Yeh, I suppose," conceded Liv, recalling the splintering crash from earlier. So, it appeared that Grace was out of the picture for a while - which was something, at least. She imagined that seeing the ghost of Monica Fisher must have been a hell of a shock to Grace too. Though Liv tossed her brick onto the sofa, she wasn't quite ready to relinquish her grip on the rolling pin. As a sort of compromise, she perched on the upholstered arm of the other armchair.

"So," she murmured, "Tell me what's going on."

Monica favoured her daughter with a faint smile.

"And you can start with why you aren't dead."

"Straight for the jugular, as ever," said Monica. "Your sharp words certainly haven't lost their cutting edge, have they?"

"The past two days might have blunted my edge a bit," conceded Liv. "Now, stop stalling and tell me why you weren't in that plane when it went down."

"Well, why would I want to be in it, dear?" asked Monica, offering a rueful smile. "After all, I paid a very large sum to arrange for it to plunge into the sea without me."

"What about your husband? Where's he?"

"Henry didn't make it. So I imagine he's somewhere in the water off Bermuda. "

"So, did you set it all up just to kill your husband?" demanded Liv, surprised at the lengths to which even her mother would go. "You'd been married for what... twenty years – why now?"

"Our marriage was an alliance, Olivia, never a love match," murmured her mother. "But you must surely have realised that."

"I was pretty sure you disliked each other," said Liv. "So, what happened? You fell out even more?"

"Yes, we had a serious falling out," agreed Monica.

"It must have been a fucking enormous falling out then," declared Liv. "Have you not heard of divorce – or separation?"

Monica regarded her daughter solemnly. "I needed a more... permanent separation," she explained.

"So, just a couple of thieves falling out then."

"Thieves?" scoffed Monica, aghast. "Kindly don't refer to us as thieves. We are – we were – business people."

"Yeh, business people who, I'm told, work for organised crime," scoffed Liv.

After a short pause, Monica allowed herself another wan smile. "It seems you've been talking to someone."

"Several 'someones' actually," replied Liv, "some of whom have, by the way, been trying to kill me."

"Well, it looks to me as if you're still very much alive."

"No thanks to you," complained Liv. "Not that it'd bother you anyway, since you never gave a shit about me in the first place."

To Liv's surprise, Monica looked genuinely aggrieved. "That's simply not true," she replied. "I am your mother, after all."

"Forgive me for not noticing."

"I kept you safe," insisted Monica. "Always."

"You think so - seriously?" cried Liv bitterly. "In my teens, you didn't even know where I was most of the time."

But Monica shook her head and smiled darkly. "Oh, no, Olivia, from the moment you were born, I always knew exactly where you were."

"You fucking didn't..."

Leaning forward, Monica met Liv's steely glare with one of her own and replied: "I fucking did. I always knew where you were because I had a tracker put in you before you even went to nursery school."

Appalled at the very idea, Liv was momentarily lost for words.

Then she muttered: "I don't believe you."

Except, despite her shock, she did believe it, because it took only a moment's reflection to see that it was exactly what her mother would have done. Monica would always want to know where all her assets were.

"Well, even if you did know where I was," said Liv, "you didn't know what I was doing. I got into regular gang fights and I was sometimes hurt – quite badly..."

"Never died though, did you?" Monica observed, with that smug, irritating smile that told Liv another revelation was coming.

"And do you know why you never died, Olivia? Because all your life, someone has been watching out for you. And, when required, he picked you up and took you to hospital. Once, as I recall, he even prevented some vile wastrel from raping you. Did you never sometimes wonder how it was that you were never arrested, why you never overdosed, or were never cut to ribbons by some drugged-up loser? Perhaps you also half-remember sometimes receiving help from a random stranger... Well, Olivia, he wasn't random and he wasn't a stranger. It wasn't blind luck that you survived. Mark's been keeping you safe since the day you were born."

"Mark?"

"Yes, that's your guardian angel's name," confirmed Monica. "And I should imagine he's the reason you're still alive now."

"Mark..." moaned Liv, letting slip the rolling pin and collapsing into the armchair.

And, not for the first time in the past few days, she wept, clutching at her cheeks as tears rolled down them. Because, if ever someone deserved her tears, it was surely Mark. Mark, who she never knew at all. Mark, who she even suspected was a threat until, as she now understood, he had given his life to save her one last time.

"He's dead," she choked out. "Mark's dead..."

"No, he isn't," said Monica. "That's absurd. No-one could ever get the better of Mark."

"They could," argued Liv. "And they did, while he was more concerned with saving someone else."

When Liv described the man who perished in the surf beneath Sunrise Heights, her mother went deathly pale and remained very still for some time, silently, but visibly, grieving his loss.

"Poor Mark," murmured Monica. "I should have told him more about what I was doing."

"Yeh, you should," cried Liv, her grief turning all too swiftly to anger. "And, right now, you should tell me, your daughter, what's going on."

"Yes, alright," agreed Monica, who appeared much subdued. "But I confess things seem to have taken several unexpected turns."

"It's all 'unexpected' for me," declared Liv. "So, just tell me. You said you had a falling out with my father..."

"Our business was..."

"Your business was making large sums of money from drug users," accused Liv.

Ignoring her daughter's interruption, Monica continued. "Our business is an unforgiving one. This house was a counting house where cash came in and cash went out. Often such places are in some seedy back room but we offered a more... superior service for our clients."

"A crime syndicate," said Liv.

With a shrug, Monica replied: "If that's what you want to call it."

"That's what it is," insisted Liv.

"Well – whatever you choose to call it - I wanted Henry out. God knows, we'd both made enough money to last several lifetimes but he told me they wouldn't just let him walk away. It turned out he was right about that..."

"So you killed him?" declared Liv, incredulous.

"Yes, I killed him because he was a self-obsessed bastard who would have killed me in a blink if he thought I was going to cause him a problem."

"But, just to be clear," said Liv coldly, "you killed him in some sort of pre-emptive strike?"

"Yes, I did, but believe me, Olivia, it was truly him, or me."

"I might not have seen eye to eye with him, but he was still my father," grumbled Liv.

In a rare gesture of emotion, her mother reached out to her and rested a hand upon Liv's arm.

"Never, for one moment," she said, "was that man your father. Mark was more of a father to you than Henry ever was. He never wanted a child at all. A child, he told me, would just get in the way. When he found I was pregnant with you, he was furious. But I never regretted bringing you into the world, Olivia... never."

"Yeh, right..." groaned Liv, struggling to cope with Monica's outpouring of maternal information after a lifetime of monosyllabic responses. She'd asked for an explanation but now she wasn't sure where the truth ended and the lies began. Because, if it was all true, then her entire childhood - her whole life - was not as she'd imagined it at all.

"I suppose it is a lot to make sense of," said Monica.

"Make sense of? Do you have any idea what I've been through in the past few days?" murmured Liv.

"I can only imagine," commiserated Monica.

"People have been coming at me from all directions," cried Liv. "And all the time, it was your fault. It was you that got me into this."

"But I tried so hard to keep you out of it," insisted Monica, "to protect you."

"Yeh? Well, good job, 'mum'".

"I'm sorry you've been caught up in it, Olivia."

That was a first, because Liv couldn't remember any other single occasion when her mother had actually apologised for anything. Just for an instant, it occurred to her that perhaps she was more like her mother than she cared to admit. But the moment passed swiftly.

Offering her a smile of truce, Monica said: "So, you had better tell me everything that's happened to you."

So Liv did, while her mother listened impassively to her tale of blood, death and torture. Not a tear, nor even a raised eyebrow from Monica, to betray her thoughts or feelings. Throughout, she sat stiff-backed and stern-faced because nothing it seemed, however terrible, could penetrate her steely carapace. Having heard it all, she made no comment, but Liv knew that she would be quietly analysing it all. How did Liv know? Because it was exactly what she would do herself. Like mother, like sodding daughter...

"So, maybe you can see why I don't trust you," concluded Liv. "And you've certainly never put any trust in me."

Monica studied her for a moment before replying: "You want some trust? Alright, How about this? In our bedroom, Henry stashed some emergency cash – and I don't mean a petty cash box. So, now you know that, you could just take it and go. But I trust you."

Suddenly Liv remembered the hidden cavity that the late Danny had partly excavated in the bedroom wall. How in God's name had she forgotten that? It was only a few hours ago – a few rather hectic hours though...

"Whereabouts exactly in your bedroom did he put it?" asked Liv. "Because I've already searched in there."

"It's not somewhere you would just happen across," replied Monica airily.

Just then her phone vibrated and she tapped on it. Whatever she saw on the screen must have unnerved her for Liv noted that she stared at it for much longer than it took to read a text.

"Now, listen," Monica said. "There's something I have to go and do. So, you need to wait here for me."

"Why would I want to wait here?" grumbled Liv. "I'm not safe here."

"I won't be long," Monica reassured her. "But, it's important I go. It's getting dark now so, even if someone's watching, I should be able to get away through the trees."

"OK. Piss off then," said Liv. "I'm hardly going to miss you, am I?"

"Be careful while I'm gone," warned Monica. "Because everyone out there is our enemy."

"Not everyone," countered Liv.

"Are you referring to – what was his name: Graham? I thought you said he was dead."

"Well, he probably is..." said Liv, surprised at the regret she felt.

"Do you like him then?" teased her mother.

"No, he's not my type," said Liv quickly. "But if you take out every man in that category, I don't think there'd be many left."

"So, he's not all cock and no brains then?"

"Fuck the hell off," snarled Liv, "He's already taken one bullet for me. And, apart from Mark – apparently - he's the only person who's actually tried to keep me alive."

26

The Pavilion Pub in Highcrest

Graham had seen many such faces over the years: men who wore an arrogant smirk and just begged to be slapped in the mouth.

Taking an instant dislike to him, Graham enquired: "Do I know you?"

"We've never met, Graham," replied the stranger.

"Yet you appear to know my name."

"Well, that's simply because, from time to time – as now, I've been your paymaster."

And then Graham understood that, though he didn't know the man's name, it didn't really matter. He was one who lurked in the shadows · rarely seen and almost never identified – which, of course, was precisely how he preferred it. And, up to now, he had communicated with Graham only by text.

"Do you have a name?" No harm in asking, he supposed.

"Charles Grey," replied the man facing him.

"You say you're my 'paymaster' but you're not the one that hired me," said Graham. Though, of course, it was hard for him to be precise about such matters.

"Let's not argue about that," said Grey. "You were approached by someone from SWROCU."

"Yes," admitted Graham, who had checked that particular 'someone' out so he knew the guy was definitely employed by SWROCU.

Grey's smirk deepened. "Yes, he's quite a senior officer actually," he confided, "and very useful he is too."

"So, I'm not working for SWROCU at all," said Graham, wondering how his short-term contract with SWROCU could be so easily hijacked.

"Well, technically, you still are, but it was me who sent them to you."

Graham had to admit that, in the past few years, it had certainly become more difficult to work out exactly who he was working for. In the end, he'd just learned to take the money and stop caring. Servicing Barbara's needs and desires had been an expensive business. Well, at least he didn't need to worry about that any more.

"What about my colleague, Mark?" he asked. "He must have been working for you too."

"Ah, yes, Mark," said Grey, the smirk turning to a frown. "I'm afraid Mark had a habit of going rather… off-piste – and this time, I fear, it killed him."

Though Graham studied Grey's expression closely, he couldn't tell whether he was accepting responsibility for Mark's death, or simply lamenting it. So, he decided to press a little harder because, by Christ, he owed Mark that much.

"He was killed protecting Olivia Fisher," he murmured.

"So I understand," conceded Grey. "But you see, Graham, that was not his brief. The fate of the Fisher woman is of no consequence at all."

"It's of consequence to her," declared Graham.

"Why would I care what matters to her?" demanded Grey. "And, for that matter, why would you care?"

"My job involved getting close to her," argued Graham.

"Not that close," grumbled Grey. "And only if it led you to the money – which it clearly hasn't."

Fearing he had struck some sort of a dangerous nerve with Grey, Graham decided to change the subject.

"How did you find me?" he asked.

Grey gave a sigh of frustration. "Please keep up, Graham. I'm the one who sent you here."

"Er, yes, I suppose..." said Graham, "but how did you find me here - in this pub?"

"Oh, you mean, in the absence of you helpfully alerting your contact to your whereabouts, or even perhaps... I don't know... reporting in - as you were supposed to. First, we tried tracking your phone and, when that failed, we got lucky, because you used the emergency bank card, didn't you? By God, it was lucky you didn't lose your trousers, wasn't it?"

"Very fortunate," agreed Graham, wishing he'd abandoned them in the sea. Except, if he had, he wouldn't have enjoyed a recuperative meal of fish and chips...

Keep your focus, he told himself, because, while Grey's voice charmed, his slate eyes were observing, analysing and calculating.

"I was concerned for your welfare," said Grey.

"I'm sure," muttered Graham.

"Especially after that wine bar fiasco. God knows what you were doing there. Not your finest moment,

Graham, I'd say. That's why I had to come down here myself. You are aware, I suppose, that your job was not to protect Olivia Fisher, but to find out what she knows?"

Graham, no longer trusting himself to talk much about Liv, let the censure pass and instead said: "Fine, so, now you've found me: what do you want?"

"Well, it's old fashioned, I know, but since you're supposed to be working for me, I'd rather hoped you might be able to tell me what exactly is going on at Sunrise Heights. Your contact at South West Constabulary hasn't heard from you. So, why haven't you reported in?"

Knowing the person sitting opposite had the power of life or death over him was a sobering experience. Graham suspected that, if he didn't tread carefully, he would soon be joining Mark.

"I lost my phone-"

"Spare me the rubbish," snapped his employer. "Just tell me what's happened."

"If you've a watcher at the house – which I'm sure you do - then you must know a lot already," argued Graham.

"What I do know is that it's been a little too exciting inside – and out," complained Grey, through gritted teeth. "You're supposed to be operating under the radar, but you seem a little too invested in Olivia Fisher. I could live with that if you were getting results but, clearly, you're not. Your friend Mark was distracted and got himself shot looking out for that wretched woman. It looks to me as if you might be making the same fatal error of judgement."

"That's not what's happening," protested Graham.

"Alright then, what have you learned from the daughter about the Fishers' accounts?"

"Nothing," declared Graham. "Because she knows nothing."

"I suppose that was always likely," mused Grey, "though I did wonder whether the mother had told her anything."

"I don't think so. She seems pretty much at sea with all of it."

"She's still alive then?" said Grey.

"She was, when I left her," replied Graham.

"Did anything suggest that she had been in touch with her mother before the plane crash?" Grey pressed him.

Graham couldn't help but chuckle at that thought.

"What so amusing?" said Grey.

"Liv Fisher truly couldn't give a shit whether her parents are dead or not," he said. "She didn't talk to them, or even see them, when they were still alive. As far as she's concerned, their passing is a happy accident."

"I suppose it always looked that way," lamented Grey. "All the same, don't let her fool you, because I think she can be a cunning bitch."

"You know her then?" said Graham.

"I've heard things," replied Grey. "But the Fishers were very organised so, you can be sure that they would have left instructions for someone – and the most likely someone is their only child."

"But we've not found anything," insisted Graham.

"We?" said Grey, frowning.

"No harm in getting her to look, is there?" said Graham. "She was bound to look around anyway, wasn't she?"

"But you said she doesn't know what to look for," said Grey sharply.

When Graham made no reply, he scoffed: "You told her - of course you did - because you're a damned fool. And now, you've left her alone in the house. She could easily have found what we're looking for while you were gone and you'd be none the wiser."

"Hardly, she's locked in the cellar," Graham pointed out.

"If you locked her in the cellar, how did you end up in the state you're in?"

"I didn't lock her in the cellar," grumbled Graham. "Grace Walter locked us both in there."

"Ah, yes, I was informed that Grace was hovering around, posing as police. I assume she's working for the cartel. So, you've seen her?"

"Seen her?" scoffed Graham. "Grace is doing a lot more than 'hovering around'. She's out of control. Look at my face. These bruises are her idea of asking questions."

"Keep your voice down," ordered Grey sternly. "We don't want to upset the good folk of Highcrest, do we? At least not any more than you've already done. Anyway, Grace must have thought there was something off about you."

"Well, there was nearly something permanently off about me," muttered Graham. "That woman's a loose cannon, I tell you."

"Perhaps, but it looks to me as if her rather direct approach has more chance of yielding results for the cartel than your soft shoe shuffle is doing for me." He fixed Graham with a fierce glare. "High stakes, Graham, makes people rather desperate – even Olivia Fisher. Perhaps Grace has persuaded the daughter to tell her something."

"Not a chance," scoffed Graham. "Liv has history with Grace. She wouldn't tell Grace anything with her last breath. Believe me: Liv's hard – and uncompromising."

"'Liv' now, is it?" remarked Grey. "Sounds to me as if you've got rather too close to her already. By God, you've made a sorry mess of this. Perhaps it really is time you were put out to grass…"

Ignoring, momentarily, the prospect of his imminent demise, Graham enquired: "So, what do you want me to do now?"

"With so many other players gathering, we need to act fast," observed Grey. "we're too far along to put anyone new in so, you need to hang in there a little longer. But get a grip on yourself and be prepared to cut Olivia Fisher loose."

But Graham knew he couldn't do that. In truth, he also realised that he couldn't hack doing the work anymore. Perhaps if he'd got out sooner, Barbara wouldn't have ditched him; then again maybe she would have ditched him even faster. Though Grey might complain, he wasn't supposed to be doing any more than investigating Liv – and certainly not dodging bloody bullets. Once, he had the nerve, guts, bottle – whatever you chose to call it – to work in the field. But not now. Whatever happened here in Dorset, it was past time for him to get out.

"What if we - I - find the cash?" he asked.

"If you find it, all well and good, but you know it's the accounts that matter. What's a few paltry thousand compared to millions?"

A sudden thought struck Graham. "Who was it did the wine bar hit?"

Grey stared him down. "I couldn't say, Graham. There seem to be more people involved in this than a bloody charity run. Someone with a grudge against the family, perhaps – or more likely against that wayward daughter. But you can forget about that now."

"Easy for you to say," scoffed Graham. "I could have been killed…"

"Daughter patch you up, did she?" remarked Grey.

"Yes, because she was the only other person there."

He could hear himself sounding more defensive every time Liv was mentioned. He needed to keep his mouth shut, or Grey would no doubt shut it for him.

"Just go back and get the job done," ordered Grey. "Persuade her, plead with her, torture her, fuck her for all I care, but don't come out of that house again without the information I need. I suppose at least she trusts you now, doesn't she?"

"Yes, she does," conceded Graham. And, of course, she did, he thought. Perhaps, even now she was expecting him to come back and free her from that maniac, Grace. Then he thought: no, Liv was utterly practical. She'd probably assume he was already dead. Either way, though, if he went back to that house, Grace would still be a problem.

"What about Grace Walter?" he asked. "Because I'm struggling to know who I can trust."

"Assume that every person you encounter is a dangerous rival – including Olivia Fisher. Tread carefully with Grace – until I know whose side she's on. Is that clear?"

"Oh, very," replied Graham, though it wasn't at all clear what he was supposed to do with her.

"You'd better take this," said Grey, handing Graham a bulky manilla envelope. "Sounds as if you might need it."

Glancing inside the packet, Graham frowned at the Glock 19 and enquired softly: "Who do you think I'm going to shoot?"

"As far as we know, Olivia Fisher is still in there with Grace and a couple of the cartel's witless lackeys. Once you've found what we need, you can't let anyone else get hold of it. No loose ends, Graham · and especially not that daughter. Use her if you like, but keep your distance."

Perhaps Graham's countenance revealed his inner feelings because Grey added: "Remember, it's me you work for. So, no loose ends at all. Just do what you're told and you can walk away from this."

Gripping the table edge tightly, Graham fought to control himself, because Grey's brutal assessment of Liv was all too accurate. She was a lifelong fuck-up. But that didn't mean she deserved to be tortured or killed. In any case, Grey's warning had, of course, come far too late. He had already gotten too close and, whatever Grey wanted, he was going to try to get Liv Fisher out of Sunrise Heights in one piece.

"No loose ends," he agreed, though his hands were trembling as he said it.

Getting to his feet, Grey said: "Now go back to that house and do what you're being paid to do. I don't want to see you again until it's done."

27

Sunrise Heights in the early evening

After her mother left, Liv just sat for a time in the living room with eyes closed, trying to absorb all that her mother had revealed. But it was too much, so she shut it all out and stared at the nearby half-brick. She'd really like to hurl that at something – or someone - right now. Instead though, she got up and went upstairs to test the extent of her mother's trust. Danny's relentless blows had revealed all but the bottom third of the wall cavity at the rear of the wardrobe but, when she peered into it, she couldn't see anything inside at all. If there was cash in there then it must be right at the bottom, but attempting to lever off the remaining plasterboard without any tools looked impossible.

A glance at the mirror on the wardrobe door gave her a start for she looked a wreck. Still wearing the torn garments plastered with the dust and dirt of the cellar, she was in desperate need of a shower and some clean clothes. Still, she reckoned, removing the rest of the wall would probably be dusty work. So, maybe the shower could wait a little longer.

From her earlier searches, she remembered seeing a small torch in one of the drawers of the bedside cabinet and quickly retrieved it. It was of limited help though since the batteries were so weak its beam only amounted to a dull glow. Nonetheless, by its dim light, she could make out some sort of object in the cavity, but it certainly didn't seem like a bundle of notes. In frustration, she kicked at the base of the wall and, to her surprise, the whole section of skirting simply popped out.

Of course, she should have realised that there would be no point in hiding cash that you could only get to by smashing down half a wall. Kicking aside the length of skirting, she pointed the failing torch at the gap and gave a gasp. There was no bundle of notes hidden there, but there was something Liv would rather not have seen.

She had never been squeamish so, neither blood nor bones held any intrinsic horror for her, but it was always a shock when you expected to find one thing and found something entirely different – especially when that something was a skeletal hand with a ring still upon one of its bony fingers. Staring at the macabre discovery, Liv observed that the finger bones of the hand appeared to be splayed out as if to exhibit the ring as prominently as possible.

Though Monica said that Henry had hidden cash there, it seemed that he had actually concealed a rather different treasure. But whose hand was it and why was it placed there? It didn't take Liv long to realise that finding it probably made things worse rather than better. Not only was there no cash, but she had unearthed part of a fucking corpse – a real person. It most definitely hadn't ended up behind the wardrobe by accident. Her father must have planted it there for a reason, of that she was in no doubt. But how should she tackle the subject with Monica, who would eventually visit the hiding place to retrieve what she expected to be cash?

Distasteful though it was, Liv forced herself to examine the hand more closely, before the torch battery gave out entirely. The finger bones were larger than hers, so very probably those of a man. Was it the hand itself, she wondered, or the ring that was significant? Perhaps the ring could identify the owner of the hand – else why bother leaving it? Carefully drawing the hand out of its hiding place, she removed the ring and was unable to stop an image of Frodo Baggins leaping into her head. She gave the object a cursory examination as she turned it around in her fingers and decided that it was white gold.

She fancied there might be an inscription on the inside, but couldn't quite make it out. Since there was little else to glean from the artefact, she replaced it and the length of skirting. She was about to close the wardrobe door when she saw the pile of clothes she had tossed onto her mother's bed during her original search. Snatching up several, she hung them up to cover the yawning gap at the rear of the cupboard.

After her grisly discovery, Liv decided that a shower was even more urgently required. Going to her own room, she stripped off and headed for the bathroom. She already knew not to expect hot water but, perhaps, in some grim way, a cold shower was exactly what she needed. Bracing didn't quite do justice to the chill blast of water Liv endured for what felt like an hour but was, no doubt, only a few minutes.

While under the brutal shower, she distracted herself by starting to consider what to do about her grim discovery. One scenario was that Monica knew it was there and had lied to her. But, if so, why bother mentioning it at all? The other, more likely, possibility was that Henry had lied to Monica and, instead of a wad of cash, had left a bony hand. But again, why? If nothing else, it was a timely reminder of just how fucked-up her parents were. But, by the time Liv turned off the shower, she had decided what to do.

After briskly towelling herself dry, she wrapped the towel around her and padded back to her room. Since she had packed a bag for only a few days, she was onto her last set of clothes. But then, she reckoned that, the way things were going, within the next 24 hours, it probably wouldn't matter much. In the mirror, she studied the cuts and bruises that now adorned her face. Some were courtesy of Grace's attentions, but one, the dark red smudge on her cheek, caused by a fragment of sandstone, reminded her of Mark. She wanted to mourn him, but how could you mourn someone you never knew?

With a sigh, she finished combing out and slicking down her hair, before donning her last clean clothes. She had decided to retrieve the object from the wardrobe and, when she got downstairs, she set it down on the coffee table so that she could challenge her mother about it when she returned. Fleetingly, she wondered what she was going to do if Monica didn't return at all. Most likely, get out of the house, she thought. Because, at the very least, Grace was out there somewhere.

The clock on the mantlepiece read 3.45pm, but she hadn't seen its hands move a millimetre since she arrived. Prising her phone out of her slim jeans pocket, she found it was after eight. How long had Monica been gone? She had no idea because judging the passage of time was not exactly one of her strengths. Maybe she should be prepared to repel more interlopers, but her weapon stock was seriously limited.

Casting about for the rolling pin, she found it still lying on the floor where she'd discarded it. Perhaps there was a women's shelter nearby... When a creak came from the dining room next door, she let out a long sigh before reaching for the rolling pin. Creeping into the dining room, Liv saw that Monica had left the door unbarred. She might as well have put up a neon sign...

Deciding that the safest course was to keep clear of the door and boarded-up window, she retreated to the living room and waited. Though she was listening, she must have dozed off because a sudden tap on the boarding in the next room woke her with a start. Crossing back to the outer door, she saw that it was Graham and hurried to let him in.

"It *is* you," she murmured. "Shit. I thought you'd be in France by now – dead, obviously."

"I can see you're disappointed," he said, with a grin.

"Come and sit down," she said, deciding that she had rather missed that nervous smile of his.

"You know the back door's unlocked," he told her.

"You mean the door next to the badly boarded-up broken window?"

"Fair point, I suppose," he agreed, as they moved out of the dining room.

In the better lit living room, Liv saw his face more clearly, her sharp eyes tracing the line of every bruise and laceration.

"Are you... alright?" she enquired.

"Just glad to be alive, Liv. I tell you: I thought I was gone. But you. How did you get out of the cellar? And where's Grace? That's why I was creeping in the back. I thought she and the others would still be strolling around."

"Yeh, as you can see, I don't need rescuing," she assured him.

"So, what happened?"

"My mother happened..." she began and then told him all that had occurred.

"It's too much, Liv," he commiserated. "And I'm glad I'm here now to help, because you don't deserve this."

"Like you know what I deserve," scoffed Liv.

"I told you: I checked you out before I even met you-"

"Oh, please, spare me any more witness descriptions of the fuck-up that is Liv Fisher."

"It wasn't just your colleagues I spoke to, but some of the pupils too."

Liv pulled a face. "What, outside the school gate? 'Cos that's not creepy at all..."

"The girls all shared the same opinion of you-"

"Yeh, I can imagine what those dozy cows said."

"The older ones were pretty unanimous."

"I'll bet they were," muttered Liv. "The ungrateful bitches..."

Undeterred, Graham continued: "No, not ungrateful, as it happens. They all agreed that you were, as one particularly forceful young lady put it, 'a fucking warrior - who fought for them no matter how badly they messed up.'"

Liv was so wrongfooted that, for once, she could find no cutting response to deliver and felt a tear attempting to glisten in her eye.

"Yeh," she conceded, "but they only said that 'cos I messed up worse than they did."

"Well, that's pretty much what they said," chuckled Graham. "But they loved that you supported the girl who was...er..."

"Raped," snapped Liv. "She was raped, Graham. But I'm surprised they told you about that."

"Clearly, they weren't supposed to talk about it," he agreed, "but I guess I came along when they were keen to vent some anger..."

"I didn't do enough," she lamented, "because the police believed *him*, not her."

She had already wrestled the whole incident from her mind once, but Graham's intrusive questions were bringing it all back. Not that it was something she was ever likely to forget.

"It was so long after, there was just no evidence... My pretty mindless rage did nothing to help her – and did even less for me. Some fucking warrior I am."

"But you *are*, Liv," insisted Graham. "I've seen that much with my own eyes."

"Whatever." Dismissing the notion, Liv decided to change the subject.

"How well did you know Mark?" she asked.

"I knew a lot about Mark so, what specifically about him?"

"Well, for example-" Liv hesitated, suddenly unsure whether she should reveal what she was thinking to a man about whom she still knew next to nothing. But then, if he truly knew Mark...

"This is a bad idea," she muttered, unable to put into words the thought which had been circling around in her head ever since she had spoken to her mother.

"What?" enquired Graham, frowning with concern.

"OK. So, for example, is there any chance at all that he was... related to me?" she asked.

For a moment Graham stared at her, open-mouthed, but then he muttered: "So maybe that was it."

"What was what?" cried Liv. "What do you know?"

"I don't know anything for certain," Graham replied hastily. "But I knew there was something Mark was keeping from me. Something personal."

"Well, did you know that he's been – that he was - my guardian fucking angel since the day I was born?" asked Liv.

"What?"

"And that's crazy, isn't it? I mean you'd only do that for... family, wouldn't you?" she continued.

"So you think he was your father," said Graham gently.

"I don't know – it's just the way his death affected my mother. Just for a few moments at least, she looked... I don't know, crushed. Not like her at all. And then she said he was more of a father to me than Henry Fisher."

"But surely that's what people say, when someone *isn't* your father?"

"So, you think I'm reading way too much into it."

"Maybe not," he murmured. "Once, some years ago, Mark asked me out of the blue, to do a DNA check for him on two hair samples. He never told me why, but it turned out they were a close match. At the time I just thought it was for another job. We were always doing each other little favours like that…"

"Not so little for me," said Liv. "Tell me: how did he look when you told him the results?"

"How did he look?" said Graham. "Oh, I don't know. Mark was always quite hard to read. But, he seemed… pleased, I suppose. Yeh, pleased."

"You're just saying that," grumbled Liv.

"No," Graham assured her. "Because it would certainly explain why, when we took this contract, Mark told me that you were to be protected at all cost. Even though, as I told you, that wasn't what we were hired to do. I didn't get it at the time and Mark wouldn't say why – but he was adamant. Mark was a good guy…"

Liv nodded. "Yeh, very good, but also now very dead."

"Why don't you just ask your mother straight out when she comes back," he said.

"Trouble is, whatever she tells me, I'm not sure I'd believe it."

Though Graham was listening to her, she realised that she no longer had his full attention. His eyes had lighted upon the skeletal hand which, she had to admit, looked significantly out of place on a coffee table.

"One of your earlier victims?" he mused.

"Listen, I'm glad you're back," she said, "but don't be a dick. It's someone I found... or at least part of someone..."

"As you do," he murmured. "Whose hand is it then?"

"How should I know?" she cried.

"I thought you might – as things seemed to have moved on a bit since we were locked in the cellar together."

Liv explained how she had found it and concluded: "It must be my father who hid it there - assuming Henry Fisher was actually my father. But who hides a hand at the back of a wardrobe?"

"But it wasn't hidden from everyone, was it?" he remarked.

"No, he told my mother he'd left some cash where I found it," agreed Liv.

"But no cash in hand," he quipped.

Liv glared back at him. "I'm starting to wonder why I was pleased to see you."

"You were pleased to see me?" he said.

"Don't get your hopes up," she growled.

But the sound of the back door slamming brought them both back to the real world.

28

It was a cool, grey, winter afternoon so Monica pulled up her hood as she worked her way cautiously through the trees on the eastern side of the house. Hopefully she could avoid any watching eyes – such as those of Grace. It could only have been the ebullient redhead who informed Ivan of her return from the dead. So, Grace might yet be an ally – or not... In the past, Monica's route out to the coast road would have been simple enough, but erosion appeared to have taken its toll in places. It thus proved rather difficult to stick to what used to be a familiar path through the trees.

Judging by the frantic manner in which Grace left Sunrise Heights, Monica thought it unlikely that she was privy to her arrangement with Gerald. Had Gerald told anyone else about their agreement, Monica wondered? Because she had come back to find a shit-show, rather than the smooth takeover she had anticipated.

And where exactly was Gerald? Because he needed to take matters in hand. Since his number two, Ivan had arranged to meet her half a mile along the road, she assumed that he at least was in the loop. Except, why was she meeting the cartel's second in command rather than its boss? And why was Ivan worried about being seen at the house if his own people were already out front? Christ, she sincerely hoped that Ivan was going to shed a little light on what was going on.

Running more or less parallel to the coast, the road itself was shrouded here and there on the landward side by a succession of small copses. Since there was little traffic on a January afternoon, it was hardly surprising there was only one car parked along it. In the circumstances, the flash of its headlights as she approached seemed rather unnecessary.

When Ivan leaned over to open the passenger door, she could see that he had come alone, for which she was grateful. Without hesitation, she got in and closed the door.

"Monica," said Ivan, "Still alive then I see."

"Where's Gerald?" she demanded.

"It's good to see you too."

"Where is Gerald?" she repeated.

After a sigh, Ivan said: "Gerald couldn't come."

"Am I not important enough to merit his attention?" grumbled Monica. "Doesn't he want to be able to access the cartel's accounts again?"

"So that *was* you," grumbled Ivan. "Gerald was livid. He said it wasn't part of your deal."

"It wasn't. It was my insurance," explained Monica. "But I'll be happy to give all the account details to Gerald."

"You can give them to me," ordered Ivan, his tone a little sharper.

"No. Only Gerald," argued Monica, leaving no room for doubt.

"Well, that's going to be tricky," said Ivan, "because Gerald's dead."

Monica was already more than halfway towards reaching that conclusion without Ivan's help. What concerned her was who was now in control of the cartel.

"So, I've stepped up," said Ivan, in response to her unasked question.

"Have you indeed?" remarked Monica, thinking that, while Ivan had been a reliable second to Gerald, he surely lacked the subtle manipulative skills of his former boss.

Perhaps her expression revealed her doubts for he asked: "Don't you think I can handle it?"

"Me? My little opinion hardly matters, does it, Ivan? But what do the rest of the cartel think about it?"

"At first, there were a few grumblers," admitted Ivan, with a dark grin. "But they didn't argue for long."

"What happened to Gerald?" she enquired.

After a pause, he conceded: "Bullet to the head."

"From you?"

"No, why would I want to kill him?"

"Well, someone obviously thought it was a good idea and since you've taken over..."

"It wasn't me," said Ivan flatly.

"Don't you want to know who?" she persisted.

"Whoever it was, they've probably already been... dealt with. I've had a bit of a clear out..."

"Very well. Let's assume that it's you I need to deal with then," agreed Monica, though secretly, she doubted that some of his most likely opponents would have succumbed quite so meekly.

"Listen, I know what you agreed with Gerald," he said. "Henry had to go and I've no problem with that. He was a miserable bastard at the best of times. But locking us out of the accounts wasn't part of the deal. So, I want those accounts – now, Monica."

Since Monica had known what he would say even before he said it, her mind was already working out her options. Something didn't feel right. If Ivan was in full control of the cartel then he could have just walked up to Sunrise Heights and rung the doorbell. Grace had told him she was there so, why the clandestine meeting? Was he worried that perhaps Grace might have told someone else – someone who was not entirely on board with Ivan's accession? He'd been suspicious enough when he was under Gerald's control. Christ knew how he would cope with being top man.

Though Monica could guess at several prominent names who might be prepared to plot against the new boss, she would gain nothing by speculating. What was clear to her, however, was that she dared not simply hand over her valuable insurance policy to Ivan. She needed to know who else was in the game.

"I'll need to get the account information for you," she told him. "Because you surely don't think I carry all that around in my head."

"By tomorrow morning then," he warned.

"Or what, Ivan?"

"I might need to have a chat with your daughter…"

"You think that'll motivate me?" groaned Monica. "She and I - we're barely on speaking terms. But don't worry, I'll call you in the morning."

Before he could say any more, she got out of the car and walked away, taking steady, confident strides to hide the concern she was feeling. Gerald was dead. Ivan was in charge. But was he? From what Olivia had already told her, she thought there had to be more than one hand at work.

29

The Pavilion Pub in Highcrest

In the end it had been a surprisingly easy decision for Brad to follow his brother to England. Failure to make his deadline at work before Christmas had lost him his only remaining client - a mortal blow to an already ailing business. So, when Hal told him that he'd found Henry Fisher's house - and very probably his daughter - he had to admit that he was desperate to know more.

Since, as Hal pointed out, all the houses in the area were large, with stunning coastal views, the Fisher property was likely to be worth a packet. And, with only, maybe one half-sister to share it with, Brad reckoned that his brother was definitely onto something real. Feeling bad that he had been so quick to pour cold water on the whole idea at the start, he was keen to help his brother now.

But, despite Brad's newfound enthusiasm, his first problem had been to raise enough cash for the flight to the UK. He'd never truly appreciated how grim it would feel being poor again after so many years putting everything into his business. Though he managed to sell the company, he was so far in debt that he recouped almost nothing from it. More desperate measures were needed if he was to buy an air ticket. In the end, only by selling some of his few remaining possessions, had he managed to scrape together the fare.

What he also hadn't considered, until he tried to book a flight, was that it was, of course, the Christmas holiday period. So, the best he could do was book a stand-by ticket and that meant waiting a long time at JFK before he got on an airplane. By then, he was so exhausted he slept most of the flight.

Communicating by text, he and Hal had agreed upon a simple course of action when Brad arrived in the UK. They would go to a lawyer together and present their claim to the Fisher estate. A simple DNA test would confirm their relationship to the deceased. By all accounts, Henry Fisher had been a successful business man, so Hal reckoned the legacy would be substantial – especially with the property he owned.

When Brad's plane finally touched down at London Heathrow, he felt surprisingly well-rested and relaxed – unlike many of his fellow passengers who had over-indulged in the New Year spirits available. Brad couldn't afford such frivolous luxuries because he needed to arrive with a clear head and what little remained of his money. For all that, he felt optimistic and perhaps his upbeat mood had a lot to do with the belief that he would finally be exorcising the ghost of his father. And, if he did, there would be plenty of time to celebrate in the coming months.

Upon entering the airport terminal, his euphoria evaporated amid the bewildering crowds of travellers and the numerous travel options he faced. The prime concern was whether he would have enough UK currency to travel south to meet up with Hal. So, he didn't take the train to Bournemouth and opted instead for the coach. There was no real urgency and it was a direct service which took just over a couple of hours.

While he was awaiting the coach, he received a text from Hal with detailed instructions about how to find the Fisher house. It brought him a surge of genuine anticipation. Because they were really doing this. They were about to set in motion a process that would change their lives forever. Though Brad was fired up, he was a little disturbed by a second text from his twin. It appeared to be a warning of sorts because Hal instructed him, on no account, to go straight to the house. They would meet first, Hal told him, at a pub in Highcrest called the Pavilion. Though a little surprised, Brad knew his brother would have a good reason for not meeting at the house and would no doubt explain all when they met.

The coach journey flew by and soon Brad was at Bournemouth coach station, scanning the local bus timetables to find out how to reach Highcrest. It turned out that there was a regular service and the nearest bus stop was only a short walk away. So, although it was close to lunch time and he really needed to eat, he decided to catch the next available bus.

Before his phone battery died, he agreed to meet Hal at 3pm at the Pavilion. In Brad's book, the sooner he got there the better and he could eat at the pub anyway. The journey took around an hour and he enjoyed the novelty of a double-decker bus ride. Since Highcrest was only a small place, the Pavilion was not hard to find and soon Brad was splashing out a little more of his precious cash on lunch.

After his meal, with time to spare, he spent the next half hour or so exploring Highcrest because, after his long journey by plane, coach and bus, he certainly needed to stretch his legs. Even before he returned to the pub at around 2.45pm, his excitement was growing. Brad only started to worry when, by about a quarter after three, Hal had not yet arrived. By 3.30pm, Brad was sweating blood because Hal was almost never late. And now he had a decision to make about what to do next.

30

Late afternoon at Sunrise Heights

Liv was relieved that it was only Monica who strode into the living room, but her mother stopped dead when she saw that Liv was no longer alone.

"You must be Graham," she said brightly but, when he stepped forward to greet her, she cracked him on the head with the butt of her gun.

"Why the fuck did you do that?" cried Liv, making a poor attempt to catch Graham as he dropped like a stone.

"You may trust him, but I've no reason to," replied Monica.

"Without him," Liv protested, "I'd already be dead. He's been on my side all along. So, I owe him."

"Trust me, the only one on this planet who's truly on your side is me," insisted Monica.

"Fuck you," muttered Liv, as she hauled Graham across the living room and laid him out on the sofa.

"We'd better tie him up," said Monica.

"Absolutely not," spat Liv. "The poor bastard's been through more than enough. If you want to tie him up, you'll need to shoot me first."

"Why do you always have to be so difficult?" groaned Monica. "What if he betrays us?"

"He won't."

"I'm telling you, Olivia, he's not your friend."

"Maybe not, but he's been my only ally so far. And I'm warning you that, if you kill him, it'll be the last thing you ever do."

"But you said he's undercover, working for the regional crime squad," said Monica. "So, even if he's not working against us now, sooner or later, he will be."

"He saved my life at the wine bar," argued Liv.

"Of course he did, because he needs you alive – they all do."

"Well, someone doesn't," Liv snarled.

"All I'm saying is don't let your guard down. You've always been streetwise, Olivia. So, trust your instincts."

"I am. And my instincts tell me that he's on the side of the good guys."

"He may well be," lamented Monica, "but the thing is, dear, *we're* not exactly the good guys..."

Glaring at each other, the two women slumped down into the armchairs on either side of the sofa. The sullen standoff continued until Monica suddenly realised what was on the coffee table. Liv wasn't sure what reaction she had expected from her mother, but it probably wasn't stunned silence. Monica simply stared at the skeletal hand for a long time, until her mouth opened, as if she was about to say something, but thought better of it. Making no attempt to touch the ring, she merely continued to gaze at it long and hard. In so far as her expression betrayed any emotion at all, Liv reckoned it was a bitter, cold fury.

Finally, it was she who broke the uneasy silence.

"Did you lie about the stash?" she asked. "Was it you that left this there?"

"Of course it wasn't!" snapped Monica.

The woman who prided herself on her calm demeanour, had cheeks flushed with anger, but she said nothing more until Liv reached out to remove the ring.

"Leave it," she warned.

"I thought it might have an inscription in it," suggested Liv, "to identify the owner..."

After another prolonged silence, Monica gave a sigh and told her: "It has, but I already know who the owner was."

"Well, who was it then?" demanded Liv.

But Monica looked away and made no reply.

"I want to know," insisted Liv.

"You don't," groaned her mother.

"Just tell me what you know about it," urged Liv. "I'm not a child."

"If I do, there's something else you'll need to know first," said Monica. "And I suppose there's no reason why I shouldn't tell you now."

"Go on then, reveal all," said Liv, waving her hands theatrically. "I'm pretty fucking shockproof now."

But it turned out that she wasn't.

"It concerns Mark," began Monica.

"He was my father," said Liv.

"No he wasn't," retorted Monica. "What made you think that?"

"The way you said he watched over me," said Liv.

"Well, he did watch over you, but you're not his daughter."

"Oh…" Liv felt the pang of disappointment, because it would have been so much better to have Mark as a father than Henry Fisher.

"You're his niece," said Monica.

"He was my father's brother?" murmured Liv. "But they seem so different…"

"That's because Henry wasn't your father."

"Then who is?" gasped Liv.

"Mark's brother, David."

"So, where's he then?" cried Liv.

When Monica glanced down at the coffee table, the not-so-shockproof Liv suddenly wanted to throw up. In the grim silence that followed, she slowed her breathing and fought to keep control of herself. But it took her a long while to come to terms with the idea that it might be her own father's hand that lay on the table before her.

Neither woman spoke until, as before, Liv capitulated first.

"This guy, David… did he know me at all,?" she enquired, in a trembling voice.

"No, he didn't. It was a… mad moment – a silly fling, if you like. I lost touch with him before you were even born."

"Then how did his… how did this… get where I found it?" whispered Liv.

Monica gave a shake of the head. "There's only one explanation," she said, "simply because the only other person aware of that hiding place was Henry. He must have known all along about David and arranged for him to… disappear. That would certainly explain why he left so abruptly."

Liv was tempted to reach out to her mother, but could not.

"All this time," continued Monica, "I believed that David was spared my way of life. I never dreamed that he.... I gave him that ring. And you're right: there's an inscription inside. But how very like Henry... determined to have the last word after all."

"So, you really think Henry Fisher killed my natural father?"

"Or had him killed," suggested Monica. "And where better to leave that little memento than in the very place I would go to when I was most desperate. Henry always knew how to wreck someone's life."

"Did Mark know he was my uncle?" asked Liv.

"Perhaps. But, if he did, he never admitted it to me."

"I think he might have compared our DNA," said Liv. "Graham told me."

"You need to stop sharing things with Graham," warned Monica.

"I'll decide who I tell what," declared Liv. "But how did you come to know the two brothers?

"Mark was a friend to me long before I met his brother David – or even Henry Fisher. He was that very rare person, Olivia: a loyal friend. He was always there to help."

Liv's customary bravado was unable to find the words to encompass the chaos of emotions she was feeling. Though consumed with regret that she had never known her real father – or her uncle, for that matter – she was also livid that her mother had concealed it all from her. Most of all, perhaps for the first time in her life, Liv felt grief. But blind grief, because she had never known her real father and the enduring memory of her uncle would be the moment his head was shattered by a high velocity bullet.

"You should have told me all this years ago," she murmured.

With a shrug, her mother replied: "By the time you were old enough, you were already off the rails. You had enough rage in your life, Olivia. You didn't need any more."

"But, since then, you could have told me any time." Liv's retort was dripping with resentment. "Admit it, if I hadn't found this, you never would have told me, because you're a cold, fucking bitch."

Monica gave a weary shrug. "Call me what you like, but you'll still need me if you want to get out of this house alive."

Liv's response was to stalk out of the living room and she would have continued on out of the front door, had there not been a better than average chance that she would follow her father and uncle into oblivion. So, instead, she paced up and down the hall, spitting fire even as she scoured the embryonic tears from her eyes. Even if she had known that night at Slough Station, she could have spent a week or two with her uncle and got to know him - at least a little....

Having never before felt such loss, nothing prepared her for how she felt about it. But, irritatingly, her hard-nosed mother was right: if she intended to live much longer, she could spare little time for grieving. What a bitter irony that, right now, she needed Monica more than she'd ever needed her before.

31

Sunrise Heights

As Hal continued his passive surveillance of the house, he couldn't help feeling unsettled. When half your attention was focussed on a nearby building while the other half was preoccupied with clinging onto a thick horizontal branch, concentration was paramount. He reckoned himself a hard man to surprise, but the redhead's abrupt departure from the house through the large side window had certainly been spectacular. He'd almost fallen out of his tree in shock. He was amazed that the bat-shit crazy woman appeared to have escaped serious injury, although he did notice a slight limp as she made for her vehicle.

It wasn't her exit, however, that made his position more vulnerable, but the fact that she was still there now outside the house. From what he'd observed so far, she was a real piece of work and not a woman whose presence should be dismissed lightly. As far as he could tell, she was still in her car, a silver saloon, a little way down the road. What worried him was that she probably wasn't alone, because he knew for a fact that two guys had entered the house with her. Not only did the presence of other watchers unsettle him, but it also meant that it would be risky now to try to meet up with Brad at the Pavilion.

When he'd summoned Brad over – and his brother had answered that call – Hal imagined there might be a few bumps along the road to securing their rightful inheritance. But this was not what he'd expected at all. The Fishers sure were a messed up family. Hal was all too familiar with a world of guns where people were killed like they were cattle, but Brad wasn't. And his brother had sacrificed all the cash he had to join Hal's quest. How could he tell his brother now to go home? But, whatever he did, he needed to keep Brad safe.

As he lay there, however, he had to admit that it was not his brother's situation that was causing him most regret, but something else entirely. He was missing Lisa more than he could ever have imagined. I mean, shit, he'd barely known the gal more than a few days, but every moment he'd spent with her was already a cherished memory. She was almost never out of his thoughts but that was a double-edged blade, because how would she react if she learned the truth about him? That he was a killer.

So, every thought born of joy ended in sorrow, because it could never work out between them. Better to hold onto the sweet memories and just let her go. Better for him – and definitely better for her.

Shifting his position slightly, as he did every half hour or so, he scanned the nearby trees yet again for any sign of life. Though he saw no-one, he would keep on doing it – as he had ever since he'd encountered the sniper on the beach. Since someone had taken out the guy lying stiff under the porch, it was more than likely that the shooter was still there... watching and waiting.

And it wasn't impossible that there were other armed men nearby.

Assuming that the young woman who had been there from the start was still alive, he estimated that there must now be somewhere between three and five people in the house. He was still pretty certain that the woman had to be Olivia Fisher – 'cos who else would just decide to stay in that god-forsaken place?

Earlier, just before the frantic exit of 'bat-shit crazy', someone else had sneaked in. Swathed in a hooded jacket, they rang the doorbell and then darted around the rear of the house so fast that Hal had very nearly missed them completely. He couldn't tell whether the newcomer was a man or a woman, but the slight, hunched figure suggested the latter. So, one woman out and maybe one woman in. But then, what had happened to the two guys who had gone in earlier with 'bat-shit'?

When the Fisher woman's male friend from the previous night returned not long ago, Hal was seriously beginning to lose the plot. It was becoming increasingly obvious that, on his own, he couldn't keep track of everyone. He was already far enough out of his comfort zone. Give him a clear sight of his enemies and he'd take them out, but he found this whole muddled situation bewildering. At least if Brad was with him he would have an extra pair of eyes.

Part of him was tempted just to walk away and leave them all to it. But what was left for him then: a life as a contract killer? He resolved that he should at least stay until he could talk it all out with his brother. But that would have to wait a little longer.

Abruptly, something drew his attention to the east of his position. Well-attuned by now to the sounds of the neighbourhood, a new but all too familiar noise had intruded: the pop of a suppressed high velocity gunshot. Beyond the deciduous trees at the front of the house stood some evergreens which could provide a suitable place for a sniper to conceal himself. Though no-one appeared to be shooting at either him or the house, that was small comfort. The close proximity of another shooter was enough of a worry in itself because someone was clearly a target. But who?

It surely had to be the same shooter from the beach on New Year's Eve. Because, Jeez, how many snipers could there be in this Dorset backwater? The more important question though was: did the shooter know Hal was there? His position was well-shrouded but, if he fired, he'd reveal where he was at once. Not that he had any intention of firing.

Very slowly he moved his position to face away from the house and towards the clump of evergreens. With suppressed rounds there was hardly any muzzle flash so he focussed his scope in close, looking for any slight movement among the branches. A thermal scope might have helped a bit but that was rather beyond his budget.

The tree upon which he was focussed in particular was, he thought, a variety of cedar - which was one of the reasons he'd rejected it in favour of his own position. Cedar branches sloped more than those in the tree he had commandeered. Staring unblinking at the tree, he fixed his eyes on the place which he reckoned was the optimum height to give a sniper maximum coverage of both the road and the front of the house.

All he had to do was wait and that was something he could do for hours if required. But on this occasion his close scrutiny paid off quite swiftly when he spotted a tiny flicker of movement. So, this guy was either an amateur or a rookie. Now he knew where the shooter was, he could get some idea of what he might be firing at. Since the sniper wasn't firing at the house, his possible lines of sight suggested a target further along the coast road. The only item of interest there was a parked car, but Hal could only see the bonnet because overhanging trees obscured much of the target area.

Deciding that the shooter had finished firing, Hal moved his position again slightly, closer to the tree's trunk. So far, he had been an invisible watcher and he wanted it to stay that way. The last thing he needed was to be seen by the sniper, but had the latter moved his position after Hal spotted him? He settled down once again to observe.

Returning to his other priority, Hal pondered his brother's imminent arrival. When he didn't turn up at the Pavilion, what would Brad do? He'd wait, because Brad was a patient man. But how long would he wait, and what would he do when the Pavilion closed?

32

Eventually Liv buried her anger and returned to the living room because, whatever misgivings she had right then – especially about her mother, doing nothing was hardly likely to improve her situation.

"Strop over?" enquired Monica.

Liv glared at her but said nothing.

"I get it, Olivia: you don't much care for me. But we need to decide what to do."

When Liv glanced at Graham, still out cold on the sofa, she felt a surprising flutter of concern. But first, she needed to confront her mother.

Sinking down into an armchair, she said: "So, let's talk then. And first, I need to know what's going on. And don't give me any shit about keeping me safe. In case you hadn't noticed, I don't feel very fucking safe just now."

"I understand-"

"You don't," barked Liv. "You hung me out to dry and now you just tell me half-truths. I can trust my instincts. I can fight, but only if I know what I'm truly up against."

Despite a grimace of distaste, Monica acquiesced. Perhaps she realised that, only if Liv was armed with the truth, would she be able to navigate her way through it.

"Well," began Monica, "the issue is that I moved all the cartel's money into new accounts and closed those we were managing."

"Oh, shit," cried Liv, because, even with her Mickey Mouse level of financial expertise, she could understand why anyone, not just a crime syndicate, might be very pissed if an account disappeared – let alone all their accounts.

"But, why would you do that?" said Liv.

"I suspected Henry was planning to squeeze me out. So, by changing the accounts, I got some leverage."

"You thought he would what... kill you?"

"Well, if he forced me out of the cartel... trust me, that wouldn't have ended well."

"So, what were you going to do when you came back?"

"I'd already made an agreement with the cartel boss, Gerald."

"Let me guess: to force Henry out? You're as bad as each other."

"It was him, or me," argued Monica. "And by changing the accounts, I made sure Gerald would keep his word."

"So, did he? Did he keep his word?"

"I never found out because, while I was gone, he was killed."

"Great... So, who killed him?"

"I don't know, but I suspect there's a coup taking place right now in the cartel. It's possible it all started when they discovered they couldn't get into the accounts."

"Yeh, I should think that might have shaken things up a bit. So that's what everyone's looking for, isn't it?" Liv had already gleaned that much from Graham though she hadn't understood why.

"Until now, most members of the cartel, except Gerald, would have believed both Henry and I were dead," explained Monica.

"So, they came looking for me," muttered Liv.

"Yes, and I'm sorry for that."

"Not as sorry as me," Liv grumbled.

"But the moment Grace Walter saw me today, everything changed. And, if I'm right about the coup, she's not the only one looking to get into those accounts."

"So, why not just give them what they want," said Liv.

"But give *who* what they want?" asked Monica. "It's likely there are only two factions but both will know that, without access to those accounts, they can't win. And you can bet that neither is going to give up without a fight."

"Where did you hide the account details anyway?" asked Liv. "I've not found them – and I've looked everywhere."

"So I see," remarked Monica, eyeing the debris strewn across the floor.

"Some of that was... collateral damage," said Liv, feeling like a guilty eight-year-old.

With a dark smile, Monica tapped the side of her head. "The accounts are in here, Olivia. They always were."

"Oh, shit, your famed memory," groaned Liv.

"One of my talents you clearly didn't inherit, my dear, was my head for figures."

"Fucking photographic memory..."

"People may call it that, but there's really no such thing. You *see* everything, but how long do you remember any of it for?"

"Mostly not very long," conceded Liv.

"Exactly. I don't see the world as you do, but I've taught myself to remember numbers – even quite long ones. In this case, it was all that kept me alive."

"And all those years you were moving cash in and out of those criminals' accounts," said Liv. "Tell me, how much drug money did I launder for you without even knowing it?"

"Just focus, Olivia," ordered Monica. "You can judge me later because, I'm sure you can see how very, very... disappointed some of my former clients are going to be if they don't get what they want."

"But, if you're right about the coup then someone's bound to be disappointed," Liv argued. "And, just to be clear, whatever may be happening in your sweet little cartel, somcone is also genuinely trying to kill me."

"No, that makes no sense," said Monica. "They're just trying to frighten you; it's not in anyone's interest to kill you."

"But someone has been trying to!" snarled Liv. "Because I'm only still alive thanks to Mark and Graham - and a shitload of luck."

"That can't be right," murmured Monica. "But let's not get distracted."

"Yeh, because being a fucking target isn't distracting at all."

"Alright, alright, I believe you. But let's put it aside - just for a moment," suggested Monica.

"OK," agreed Liv. "Back to the cartel. Now tell me who you went to meet just now. Because I can't trust you."

"But I'm your mother," said Monica.

"Yeh," growled Liv. "Mother of the fucking year..."

"I was meeting the man who claims to be bossing the cartel now," confided Monica. "Ivan Turner."

"But you don't think he is?"

"I think he has rivals," said Monica. "He more or less admitted as much. There's a car outside and I think Grace is in it. But there are certain to be others."

"Awesome," breathed Liv. "So, we can't just walk out of here."

"No. And we don't even know which faction Grace is working for, let alone anyone else."

Glancing down at the unconscious Graham, Liv murmured: "I wonder how much of this he knows."

"If you're such firm friends, I'd have thought he would have told you all he knows," remarked Monica.

"He's told me a lot," insisted Liv, darting a fiery glare at her mother. "He's an investigator with SWROCU."

"So he told you," scoffed Monica. "But perhaps it's time we woke him up to find out exactly who he is working for."

"You shouldn't have hit him so hard," complained Liv.

"I'm sure he's fine," replied Monica, tossing a glass of water onto Graham's face.

"Mother!" protested Liv.

"Well, you said we needed him awake, didn't you?"

Graham, recovering surprisingly swiftly from his cool awakening, wiped a dribble of water from his face and stared at Monica. "So, it *is* you?"

"Yes, Olivia's mother," replied Monica, forcing a smile. "But you can call me Monica."

"But you're not‑"

"‑not dead?" said Monica. "No, I'm not dead – at least, not yet."

"And your husband... is he alive too?"

"I very much hope not," retorted Monica, with a smirk.

"Right," said Graham, clearly wrongfooted by this unexpected development. Looking at Liv, he asked: "Did you know?"

"Of course I didn't know," retorted Liv. "I'd hardly waste my time looking for stuff, if I knew she was still alive, would I?"

"I don't know," said Graham, "'cos I'm never sure what you're going to do next."

"Maybe not," agreed Liv, "but I wouldn't have lied to you about that."

Graham, she thought, still looked unconvinced but she imagined the small lump on his temple wasn't doing a lot to help her credibility.

"It wasn't me that hit you."

"I know," he conceded. "So, would either of you like to tell me what's going on?"

"We appear to be trapped here between two factions of my mother's former friends and colleagues," explained Liv.

"There are two factions?"

"Yes, keep up Graham," admonished Monica.

There was a sudden almighty crack and Liv felt a shiver pass through her from head to toe.

"What was that?" she gasped.

In response, a low rumbling growled up through the very floor causing the whole house to shudder. A moment later, however, there was silence and all was still once again.

Finding that she was gripping Graham's arm like a vice, Liv released it at once, muttering to herself: "Wimp..."

"That didn't sound good," observed Graham.

"Coastal erosion," remarked Monica, dismissing his concern. "Don't worry, they've been telling us we're going to drop into the sea for the last ten years. I'm sure it'll wait another few days."

33

For a long while, Hal remained prone on his branch, continuing his observation of the front of the house, whilst occasionally keeping an eye out for his fellow sniper. It had already been a long day and in the cool of the late afternoon, he could feel his concentration flagging.

Shit. Suddenly, he was staring at the guy in his scope – a man who looked just as surprised as he was. If it came to a shootout, each man knew the odds. They would probably get one shot – two at most. That meant it was pretty much a lottery who nailed their opponent first – and Hal had never yet possessed a winning lottery ticket.

Habit told him not to let another sniper get the drop on him and instinct urged him to open fire. Except... the shooter in the cedar hadn't yet fired and he must have had Hal in his sights for at least thirty seconds – maybe more. Hal could think of only one reason why the other man hadn't taken him out. It could only be the same reason that he too had hesitated: neither man had the remotest idea who the other was.

The other rifleman must know he'd been spotted but he appeared content, for the time being, to prolong the stalemate. He would be considering his options, but his options probably differed from Hal's in one important respect: he could presumably ask a superior what he should do. In war, Hal wouldn't have wasted a second and the other sniper would already be dead. But shit, this was Dorset, not some far off battlefield. He couldn't just take someone out – well, not without a contract at least. A contract though, didn't make it less of a crime. Because it was still murder.

Since he'd first seen the shooter, Hal had given a lot of thought to why exactly the guy was there – especially after he'd fired some shots down the road. But, with all the comings and goings at the house, not to mention random shots fired, Hal had to accept that he still had absolutely no idea what was going on. The trouble was that, even if he didn't have a reason to open fire, he couldn't lie there completely exposed for much longer.

For a moment he remained absolutely still with his shoulders relaxed, slowing his breathing to less than a murmur as he studied his opposite number carefully. Then instinct kicked in and he rolled along the branch to his left, sensing, rather than hearing, the suppressed report of his opponent's weapon. His sudden manoeuvre was vindicated when a slug thudded into the tree trunk to his right. Shit, welcome to the lottery, Hal....

At once he loosed off two rapid suppressed rounds and would have fired again, but the impact of a bullet all but swept him off the branch. In his shock, he almost slid off because, Jeez, he was hurting. What a nightmare. But he realised he could only have been hit by a bullet fragment. Else he'd already be dead. His covert vest had absorbed most of the impact, but an entire bullet at full velocity would have passed straight through it.

So, he wasn't dead... but first things first. If his opponent had also shifted his position, Hal had very likely missed him. Swiftly he focussed his scope on the cedar and found the shooter at once. It turned out that he hadn't moved – and never would again.

Hal's relief was short-lived because he still needed to deal with the bullet fragment that had pierced his Kevlar. Knowing that he had taken out the perpetrator didn't stop the wound from hurting like hell. Very likely it had penetrated only an inch or two into his flesh and his first instinct was to rip off his jacket and vest. Bad idea though, because there might be other hostiles close by. The best he could manage in the circumstances was to check it with his fingers to discover how bad it was.

When he did so, he was encouraged to find that the stray chunk of metal had caused a fairly superficial wound. So, pulling out the offending piece of shrapnel wasn't going to damage anything vital. On the other hand, if he couldn't shift it easily, it would be safer to leave it where it was. Only in Hollywood did they insist on retrieving every bit of every bullet and in the process tearing more holes in the poor victim's flesh. In the end, he found it easy, if painful, to remove. Since no sudden lake of blood pooled in the wound, he reckoned he could put a small field dressing on it and deal with it later.

When he had finished treating the wound, he glanced at his watch. It was thirty after four and he was already very late for the meeting with Brad. Not for the first time, he wondered how long his brother would wait. After what had just occurred, his own safety required him to lie still and silent. But the moment Brad left the pub, his life would also be in jeopardy. Deciding the small risk was worth it, Hal rummaged in his jacket pocket for his burner phone. After all, he could send a text silently enough. Except, how in hell could he explain in a few words the shit that was going on at the house? He couldn't. Better to keep it simple rather than scare the shit out of Brad with a half-arsed attempt to explain all that had happened.

In the end he just texted: "Stay put."

34

Liv felt Graham's eyes upon her when he said: "I told you there was something off about those accounts."

"What's off about them is that Monica decided to close them all," declared Liv.

"Tell me about those accounts, Monica," invited Graham.

"Why would I do that?" said Monica.

"She has all the new account numbers in her head," Liv informed him.

"Really?" said Graham.

"What did you tell him that for?" snapped Monica, glaring at her daughter.

"Because he's risking a bullet too," retorted Liv.

"So, there are two cartel factions now," he said thoughtfully. "But do we know exactly who's outside?"

Monica, eyeing him warily, replied: "I don't think it stretches credulity to assume that both factions are represented. But, never mind who's outside. I'm more concerned right now about who's inside."

"Really, mother?"

But Monica seemed determined to press Graham harder on his involvement. "The only reason you're still alive," she told him, "is that I need to know where you stand."

"Where I stand, Monica? I want those cartel accounts," he declared. "And I can call for back up anytime. How many allies can you summon up?"

Though Monica grilled him with a lingering look, she made no reply.

"Alright. Cards on the table," he said. "What do you actually want?"

"That's simple enough," replied Monica, "I want to get out of here with my daughter."

"That's all?"

"Works for me," muttered Liv.

"No, of course that's not all," declared Monica. "I also want us to have what should be ours."

"And, by that, I assume you mean the cash you've taken from the profits of crime," said Graham.

"I earned every penny of that money," protested Monica.

"Yeh, right," groaned Liv.

"Listen," said Graham, "I can get us all out of here, but only if you give me the cartel's accounts first."

"Not a chance," Monica replied flatly. "I'm still not sure you're even who you say you are. We'd have no guarantees."

"When are there any guarantees?" argued Liv. "Just ask Mark about that."

Monica, she observed, winced at the mere mention of Mark's name.

"You have to trust someone," urged Liv.

"No, I don't. I don't have to trust anyone," said Monica, "I just have to make a deal with one party or the other."

"Yeh, but which party?" asked Liv.

"You can make your deal with me," suggested Graham.

"You seriously think that SWROCU can protect either me or Liv from the cartel?" cried Monica.

Liv noted the shadow of doubt that passed swiftly across Graham's face.

"Alright," she said. "Let's, just for a minute, assume Monica gives you all the cartel accounts. What would happen next?"

"I'd call for a tactical firearms unit," he replied.

"And, how long after you call, before they get here?" said Liv.

"If they're close, fifteen minutes max."

"Are they likely to be close?" asked Liv.

"Er no, probably not," he replied sheepishly. "And, if they're in west or north Dorset, it'd be more like forty-five minutes."

"Compared to the few minutes it would take someone to get into this house, that's a very long time," remarked Liv.

"I know that," he conceded. "So, we'd have to stall the cartel somehow..."

Graham's vague response worried Liv but not as much as it appeared to concern Monica who took out her gun and pressed it hard against his forehead.

"What are you doing?" cried Liv.

Ignoring her daughter, Monica focussed solely upon Graham.

"Truth or die time, Graham," she said flatly. "Whatever my daughter believes, I know how things work. So, I'm guessing that, while you probably are working for the SWROCU, they're not your only masters, are they? And be very sure I'll pull this trigger if I don't like your answer."

Just deny it, Liv pleaded silently. Just deny it and I'll believe you…

But one look at his face told her that he couldn't. She turned away in disgust, because there it was again. Every time she was tempted to put her faith in him, he came up short. But it was her own stupidity, of course, not his. And he was just one more in the long procession of men who'd disappointed her. If she didn't know any better by now, perhaps she deserved to be comprehensively screwed again.

Monica, her weapon still jammed against Graham's brow, barked: "Who is it? Who are you going to give those accounts to?"

"The truth is," Graham began.

How many lies started with those three words, Liv wondered.

"I don't actually know," Graham told Monica, but it was Liv he was watching. "I was just paid to get the data and pass it on to my contact at SWROCU."

"A rather bent contact, I presume," said Monica.

"I suppose," he said. "But I only knew that for certain today."

"Stop with the bloody beige answers," snapped Monica. "Just tell us all you know now, or I will shoot you. Are you working for the cartel?"

Still staring miserably at Liv, Graham said nothing.

"Pick a side, Graham," growled Liv. "Or I'll fucking shoot you myself."

"Alright, alright," he agreed.

"So, who actually hired you?" demanded Liv.

"I thought at first he was a sort of middle man," he told her. "But now I'm not so sure. He calls himself Charles Grey."

"Charles Grey..." muttered Monica glumly, lowering her pistol.

"Who's Charles Grey?" Liv asked.

"Truly, Liv, I don't know," said Graham, "and I'm not sure I want to know."

"Great. So you'll work for anyone as long as you get paid."

Liv poured out her scorn because it turned out that he was just a grubby little investigator after all.

"Charles Grey," announced Monica softly, "is a prominent member of the cartel..."

"Of course he is," muttered Liv. Then, stabbing a finger at Graham's chest, she asked: "Did you know there was something 'off' about the cartel accounts *before* Grey brought you in?"

"No, it was he that told me," he admitted.

"Then he's the one behind the coup," said Liv simply.

"Yes, it has to be him," agreed Monica.

"So, who is he trying to remove?" asked Graham.

"Ivan Turner," muttered Monica, "who doesn't even seem to know."

"Alright. So, now we reckon we know who heads each factions" said Liv, "where does Grace Walter fit in to this?"

"Grace hasn't been working for Grey," said Graham. "Because he asked me about her."

"So Grace must be working for Ivan," said Monica, "which fits because she was the only one who saw me here and could have told Ivan I was still alive."

"So, to sum up," said Liv icily, "Graham is supposed to be feeding the accounts data to Grey and Grace was searching for it to hand over to Ivan. And we can't please both factions."

"As I told you to start with, we just have to make a deal with someone," urged Monica. "Then they'll protect us."

"But would they?" asked Liv.

"Yes, they would," said Monica. "Don't forget I've already spoken to Ivan. I had an arrangement with his boss Gerald and he told me he'd honour it. I think we can trust him."

"Yeh, but I doubt your original 'arrangement' included denying the cartel bosses access to their own accounts, did it?" said Liv. "So I'd say all bets are off with this Ivan character."

"But what choice do we have?" protested Monica. "He and his friends are right outside. If we don't deal with him, we're dead."

Liv grimaced. "But they're not going to let us go anyway, are they?"

"It's our best chance," insisted Monica. "You surely don't want to deal with Charles Grey through Graham when you've just heard how much he's deceived you."

Unwilling to reply, Liv stared at Graham, trying to decide whether, when it came to it, she could trust him.

"Liv, I swear-" he began.

But, riding roughshod over his words, she warned: "Please, no more professions of faith. But, mother, if it comes down to who do I trust more: anyone in the cartel, or Graham, I think he just about edges it."

"But Graham *is* part of the cartel," argued Monica.

"Not exactly," said Graham, earning himself another withering glare from Liv.

"Well, I can only trust the man I've spoken to face to face," said Monica. "And that's Ivan Turner. I'm going to offer him access to one of the cartel accounts - as a sign of good faith-"

"Good faith?" scoffed Liv. "Do you even know what that means?"

"Anyway, you've spoken to me face to face too," argued Graham.

"Yes, but it didn't persuade me to trust you," said Monica.

Liv was thinking that she didn't trust any of those involved. "Perhaps," she suggested, "we could do a deal with both parties."

"What?" said Monica.

"Well, they're already fighting one another, so, I say let's add a bit of fuel to the flames. Play them off against each other."

"How exactly?" asked Graham.

"Anything you tell SWROCU will also go to Grey, won't it?" said Liv. "And, if Monica's right that he's controlling one faction of the cartel, we'll be offering him a small bone. So, we offer the same bone to his rival, Ivan. So, we not only play one faction against the other, but we also alert SWROCU and they send out the cavalry."

"It's not that simple," said Graham.

"Oh, really?" said Liv, with a scowl. "Well, go on then, do explain why not to the fucking idiot woman."

"Turner and Grey will try to empty the account at once," he said.

"So what? I don't care about the money," retorted Liv. "As long as SWROCU is alerted and comes to get us."

"How many new cartel accounts did you set up, Monica?" asked Graham.

Monica hesitated.

"Just tell him, mother," growled Liv.

"Five," muttered Monica.

"All with similar balances?"

"No, one is very much larger than the other four."

"So, we could give Ivan access to one of the small accounts and Grey access to a different one," said Liv. "That way, neither will know the other has gained any access."

"But how does that help us?" said Monica. "They'll both just want more."

"It gains us some time while SWROCU send some help," said Liv.

"Could that work?" Monica asked Graham. "Might it get us enough time?"

"I'm not sure," he said. "I suppose when I give that first account data to my contact at SWROCU, I can ask for immediate backup on the promise of the remaining accounts when we're rescued."

"But what if your contact just passes on the account details to Grey and keeps SWROCU out of the loop entirely?" enquired Monica. "They wouldn't get the call for backup at all, would they?"

"No, they wouldn't," agreed Graham.

"How likely is that?" Liv pressed him.

With a shrug, he replied: "About fifty-fifty, I'd say."

"This would only work if we can play one faction off against the other while we wait for backup," said Monica. "But if there's no backup..."

"Then we're totally fucked," muttered Liv.

When neither contradicted her, she added: "Yeh, that's what I thought..."

"Whatever we're going to do, it had better be soon," said Monica bleakly.

"OK," sighed Liv. "Let's do it. I suggest you each set up a text with the data for the account you're giving them: Monica to Ivan and Graham to his contact. Then you both tap send at the same time.

A reluctant Monica dictated to Graham the account data he needed to send and then keyed in her own message to Ivan.

"Why does it feel like we're taking the pin out of a grenade?" murmured Graham.

"Because we are," said Liv. "Now, just press send."

35

Outside Sunrise Heights

Grey resented having to drive. That was George's job, though he had to admit that George had rather a lot of jobs and was perhaps spread a little too thinly these days. But that was only temporary - while there were so few people he could really trust. Allowing the black Mercedes to roll to a halt behind another vehicle not far from Sunrise Heights, he expected to find George waiting for him. But instead, it was a redheaded woman who approached his vehicle from the cover of the trees. She must be one of Ivan's little helpers and he had a fair idea which one.

Ensuring that his pistol was close by, he reached across to open the passenger door.

"I'm guessing you must be Grace Walter," he said.

Beyond a tight smile, her countenance revealed nothing as she replied in kind: "Charles Grey?"

When he nodded, she got into the car beside him.

"Ivan got your message," she told him. "The bullet to the head, that is..."

"Ah yes, George is a man who possesses many skills," he replied, unable to keep a trace of satisfaction from his tone.

"George *was* a man of many skills," said Grace, as she made herself comfortable in the passenger seat.

"But right now, George is lying up a tree with a hole in his head."

"You had him killed?" growled Grey, closing his hand around the butt of the pistol beside his seat.

"No, I didn't," said Grace. "That was someone else."

"Who then?" enquired Grey sharply. "Another of Ivan's?"

"Unknown for now," murmured Grace.

"So, what do you want?" he enquired.

"Well, Mr Grey, I'm now lacking an employer, while I believe you now have a vacancy, eh?"

Grey, still reeling from the shock of losing George, kept his expression taut and devoid of emotion. Admittedly, George had lost some of his touch of late and his judgement had been a little awry to say the least. He had started to make decisions for himself – a dangerous trend which had led to the whole messy wine bar episode. Nonetheless, George would have been a damned hard man to kill so, whoever had done so, was a person to take seriously.

"Another sniper took him out?" he asked.

"I believe so," said Grace, clearly enjoying her moment.

"But you don't think it was one of Ivan's men?"

"No," said Grace. "I would have known if it was. But, putting the late George aside for a minute, what can you offer me?"

Grey had to admire the woman's resilience, because she must only just have heard about Ivan's demise. It confirmed, however, all that he had heard about Grace Walter. She was uncompromising and could be effective, as long as you kept her on a tight leash.

"Why do you want to work for me?" he asked.

"You're taking over the cartel and I want a piece of that," said Grace.

Grey said nothing.

"I want-"

But Grey held up a hand to silence her because he didn't much care what Grace wanted. He did, though, need to replace George.

"How advanced is your driving?" he enquired.

"What?"

"Your driving."

"I can get from A to B faster than most and usually without killing anyone," said Grace. "Why, do you want to go somewhere?"

"Not just now," he replied, "but when I do, part of your duties will be to drive me."

"Get yourself a chauffeur then," retorted Grace. "I'm not looking for a job as a driver."

"George wasn't just a driver," explained Grey. "He had my trust. But if you want that, you'll need to earn it. And, if you work for me, you can have only one master..."

"Fair enough," agreed Grace.

"Good. That's settled then. Now, I'm concerned about this sniper, because I don't understand how any third party could have gotten involved."

"All I know is that he's good," said Grace.

"Perhaps it's my fault," conceded Grey. "George warned me about his presence and I should have paid more attention. Is he close to the house?"

"I think so, but I'm not sure where he is – at least, not exactly."

"Then we must assume he's still active. But who is he working for? If it isn't me and it wasn't Ivan…."

"Could he be police?" suggested Grace.

"On his own? It's possible though unlikely," muttered Grey. "The only police interest in the Fishers is from SWROCU and I've got that covered. Could he be working for Olivia Fisher?"

"If he was working for her, I'd have thought he'd be in the house rather than freezing his arse off in a tree somewhere," observed Grace.

"Well, whoever he's working for, he has to go."

"I'm a bit short-handed at the moment," said Grace.

"Trained snipers are a whole different breed," mused Grey. "We'll need more men, but they can be here by morning. I'll let you know when they arrive."

"Alright," agreed Grace, "but there's something else you need to know."

Though Grey was already beginning to think that Grace was going to be a rather irritating employee, he said: "Well?"

"The reason I'm out here rather than still in the house," explained Grace, "is that another woman has arrived."

"And you were spooked by another woman?" scoffed Grey.

"Not just any woman. Monica Fisher."

"Truly?" he said.

"Definitely," replied Grace.

"You're absolutely certain?"

"Yes!" Her sharp response revealed a degree of resentment that he dared to question her word. She was certainly a little volatile, he thought. But that might make her an even more useful tool.

"Well, well…"

"You don't seem very surprised," remarked Grace.

"Gerald always used to say that Monica Fisher was a survivor," he said. "Well, she's certainly survived him."

"So, what do you want to do about her?" she asked.

"Well, it's good news for us," he told her, "because if Monica is here then perhaps we can finally sort out this unholy mess quickly rather than dancing around that wretched daughter. Who else is in there with them?"

"Only Graham I think."

"Good, because he's on our side," said Grey smugly.

"Are you sure about that?" enquired Grace.

"Yes," declared Grey, though of course he wasn't.

Nonetheless, Grey was exultant. It was going to be so much easier to discover the account details now because a human computer like Monica would undoubtedly have all that data stored in her treacherous little head. But she should have learned that you can't mess with the cartel and survive. Even so, in the short term, it required a change in his strategy. Grace's soldiers would have to be more careful and ensure that Olivia Fisher didn't catch a stray bullet - yet. Because, once they had Monica under duress, she would be forced to negotiate to save her worthless daughter.

Grace Walter's defection was a welcome windfall if only for that vital piece of information about Monica. She was efficient and succinct though, which also met with Grey's approval. Though her body count was far too high, Graham was wrong about her. She wasn't a loose cannon at all – more of a barely-trained attack dog. Graham himself was, however, a considerable disappointment and, though he was still inside the house, Grey was beginning to doubt that he could rely solely upon the washed-up investigator.

So, yes, the capable Grace was going to be a valuable asset. Even so, he suspected that skilful negotiation was one attribution which Grace lacked. He would have to oversee that delicate process personally which did mean exposing himself a little more than he would have preferred. But, if you wanted to exert control, sometimes you had to show your face.

When a mobile phone sounded, Grace gave a start though it was in the pocket of her own trousers.

"I found it," she explained. "Just after I found Ivan. Seemed like a good idea not to leave it in the car..."

"You'd better answer it then," he instructed, eager to determine how many Ivan loyalists might still be in play.

But Grace regarded the phone suspiciously. "There's no caller ID," she observed.

"Hardly unusual," muttered Grey. "Just answer it."

Grace did so and, after listening for only a few seconds, she wore a broad grin on her face.

"Hold on," she said, covering the handset.

Turning to Grey, she whispered: "It's her. Monica Fisher."

Grey gave her a nod to continue the conversation. It made perfect sense to him that Monica was contacting Ivan because she had something to sell. She was putting out feelers to him – or at least she thought she was.

When Grace covered the phone again, he enquired softly: "What is she offering?"

"Access to one of the cartel's accounts · to show good faith, she says."

"Good faith," scoffed Grey. "That's a rare commodity. So, I imagine she's offering him the one with the smallest balance."

"So, do I pursue it?" asked Grace.

"Of course. Explain that Ivan has just stepped out of the car, but she should send the details at once. Tell her that Ivan will want the rest of the accounts and then hang up."

Moments later, as Grey was logging into the account on his tablet with the password supplied by Monica, his own mobile vibrated to announce the arrival of a message. Recognising the call sign of his tame SWROCU officer, he laughed out loud when he read the text.

"What's funny?" asked Grace, as Grey began tapping once again on his keyboard.

"Courtesy of dear old Graham, we now have access to two accounts," he told her. "They're trying to play me off against Ivan. But that's not going to work very well for them now, is it? At this rate we might get all the accounts without even getting out of the car."

"How many accounts are there?" asked Grace.

Grey's smile withered. "When you need to know something, Grace, I'll be sure to tell you," he growled. Because, however useful Grace might be, there was never any harm in pulling hard on the leash. The pack sometimes needed a reminder who the alpha male was.

"So, Graham's got access to the accounts too," mused Grace.

"Only because Monica Fisher's allowed it," he explained. "The pair of them are trying to start a little bidding war. And meanwhile, Graham's asked for backup from SWROCU."

"Will he get it?" asked Grace.

"Sadly not until long after he needs it," said Grey. "I fear his request will simply disappear into the digital ether."

"So, what will they ask us for?" asked Grace.

"Safe passage out, I imagine, in return for the rest of the accounts," replied Grey.

"Will you agree?"

"I want all those accounts as fast as I can get them," he declared. "My grip on the cartel demands it. So, I'll promise her anything to achieve that. But Monica will hold on to the biggest account to the bitter end. So, we may well need to apply more direct pressure. The daughter is the key."

"So, at the end, we put Graham down and wing Monica if we can." said Grace. "Then she'll have to trade that final account to save her daughter."

"Indeed."

"Will she trust you to keep your word?"

"My solemn word?" Grey chuckled grimly. "It hardly matters because, is she really going to watch her daughter die... possibly quite slowly?"

"You shouldn't underestimate Liv Fisher," said Grace.

Grey smiled. "I can hardly just let her go though, can I?"

"No, because the bitch wouldn't leave it there."

"I'm sure you're right about that. So, can I rely upon you to deal with her when the time comes?"

"Definitely," Grace replied, without even a flutter of doubt in her voice.

"Then we have a plan," he said. "Once our reinforcements arrive, we take out the sniper and go into the house."

"There'll be shooting," remarked Grace. "What if some residents report hearing gunfire to the local police?"

Grace wouldn't have known that several such reports had already been called in. But, fortunately, the local police had already been informed by an officer from SWROCU that there was an ongoing security operation in Highcrest. Hence, all law enforcement and the general public had been warned to keep well clear of Sunrise Heights.

"You let me worry about the police, Grace – the real ones, I mean. We'll let those in the house stew overnight and just before dawn we'll ask for the remaining accounts. They won't give them all so, we'll have to go in at some point. Be ready."

"How many guns are coming in the morning?" asked Grace.

"There'll be three more men here by the early hours," he replied.

"Is that all?" she protested.

"It's all you're getting, Grace," he chided. "This isn't London. So, don't squander them this time."

36

Early evening at the Pavilion Pub in Highcrest

So, Brad's brother was telling him to 'Stay put', which was damned frustrating when he'd just flown thousands of miles to get there. But Brad knew Hal must have a good reason why he couldn't meet up. Still, how long was he supposed to 'stay put' for? If Hal didn't appear in the next few hours, he was going to need a place to sleep that night – and he had barely any cash to pay for it.

Before Brad left New York, Hal had given him the Fisher's house address and he had printed out a map showing its location in Highcrest. In Hal's absence, it was all he had. But Hal's message was unambiguous. He clearly didn't want Brad to go to the Fisher house before they had talked.

But what if Hal didn't arrive at all during the evening? He might even be in some sort of trouble. Then the house was surely the only place Brad could go – because how else would he find his brother? However, reason prevailed and he persuaded himself that, most likely his brother was still there and simply couldn't get away. All the same, he resolved that, if Hal didn't arrive that night, he would go to the house first thing in the morning. Not now though because he wasn't stupid enough to blunder around looking for a house in the dark.

Going to the bar, he enquired whether they had a room for the night. After the New Year's Eve rush, they did have one double room available but Brad knew it would take every last penny he possessed. Still, after a good night's sleep, he could set off early in the morning to find Hal. Then, together, they could sort out what to do next.

37

"There's no point in all of us staying awake," said Liv. "I can mind both phones and still keep a look out in case anyone tries anything. You two might as well try to get some sleep."

But Monica, though she certainly looked exhausted, said: "There's one thing we haven't discussed. If it comes to it, we may have to defend ourselves and they'll have guns. Have you got a weapon, Olivia?"

"Other than the rolling pin?" Liv chuckled darkly at her mother. "No, there's the odd kitchen knife, but that's about it."

Gazing at her daughter for a long moment, Monica said: "I may have something in my bag."

"I don't really want a gun," said Liv. "Last time I held one I almost killed Graham."

"Better luck next time," said Monica, "but I think you might find this more to your liking."

Reaching into her small holdall, she retrieved a leather-wrapped pouch and held it out to Liv. "I hope you're still a fast learner. Because you'll need to be..."

With a little apprehension, Liv accepted the package and unfolded the leather to reveal a set of five identical knives – each in its own narrow sheath.

"They're throwing knives," explained Monica.

"Yeh, I sort of worked that out," said Liv, "but I feel I really ought to ask why you would have these in your bag?"

"Contingency…"

"OK. Well, I suppose I am, at least, better at throwing things…"

"Can't argue with that," remarked Graham.

Despite herself, Liv couldn't resist a smirk in response.

"It depends how fast and straight you can throw them," replied Monica. "But I seem to recall you used to be pretty good with a javelin. County champion, weren't you? I remember being so proud of you that day."

"Really?" said Liv, genuinely surprised. "Pity you didn't share that with me at the time."

"Yes, alright, perhaps," agreed Monica, "but my father brought me up without praise and I suppose I did the same with you…"

Eyeing the slim steel blades, Liv said: "I can't remember ever throwing anything this small."

"I thought practising might help you to stay awake."

"Yeh, very likely…"

"They're eight inches long. So, quite long enough," said Monica. "Just hold one first and feel the weight of it in your hand and then… try it."

"So, how?"

"First, relax your body," said Monica. "You're inexperienced but the distance will probably be quite short, so you'd best try a half spin."

"A what?"

"Which is your stronger arm?"

"The right – but only marginally."

"So, face your target head on and maybe put your right foot forward half a step," instructed Monica.

"Hold it by the point or hilt?" asked Liv.

"A half-spin will work for a distance of a couple of metres and for that you hold the blade between thumb and fingers, handle pointing at the target. After that, it's like throwing any object. It just takes practice."

Liv, eyeing the living room door, noted the cracked paintwork in places and decided to aim for a slightly discoloured patch in the centre of the door. Only as she hurled one of the blades, did it occur to her that, if she missed, Graham was standing rather close to the door. He froze as the blade fizzed past his left ear and impaled itself in the door frame next to his head.

Staring at the narrow carbon steel shaft quivering in the architrave, he muttered: "I take it you still don't trust me..."

"Just practising," replied Liv, with a wry grin. "Sorry..."

"Don't forget: I've seen you throw stuff," he reminded her. "And, believe me, you don't need much practice."

"Yeh, but I probably won't be able to hit anything with these," complained Liv.

"Maybe not but, judging from my recent personal experience, you'll very likely scare the shit out of them."

Monica appeared satisfied, however, and moved to go into the hall. But, at the threshold, she warned: "Don't leave Graham on his own with those phones, Olivia."

"I won't, mother," Liv reassured her. "Now go to bed. I'll wake you in a couple of hours.

You should go too, Graham."

Though he nodded in agreement, he showed no inclination to leave and she knew that was probably because he wanted to talk. But Liv wasn't sure she wanted to talk to him. True, Graham had come back, but why? Was it for her, or to fulfil his contract and acquire the elusive cartel accounts? Of course, the two motives were not entirely incompatible.

"Go and get some sleep," she told him.

"I just wanted to say I was sorry," he murmured.

"Yeh, but exactly what are you sorry for?" she asked.

"This whole mess..."

He clearly intended to say rather more but Liv, having no desire to hear any more weasel words, replied: "I need to practise, so be careful you don't provoke me."

"But I *am* sorry," he insisted, though she noted that he moved away from the door.

Though Liv was sorely tempted to use him as a handy target, she hurled her second blade at the door frame - this time deliberately. Because, whatever else he had said and done, he had saved her life at least once, probably twice. And that had to count for something. Genuine trust though, was such a rare and fragile thing...

"Liv, I-"

"Oh, just stop talking," she warned, as she lined up another throw.

It was really all her own fault. Her Uncle Mark had expended his last few words warning her to get out of Sunrise Heights. But she hadn't.

Her next blade struck the door frame immediately below its predecessor which seemed vaguely encouraging.

She should've listened to Mark, but she hadn't. So, all that came after was down to her, not Graham. For the final two blades, she focussed her eyes upon a specific target and released them in quick succession. Assessing the results with an objective eye, she concluded that she was more accurate when she wasn't so annoyed. You have to focus the anger, Liv, she told herself – as if she didn't already know that....

"Tell me about Mark," she asked abruptly. "You were close to him?"

"As close as anyone, I'd say," replied Graham, who seemed relieved just to be able to talk to her. "I've known him since we were both a hell of a lot younger. He was a very... self-contained guy, but someone who'd always have your back, you know."

And Liv did know because he'd had her back more than once.

A sudden thought struck her.

"Did you ever meet his brother, David?" she asked.

"Meet him?" laughed Graham. "Mark and I used to go down the pub with him for a drink or two – every so often."

Learning anything about her true father could only ever be bittersweet, because she didn't know him at all, had never known and would never know him. Nor would she trade memories with her uncle. who had looked out for her all her life. It was all just... too much to bear. And thinking about it only made her wild with anger.

"So, even you knew my father," she groaned.

"I thought you said Mark was your father," said Graham.

"Oh yeh, I forgot. While you were out of it, Monica gave me a bit of an update on that. Seems his brother David was my father."

"David? Well that makes a lot more sense," he told her.

"Why would you say that?" she demanded.

"Because David wasn't like Mark," he explained. "Mark was quiet and kept his thoughts to himself. But David was full of life and didn't hide his emotions very well, you know. Like..."

"Like me?" breathed Liv.

"Yes, very much."

"Shit."

"It'd be a lot to take in at the best of times, Liv," consoled Graham. "And this is hardly that..."

Flopping down into an armchair, she closed her eyes because in the past few days all the constants of her life had been ruthlessly ripped away. Now she could put her childhood angst and teenage rants against Henry Fisher in a completely different context. And, it seemed that she took after her real father... whose skeletal hand she'd stumbled upon stuffed down the back of a wardrobe. If Henry Fisher wasn't already dead, she would have taken great pleasure in bludgeoning him to death herself.

38

Just before dawn, January 3rd outside Sunrise Heights

As the night wore on, Hal must have fallen into a deeper sleep than he intended for he gave a start as he came to, relieved at least still to be perched on his chosen branch. As he came fully awake, his first thought was of Lisa, rather than Brad. At once, he felt a pang of guilt because his brother must be worried sick about him. Maybe he was just feeling at a low point and needing some tlc, which Lisa was certainly much better equipped to provide than Brad.

His side ached a little but a swift examination of the field dressing revealed no cause for concern. Shifting his position to get a clearer view of the road, he was surprised to find that there were now four vehicles parked there. Where there had been two together, another had pulled up behind and a fourth now sat about thirty metres further back. A car door slammed and muttering voices drifted up to him. It occurred to him that perhaps a car door closing was what had woken him. Several shadowy figures were visible, milling about beside the cars in the cold early morning air.

Since none of them were close by, he retrieved his mobile and risked switching it on. Inevitably perhaps, there were three missed calls and several more texts from his brother. There was nothing from Lisa, but that was to be expected since he'd explicitly warned her not to contact him.

Working his way through Brad's texts he could almost feel his brother's rising panic. He was relieved that Brad had found a room for the night and was just considering how he could arrange to meet him when he realised that the last three texts were less than an hour old. Shit. Despite Hal's clear warning the previous evening, Brad had decided to come to the house after all. And, of course, Hal had sent him the address the moment he found the house.

It wasn't only the chill air that sent a shiver through Hal when he read the most recent text: "Almost there now, bro.'"

Shit. It was barely even light. Why hadn't he waited? Because the very last thing Hal needed right now was Brad stumbling into the increasingly volatile situation outside Sunrise Heights. If he was coming up from the Pavilion pub, he'd likely approach the house from the east... where all the cars were parked.

At once, Hal texted back: "Don't come to the house, bro'. Not safe. Wait back along the road out of sight. I'll come to you. Soon."

To his almost tangible relief, Brad texted him back almost at once. "OK. Waiting on the east side, bro'. You OK?"

"Yep. Stay there," replied Hal.

He needed to get out of his tree fast and find Brad before someone else did. Easier said than done though, because there had to be four or five of them out there by the cars. But what were they all here for – and so early? Everything that had happened so far persuaded Hal that the new arrivals meant only more trouble for Olivia Fisher. When, using his scope, he focussed on one or two who were not obscured by the branches, his heart sank. All appeared to be armed and they made no attempt to hide it.

Yet, armed or not, he tried to remind himself that these people need not be his enemies. He was just an interested observer - or at least he was, until he shot and killed the sniper. Yep, that's when his neutrality ended. And now they surely must suspect that he was hiding somewhere near the house and they wouldn't want to move in on the house till they had taken him out.

The safest option for Hal was to abandon his position – fast - and make for Brad. He needed to get his brother as far away from that house as he could, before the hostiles moved in. Just as well stealth was his middle name. But, before he could move a muscle, another car door banged shut. Jeez. These guys didn't seem to care that they were announcing their presence to those in the house. Quickly, he checked his rifle and Glock 19 handgun. Full mags in both. He was just picking up his pack when he saw several of the gunmen set off into the trees. His trees. Because, of course, they knew he was in there somewhere.

As three men threaded their way cautiously between the grey trunks, Hal took out his handgun and checked it yet again. All good: suppressor in place and eleven 9mm bullets at his disposal. But, as long as he thought they might pass him by, he wasn't going to open fire. Still, they were coming dangerously close and Hal froze because suddenly, at the base of the tree next to his, one of the gunmen was staring up into the dark, leafless tree canopy. If they were inspecting each tree in turn to pinpoint where he was hiding, his time would soon run out because there were only so many trees...

Holding his breath, he remained rigidly still on the thick branch. A tense silence lengthened as his opponents remained motionless, listening for the slightest movement. Damn, they were good. But Hal was too experienced to panic. Better opponents had tried to take him out and failed – to their mortal cost. Though he was certainly concerned about those stalking him, it was hardly a new experience for a shooter. However, with dawn fast approaching, there was, he thought, a better than even chance that they would find him.

A moment later, below him, dry dead leaves crumpled under someone's feet, but still Hal waited · right up until the moment he was spotted. Then he shot the man below him in the head before flattening himself against the tree's trunk. Even with a silencer, his muzzle flash must have shown up like a torchlight and he spotted the second gunman too late. In their rapid exchange of shots his two suppressed rounds were drowned by the crash of his opponent's unsilenced weapon.

Though his second adversary was down, Hal was grunting with pain. His aramid vest would stop a bullet from most handguns – unless of course, the bullet evaded the Kevlar and struck him, say, in the thigh... Quickly, he assessed that, though the wound was bleeding, it couldn't be arterial because, if it was, he'd already be dead. All the same, it was bad news because the bullet was still lodged somewhere in his leg. He needed to get some pressure on it, or the remaining gunman would be able to follow the dribble of blood right to him. But first, soldier, follow procedure: take care of the immediate and present risk.

The two bodies now lying under the tree made his position kinda obvious. But after a few moments, he heard the third man retreating noisily through the trees and breathed more easily again. It seemed that, though his position was utterly compromised, the enemy lacked the nerve to take him on a second time. Well, their reluctance wouldn't last forever....

The shots had shattered the peace of the early morning, so Brad must have heard them. Hal was about to send a reassuring text to his brother, when he realised that his new wound was bleeding rather more than he first thought. Shit.

39

At Sunrise Heights, just before dawn

"You should have woken me sooner," complained Monica. "It'll be light soon."

"Why? What were you thinking of doing?" enquired Liv gruffly. "Going for a run?"

"It sounds as if someone didn't get any sleep at all," remarked Monica.

"I never sleep much," lied Liv.

In fact, she had only caught a little sleep at all because Graham had stayed awake. But Liv decided not to reveal to Monica that, against her express instructions, she had left Graham with unsupervised access to the two phones.

"What was that?" said Graham, abruptly getting to his feet.

"What was what?" asked Monica.

"I thought I heard something outside," said Graham. "A car door maybe?"

All three fell silent to listen and Liv thought she heard something too, something indeterminate... Getting up, she moved to the living room door but whatever the faint sounds were, they appeared to have stopped.

"Nothing now," said Graham.

"I'll take a look anyway from the study window," she told the others.

"Be careful," warned Monica. "You'll be very exposed in there."

Liv knew that well enough, which is why she'd been reluctant to go in there after making her initial search. But, if there was movement at the front of the house, she was more likely to see it from the study than anywhere else. The door, she recalled, was stiff and needed a hefty shove before it could be persuaded to open enough to allow her inside.

Treading with care, she crept towards the bay window, which was adorned by several spectacular cobwebs. Tearing her attention from the admirable feats of web engineering, she anxiously inspected the window for any sign of a large spider. Relieved not to find one, she unleashed her wide eyes upon the trees outside.

Over the years, she'd learned that everything appeared grey to her at night, except for people and animals, which took on a darker hue. Among the nearby trees, she soon picked out several walking shadows, that moved as if stalking a prey. Yet, unless it was her imagination, their faces were looking up, not down at their feet. Shit, they were searching for someone in the trees... Directing her gaze upwards, she scoured the unclothed tree canopies but saw nothing.

Tracking their progress, as they edged ever nearer to the house, her eyes began to ache with the effort of concentration. Then, in quick succession, a series of flashes assaulted her eyes, followed by loud reports of unmistakable origin. Slamming her scarred eyes shut, she drew back from the window pane and took several sharp breaths. Get a grip, Liv, she scolded, because they're not sodding shooting at you, are they? Of course, there were two factions, weren't there? Two factions she had suggested should be pitted against each other. Well, it seemed that they were.

Once the firing stopped, she risked another look outside but opened her eyes only very slowly. Adjusting all over again for night vision, she inspected the trees one by one and, finally she observed a figure moving on one of the larger branches. So, someone had survived, but she could see enough to know that he was trying to strap up a wound.

"Can you see anyone?" whispered Graham.

"Fuck!" cried Liv. "Why did you creep up behind me like that?"

"I heard the shots," he said.

"Well, you might've warned me," she growled.

Gazing out of the window, he asked: "Can you see anything at all?"

"Of course," confirmed Liv.

"How?"

It occurred to her then for the first time that Graham had never witnessed her visual acuity in action.

"I'm tetrachromatic," she said.

"OK..."

"And also... my eyes and brain have the capacity to manage more visual data than... usual."

"OK."

"Stop saying OK," she snapped.

"But what does all that mean, Liv?" he asked.

"I guess it means I can see more than almost anyone."

"OK – er, excellent... Well, can you see anyone out there now?"

"One in the trees, alive just about. Two on the ground, most probably dead. There was another, but he fell back towards the road."

"Christ, no wonder your hand-eye co-ordination is so bloody good," he said. "I mean... how do you? Does it hurt?"

"Only when it's really bright..."

Crushed by Graham's sympathetic look, she said briskly: "We should get back to Monica, or she'll think we're plotting behind her back."

When Liv reported what she had seen to her mother, Monica turned at once to Graham and asked: "Are there any SWROCU officers out there?"

"There won't be till I contact them," he replied. "If they were out there, they'd already have blown the operation, wouldn't they?"

"Perhaps they just did," suggested Liv.

"No, they wouldn't move in unless I called them," he insisted. "And I haven't, have I?"

"Someone's still alive up in one of the trees," said Liv. "Someone I think the others were hunting for."

"As long as he's in the trees, we need to stay away from the windows," advised Monica.

"But we don't know whose side he's on," pointed out Graham.

"Whoever's side he's on, it's not ours," said Monica.

When her phone started vibrating on the coffee table beside her, all three stared at it for several moments. Then Monica picked it up and glanced at the screen.

"It's Ivan," she murmured. "Or perhaps Grace."

While the phone continued to vibrate like a bee climbing laboriously up a window pane, Liv turned to Graham.

"Have you heard from your contact at SWROCU?" she asked.

He shook his head.

"Has he even acknowledged your request for backup?"

When he gave another shake of the head, Liv told Monica: "You'd better answer that then."

"We know what they'll ask for," said Monica. "So, what do we do?"

"If it's still Grace, ask to talk to Ivan," advised Liv. "I don't trust Grace."

"I don't trust any of them," muttered Graham.

"You're in no position to question anyone's reliability," scoffed Liv.

Answering the phone, Monica listened for a minute or so before replying: "I'll think about it."

"Was it Ivan?" demanded Liv.

Monica shook her head. "Still Grace."

"That's not right," said Graham. "Would you let Grace keep your phone even for a few minutes?"

"Nope," said Liv. "And definitely not all night."

"So, what are we saying? That Ivan's no longer in the contest?" asked Monica. "But, could Grace really have taken over from him?"

"Fucking Grace Walter," grumbled Liv. "I really wish I'd ended her on the hockey field."

"So, what did she want?" said Graham.

"Another account, of course," replied Monica.

When Graham's mobile bleeped, he observed: "We're going to run out of accounts pretty damn quick."

Reading the text, he announced glumly: "Grey's SWROCU man is also asking for the other accounts."

"Ask him if a tactical unit is on its way," ordered Liv. "And lay it on thick – tell him we're under fire."

After Graham sent his text in reply, Monica asked: "So what do we do about Grace?"

"Nothing until Graham's man gets in touch again," said Liv. "Because, before we give any more accounts away, we need to know whether backup is on its way or not."

"But should we give Grace another account to hold her off?" asked Monica.

"No," replied Liv. "We're not giving Grace another thing."

"But what if she comes in here for us?" said Monica.

Liv gave a bitter smile. "I think Grace is going to come for me sooner or later anyway."

"What about Grey though?" asked Monica. "Graham's text might just piss him off."

"And, if there's no backup coming?" asked Graham. "What then?"

"We give one faction or the other access to all the accounts bar one," said Liv. "and we bargain with them alone."

"But which one?" said Monica.

"Here's a clue," murmured Liv, "Grace will kill me without a second thought."

"So, it has to be Grey then," said Graham at once. "He's got no personal axe to grind with either of you. If we don't hear anything soon, I'll send him the other account details – except the biggest one and try to broker a deal with him for safe passage out."

"That's a big risk," argued Monica.

"I'll grant you that," conceded Graham, "but I reckon dealing with Grace Walter would be a bigger one."

"No, we give SWROCU – Grey, that is - all but the richest account," insisted Liv. "That should be enough of an incentive so, we tell him he needs to remove the threat from Grace before we can negotiate with him any further. After all, it's in his interest to get rid of Grace anyway. So, that's our plan."

Having a 'plan' didn't help Liv, or anyone else, much because the waiting was still stressful. Would a tactical unit arrive, or a text or neither?

It was around 8am that Grace texted simply: "What's it to be?"

"We need to give her something," urged Monica.

"Yeh, a bullet," grumbled Liv who, snatching Monica's phone, sent the reply: "We need more time to decide."

And then they waited once again. But no more came from Grace.

"If both Grace and Grey are still able to negotiate," said Monica, "then it appears that those shots outside settled nothing."

While Monica's observation hung in the air, Graham's mobile suddenly sounded. But, as he listened to the caller, his face clouded in dismay. Ashen-faced, he pocketed the cell phone.

"Well?" demanded Monica. "Who was that?"

"That was Grey," he replied. "And it seems that Grace is now working for him."

"Shit," said Monica.

"So much for playing one against the other," observed Liv who, since she always expected the worst, was probably the least surprised of them all.

"They're both outside the house now," reported Graham.

"But, if they're working together, who was shooting at who outside?" asked Liv. "Who else is out there?"

"It doesn't matter," said Graham, "because, unless we give them the final account details, all bets are off and they're coming in. We've got fifteen minutes…"

"Could your firearms unit get here in that time?" asked Monica.

"I'm afraid that Grey made it very clear to me that there's no backup coming," said Graham.

"Wait. Even though the armed unit isn't coming, why don't we just call the police on the phone?" asked Liv. "We could just dial 999 and say we're under fire here."

Graham looked doubtful. "I think we're way past that, Liv, but you could give it a try."

As Liv dialled 999, she asked: "What do you mean: 'way past that'?"

But only a few moments after her call was answered and rerouted to the police, she had hung up.

"Let me guess," said Graham. "They said they've had several calls already and there's a team in the area dealing with the incident. It's now under control so, there's nothing to worry about, madam."

"Almost word for word..." she muttered, grim-faced. "How did you know?"

"Experience," he sighed.

Staring at Monica and Graham, Liv growled: "Why was I stupid enough to think that either of you two could actually negotiate a way out of this shit? Well at least we know now that we're not getting out of this house alive."

Grace's next text was curt: "You've got five minutes. After that, we're coming in."

"Let them come," growled Liv. "They still need to keep us alive."

"You two perhaps, but not me, they don't," argued Graham.

"Shame," groaned Liv, giving him a twisted smile.

"Once they come in, any one of us could take a bullet," said Monica. "We lose control."

"We never had control," snapped Liv. "And don't forget, it was you that started this whole shitstorm."

Ignoring Liv, Monica gripped Graham by the arm. "When they come in," she told him, "you need to look after my girl. Stay close and keep her safe."

"I don't need Graham to 'keep me safe'," retorted Liv. "I've been doing that well enough since I was eleven."

40

Pressing a firm hand against his thigh wound, Hal rummaged in his bag for one of the two Israeli bandages he had. Best emergency bandage out there - if only he could find one of the damned things. Keeping the pressure on was difficult when you were distracted, so he forced himself to take slow breaths and calm down. It wasn't the first such wound he'd encountered, though it was the first one he'd treated on his own body…

Finally he hauled out the bandage, split the pack and began to wrap the sterile pad around the wound. Occasionally, he glanced below in case anyone was creeping back into the trees, but he saw no-one. Once the pressure applicator was tightened up, he finished wrapping the bandage and secured it. Assessing his work, he reckoned it would do for now but, sooner or later, that bullet would need to be dealt with - one way or another. For all he knew, it was resting right up against his femoral artery just waiting to punch through it.

With a sigh he lamented that, after surviving two tours of Afghanistan without a scratch, he'd been wounded twice in England – in peaceful Dorset. Still, there was no time for self-pity because he had a brother to find. Hastily, his bloodstained fingers tapped out a text: "I'm coming to you now, bro.'"

Saying that was one thing, but doing it was a whole other matter. The first rays of dawn were visible on the horizon to the east so, yeh, the name Sunrise Heights was, he supposed, apt enough. At least he could now see more clearly what – or rather who · he was up against. Observing no movement near the cars, he decided to seize the moment. His time was limited because, once it was fully light, they would come for him again and he wasn't exactly at his best right now.

Picking up his pack, he dropped it onto the ground beside the tree's trunk, then with the handgun in his jacket pocket, he shouldered the rifle and began to clamber awkwardly down. The body wound hardly hindered him at all except, when he stretched out his right arm, the flesh pinched a bit. But that was tolerable. It was the thigh wound that hurt like hell and caused Hal to reflect that perhaps his pain threshold was not quite as high as he always imagined.

Long before he reached the ground, he knew the left leg was going to be a problem and hardly dared put any weight on it at all.. Since he was dog·tired anyway, he almost lost his footing several times until, when he was about five feet off the ground, he fell. As bitter luck would have it, he couldn't avoid landing heavily on his damaged leg which sent a lance of pure agony right through him. At once, he rolled off it to prevent any further damage to the limb and then just lay there beside the tree, waiting for the pain to subside and praying no·one would happen along.

He didn't dare examine the leg because, if the bullet had been driven into his artery, blood would already be spurting everywhere. Better to leave the

Israeli bandage in place and hope for the best. Anyway, he'd know soon enough if the pressure it was exerting on the wound site wasn't sufficient...

When he finally felt like trying to get to his feet, he used a combination of his rifle and the tree, to help him up. Once he was standing, he employed the rifle as a crutch – albeit a short one. In that awkward manner, he managed to limp slowly through the trees, away from the house.

With any luck, he should locate Brad almost immediately. And he did, but not where he expected to see him. His brother was walking towards one of the parked cars – the last in the line – which was pretty much the opposite of what Hal had told him to do. Momentarily non-plussed, Hal couldn't decide what to do. Why had Brad broken cover? If he called out to him now, others were sure to hear. Yet he couldn't just let him walk straight into trouble. Peering out from behind one of the broader tree trunks, he tried hissing his brother's name. To his immense relief, Brad stopped and looked around, but he was already worryingly close to the vehicle.

When Brad spotted him, Hal gesticulated wildly, urging his brother to come across to him. But Brad seemed strangely reluctant to move. Next moment, the bat-shit redhead clambered stiffly out of the leading car and proceeded to bang on the roof of the vehicle behind to urge the occupants to get out.

Suddenly, Brad was faced by the woman and two men – all three brandishing firearms. Hal watched aghast as Brad tentatively raised his hands before glancing across at his brother.

Shit. Thanks, bro'," muttered Hal.

Following Brad's gaze, the redhead must have glimpsed Hal at once and loosed off two shots in quick succession. Knowing he had five bullets left in his Glock, Hal expended one of them in Grace's direction. It was a snapshot while he was taking evasive action and, at forty metres, it was never going to do much more than discourage her. As Hal expected, it flew wide, smashing into the side window of the car a few yards from Brad.

Staring at the broken car window, Brad seemed utterly transfixed. Without warning a pistol poked out of the shattered window and shot him twice, in chest and head.

At first, Hal couldn't move. It was the shock, because why would they shoot Brad, when he was clearly unarmed and had his hands raised? Then, in his blind fury, Hal darted out from behind the tree, driven by his natural instinct to go to his brother's aid. But, when several more shots rang out, he was forced to step back again. Brad lay still, where he had dropped and Hal knew in his heart that there was nothing to be done. His poor brother didn't have Kevlar, so the close range chest wound would have ripped him apart. Deadly enough, without a bullet to the skull.

Hal was truly bewildered for his world was turning to shit while he looked on. The car door with the smashed window was thrust open. The sudden movement fired his anger because, whoever was getting out of that vehicle had just murdered his brother in cold blood. Hal fired twice at the car door and sent another round at the redhead. But when others fired back, he had no choice but to retreat. Despite the white-hot rage consuming him, he fought to regain control. Wild emotion would just get him killed too, so he had to be smart and patient. Let them come to him and see what it earned them.

His gait was ungainly as he stumbled towards some undergrowth for better cover. Once there, he swiftly reloaded the Glock and waited. They had shot Brad down like a dog, put two bullets into him... And for that crime, he would make every last one of them pay with their blood. It was agony having to leave his brother lying there out in the open, but there was nothing to be done about it. Even without the hostiles around, his thigh was already pounding from the exertion so, wherever he was going to go, he would have to go there slowly, conserving what little strength, and blood, he had left.

While the redhead and her confederates retreated behind the cars, Hal started to weep. He'd seen his share of comrades fall, but this was his brother, his twin, and it felt like he'd been torn in half. Added to his grief was the knowledge that it was all his fault – squarely his fault. Without his insistence and guilt-tripping Brad into coming over to the UK, his brother would still be alive, with the rest of his life ahead of him. He should have abandoned the house when it became clear how dangerous it was. But, of course, macho Hal hated to admit that any fight was beyond him.

Pocketing the Glock, he lay down on his front, cradling the rifle because those murderers had no idea what was gonna hit them now. In the light of the dawn, he reckoned it would be a turkey shoot.... Several hunched figures were hiding behind the vehicles, some more effectively than others. He picked out one whose shoulder he could see clearly and, without a second's hesitation, fired. At such short range, fifty metres or so, the bullet would have shattered the shoulder bone and probably sliced through the artery whilst the impact alone spun the victim backwards to sprawl in the road.

Though one was down, it seemed to encourage the dead man's companions to remain rather better hidden. There were still four more but it was only a matter of time before he picked off every last one of them. From experience, he knew that it was near impossible to conceal all your body behind a vehicle. Besides, one of his bullets would go straight through a car's thin skin. He just prayed that his work would be done before he bled out.

Already, he could feel that the leg wound had worsened. But, so be it. The dressing would hold it for an hour or so and that would be plenty long enough. While he waited, he reloaded the Glock and then focussed again on the cars. He sensed their frustration because they clearly wanted to get into that house, not linger outside waiting to get shot. On the far side of the middle car, a door was opened but Hal couldn't tell in the shadow of the interior what was going on. But one glimpse was all he would need...

Just then, his mobile buzzed and a swift glance told him it was Lisa, which threw him into confusion. He had told her not to contact him. Yet, given what had happened, it would be good to talk to her one more time. Not to explain though, because that would be too much. But to say goodbye...

Before he could even answer it, however, a hail of bullets crashed through the undergrowth around him but, mercifully, all above his head. Shit, an assault rifle. So, they'd found a weapon to flush him out, though they hadn't counted on him shooting prone. They'd learn fast enough, he reckoned. But then, to his surprise, he realised that the sudden burst of fire was merely a distraction to keep his head down. Instead of lingering to smoke him out, the redhead and two men, keeping low and running zigzags, were making straight for the house.

Having left his original position to move to the east end of the copse, he could no longer see the house door but they must have made it there. Angry and frustrated, he pocketed his phone. Lisa had rung off anyway and perhaps it was just as well. So, three had gone to the house and one he had already taken out. But was there another – the one who had shot Brad from the rearmost car? Or had he killed him already?

Unwilling to leave his brother's body out in the open, he got gingerly to his feet, stashed the rifle with his pack and took out the Glock, which still had a full mag of 11 bullets. He was relieved to find that he was able to walk - albeit slowly - as long as he bore almost all his weight on his right leg. Limping past Brad's still form, he approached the car warily with the Glock held out in front of him.

The front seats looked empty but it wouldn't be the first time he was wrong about that. Taking a pace to the right, he wrenched open the back door. The back seat was also unoccupied, so he circled the vehicle and stared at the other cars some yards further down the road. One body lay in the road along with a smattering of glass fragments and exterior vehicle parts. He'd have to take a closer look, but for a moment he paused to glance down at Brad. His brother, whose face was already a pale mask, lay in a darkening pool of blood.

Hearing the scrape of a shoe on tarmac, he swivelled around fast, intending to drop into a crouch. But, of course, his left leg wasn't having that at all and he ended up in an untidy heap on the grass. The clumsy manoeuvre saved his life as two shots whined over his head. Seeing a figure scuttle away from behind the bonnet of the front car, Hal snapped off two shots, but his target escaped into the trees near the house. Shit.

Bending down, he rested a hand on his brother's forehead where the second bullet had left a dark, ugly wound.

"It won't help you now, bro'," he murmured, "but I swear, those bastards are gonna die real soon...."

41

Sunrise Heights

"Oh, shit, they're shooting at each other again," gasped Liv.

"But Grace is working with Charles Grey, so... why?"

"A splinter group, most likely," suggested Monica. "But it doesn't change our situation, does it, because soon enough they'll be coming for us. So, we'd better get ready. They'll likely come in the back."

Graham nodded. "Right, I'll take the back then," he told Monica, "that is, if you're prepared to trust me out of your sight."

"Olivia says you're trustworthy," said Monica, "so, I suppose I have to accept that. I'll stay in here. Liv, you take the hall."

"But no-one can get in the front door without a battering ram," argued Liv. "I'm wasted there."

"You're our backup," said Monica. "Graham falls back to me and we both fall back to you in the hall. Then we have a choice: make a run for it out of the front door, or go upstairs and defend the first floor landing, then the second, until..."

"We run out of landings," observed Graham.

"By then we might not be around to care," said Monica.

"Good pep talk, mother," said Liv. "I'm going to get a bigger knife from the kitchen…"

"I'll take a quick look from the landing upstairs," said Monica. "See what's brewing."

While Monica slipped upstairs, Graham followed Liv into the kitchen.

"Do you think there's anyone out there who can help us?" Liv asked. "If they're shooting at each other…"

With a brisk shake of the head, he said: "I'd guess that a combination of Grey and Grace will outweigh any other faction. So, it's just us, Liv. All we have is a couple of guns - for which we have not much ammunition – and a set of throwing knives."

"And this rather blunt kitchen knife," added Liv, with a grim smile.

"I'm sorry, Liv," he said, mumbling his words. "I should have gotten you out of this place sooner."

"You look tired," she said softly. "Let's just hope all of us can make it out of here."

"Even untrustworthy me?" he said sheepishly.

"Yeh, even you – though I think you're running out of time to wheedle your way into my…."

"Affections?"

"I was going to say knickers," groaned Liv. "Not that you've managed to get into either so far…"

"Harsh," complained Graham.

"A little harsh, but very true," she said. "Thing is, Graham, I like to know where I am with people and I never know where I am with you - or my homicidal mother for that matter."

"You haven't given a toss about your mother for the past ten years," retorted Graham. "You told me you were actually glad when you thought she was dead."

"Yeh, she's still my mother though," argued Liv.

"Are you talking about me?" enquired Monica, descending the stairs.

"Piss off!" chimed Liv and Graham together.

Both fell instantly silent and exchanged a conspiratorial grin as they recalled the last time they had responded in such a manner.

Monica stared, uncomprehending, at the pair of them. "I don't know what you find so amusing."

Liv tried to look penitent and failed. She always liked to know what the stakes were and, now she knew, she felt somehow a little more at ease. Faced with the worst possible outcome, even her mother's secrets and Graham's lies seemed remarkably unimportant. But fighting for her life? Now that was something she understood perfectly.

"Alright then," she said with a savage grin. "Let the games begin..."

"Remember, we defend the ground floor doors and then move upstairs," replied Monica, as she checked how many bullets remained in her gun.

But all colour drained from her face as they all turned, as one, to face the front door.

Because someone had turned a key in the lock.

As the heavy door began to ease slowly open, Monica recovered her nerve and hissed: "Up the stairs now - first floor landing!"

Liv scrambled up the stairs after her mother, with Graham following on their heels. At the top of the first flight, Liv dived behind the panelled landing balustrade and Graham followed. By contrast, Monica crouched by the newel post and peered back down into the hall. They heard the front door swing wide open with a crash and, a few moments later, Monica reported softly: "It's Grace. But how in God's name did she get hold of a key?"

Liv couldn't see that it mattered much how Grace had gained entry, just that she had. And, though no voices drifted up from the ground floor, Liv was certain that Grace would not have stormed into the house alone. So, there must be several with her. Three · or two, if they were lucky. But Liv wasn't feeling especially lucky.

"It won't take them long to realise we're not downstairs," muttered Graham.

"No shit," groaned Liv, shifting her position so that she could retrieve the knives Monica had given her · just the average Christmas present from your psycho mother...

"Won't you have to stand up to throw one of those?" whispered Graham.

Liv shrugged. "I guess. I suppose I'll find out soon enough."

"How's your knee?" he asked. "Do you need any help?"

"I'm fine," said Liv. Because that's what people said when they weren't at all fine.

Though Graham said nothing more, his despairing shake of the head was not lost on her. Would one tiny moment of intimacy have hurt her? She supposed not and patted him gently on the shoulder – which, by Liv's standards, amounted to a show of affection. But instantly, she regretted the moment of weakness and snapped: "Keep your hands on your gun."

For the first time, she heard low voices which suggested that the intruders were gathering near the foot of the stairs. A single creak marked the moment that someone put their foot on the bottom step. Liv realised she was holding her breath. Breathe, you idiot, she told herself. But what little breath she had was expelled the moment Monica abruptly stood up, fired a single shot down the stairs and bobbed back down again out of sight.

At an anguished cry from below, Liv's spirits rose – only to plummet a moment later when multiple bullets raked the top of the stairs and landing. Shit. The introduction of a rapid fire weapon rather tipped the balance, she thought.

"Bugger," groaned Monica. "Anyone hit?"

Liv didn't waste her breath on a reply, reckoning that her mother could see for herself that she and Graham were still alive. Nonetheless, she had never seen bullets fly so close to her before. It was too much. But then her eyesight was surely the definition of too much.

"What now?" asked Graham. "Because, much more of that and one of us is bound to catch it."

Liv was about to say how glad she was to have those puny knives when their conversation was cut short by Grace, shouting up the stairs.

"Time to let it go, Monica Fisher. Your only way out of here alive is to surrender and give us that last account. I'll give you five minutes to think about doing that."

Glancing across at her mother, Liv detected no hint of submission in Monica's eyes.

"We could still do that," said Graham beside her.

"We're not doing that," said Liv, in a tone that left no room for misunderstanding. "No more negotiation. No more pissing about."

"Move further along the landing," advised Monica, in a whisper. "There's less chance of you being hit. And, sooner or later, they'll have to come up. Our best play is to take them out as they reach the top few steps."

Which meant, thought Liv, that their 'best play' was one which offered a remarkably small chance of success. Briefly, she questioned how qualified her mother was to determine their strategy, but let it pass because clearly, an established gun owner trumped a complete novice every time.

"Take a doorway each," ordered Monica, sitting down with her back against the closed bathroom door. She would be the most exposed because she was poised at the top of the stairs. But Monica must think she was the one least at risk – if their opponents still wanted that last account.

Sidling across to sit beside Liv, Graham whispered: "Where you going to be, Liv?"

"Why, do you wanna hold my hand?"

"I can if you want," he murmured.

Still seated on the floor, Liv shook her head but then, on impulse, reached up a hand to grasp his to feel the warmth of him – just for a moment. Surprising, she thought, what the proximity of mortal danger made you do.

"See you on the other side, as they say," he told her, with a grim smile.

Releasing his hand, she replied: "Yeh, fuck knows why they say that when there is no other side."

While he positioned himself in the doorway, she extracted two of the slender throwing blades from their sheaths. She couldn't help but admire the sleek, crafted lengths of steel. Feeling their perfect balance, she cradled one hilt in each hand, while she considered where best to throw from. As Graham had pointed out, she would be better off standing and she quickly realised there was only one place that she could do that. A moment later, she was crouching between two bedroom doorways, with her back to the wall. Already her leg was complaining because that's what it did. As limbs went, her left leg had turned into an idle bastard.

From the hall below, an impatient Grace shouted up: "Have it your way then."

Surely it wasn't five minutes yet, thought Liv – barely even two. So, Grace was keen – maybe too keen.

On the carpeted landing, she crouched on her haunches ready to rise up as soon as their assailants appeared. But, since her leg already felt as if it was on fire, God knew what it would feel like when she actually drove all her weight down hard upon it.

Opting for speed and surprise rather than stealth, a pair of their adversaries thundered up the stairs. Liv, calves and thighs tensed, prepared to spring up, She reminded herself that Graham, who was crouched close by in another bedroom doorway, had been wounded far worse than her. If he could be so damned stoic, then so could she.

As soon as a head appeared above the banister, Liv gritted her teeth and thrust herself up to her feet. The instant she was upright, she let fly with her right hand and almost simultaneously with her left. By the time the fingers of her left hand released the second blade, she had two throats to aim at. The first knife flew wide to thud into the diamond-patterned wallpaper. When her target swivelled around to turn his weapon in her direction, her second blade struck him in the eye. Liv dropped to the floor seconds before a spray of bullets arced crazily across the landing to punch lumps out of walls, doors and finally ceiling, before the gunman tumbled back down the stairs.

His comrade, armed with a handgun, must have fired at least two shots, perhaps three. It was hard to tell in the cacophony of sound that echoed around the landing. Monica loosed off several shots before she dropped down again. As Liv fell, with her eyes slammed shut to cut out the myriad flashes, she felt a sharp tug on her left shoulder. At first she thought it was Graham pulling her but, as the numbness crept down her arm, she knew she was hit. At least it wasn't in her sodding leg though...

42

Sunrise Heights

Once the shooting stopped, Liv opened her eyes a crack to take a look around the landing. One of those who had mounted the stairs lay very still on the top step, with a neat, black bullet hole in his forehead. Since Graham was already at her side, she assumed he must be unhurt.

Craning her neck around from her position on the floor, she tried to get a glimpse of her mother. Monica, she saw, was still seated with her back against the closed bathroom door but it didn't take Liv's exceptional powers of observation to notice the smudge of crimson on her chest.

"Lie still," warned Graham. "You're hit."

"Yeh, so's Monica. Like mother, like fucking daughter..."

"I'll tear off some cloth to bind up your arm," he said.

But waving him away, Liv muttered: "See to her first."

"I don't care about her," he hissed.

"Yeh, but she knows that last account number," growled Liv, "so, we sort of need her alive, don't we?

"I'd rather make sure you're alright," he insisted, pressing a wad of cloth to her shoulder.

But, resting her hand upon his, she looked him in the eye and said: "Your scrap of cotton isn't going to make much difference. If the artery was cut, I'd be bleeding to death. But I'm not, am I?"

"There could be internal bleeding," he argued, his concern evident in his doleful expression.

"It's just my arm. Monica's got some sort of chest wound."

"But–"

Gripping his hand, she prised it off her shoulder. "Go see to her... I still have three blades left. So, go and help her, or I might have to use one on you."

"Alright," he conceded, but removing his hand from her arm, he added: "Please don't bleed to death while I'm gone."

"You should be more worried about their next move. If they're happy to shoot Monica then we're all dead."

"They weren't trying to shoot her," he replied. "I reckon Monica was just hit by the random spray of bullets."

While he moved across to examine her mother's wound, Liv suddenly eased her phone out of her jeans pocket and took a picture of her bloodstained mother. Typing the caption one-handed was a struggle, but finally she sent it winging out into the ether. Would anyone see it, believe it, or do anything about it? Unlikely, but still...

Graham was helping Monica to move over to where her daughter sat. Then he roared down the stairs: "You messed up, Grace. Monica's hit and, if she dies, you'll get nothing."

Soon after, a male voice, filled with fury, echoed around the hall below: "I told you not to kill Monica!"

"That's Grey," murmured Graham, "the one who hired me."

At that moment Liv was wishing she had stayed in Reading – and not many people would say that. But her brief foray into self-pity was interrupted by a dull crack from somewhere below her, followed by a low growling and grinding sound. Then suddenly, the whole house was vibrating, as if it might shake itself to pieces. Monica reached out to clasp Liv's hand but, after a few minutes, all was still and silent once more. Well, as silent as anywhere could be with Charles Grey and Grace Walter arguing furiously downstairs.

"We should go upstairs," suggested Monica. "Make them come up to us."

"Upstairs?" gasped Liv. "You can barely stand, never mind climb the stairs."

"But they might not follow us up if they're worried about having a safe way out of the house," said Monica.

"You think?" said Liv.

"If this place slides off the cliff, we're all dead," said Graham glumly.

"To state the fucking obvious," growled Liv.

"But we have to get them to come up after us," insisted Monica.

"They *are* coming up after us," said Graham.

"We're not in any state to go up any further," declared Liv. "We'll go to your bedroom, mother. It's the last room they'll get to from the landing."

"True," agreed Graham. "We can draw them in there and there's only one entrance."

"And one exit," grumbled Monica. "But, you're right, Olivia. I'll not get much further than that. Come on then Graham, help me up, will you?"

When Graham did so, Liv noted the grimace of pain on her mother's pale face and saw the stain of blood she left behind on the landing carpet. But Liv made no comment as she levered herself up to stagger after them into the master bedroom. Graham, having assisted Monica, returned to help her.

"You're a real trier," she told him, with a grin. "But, instead of putting your arm round me, go and close all the other doors, so they don't know which room we're in."

With a nod of respect, he replied: "Good idea."

Under her breath, Liv muttered: "Yeh, I get those sometimes – though not often enough, it seems..."

"Graham," hissed Monica, "we need some warning when they're coming up and since you're a bit more mobile..."

"Yes, of course," said Graham. "I'll listen by the top of the stairs."

"Come sit here with me, Olivia," said Monica, sitting down in front of the wardrobe.

When Liv joined her, Monica thrust a bloodied scrap of paper into Liv's hand and murmured: "Here, take this – it's your legacy."

"Is it the last account number?" gasped Liv.

"No, if you get out of this house alive, the last thing you'll need is the cartel snapping at your heels. The accounts are going to die with me."

Monica's breathing was already ragged which did not augur well.

"I'm sorry It's all I have left to give you. And it's something, at least. Memorise it, then destroy it."

"Did you get that line from an old movie?" said Liv. "Can't I just put it in my phone?"

"Anyone could get your phone," croaked Monica. "So, just do it, Liv, please..."

Liv realised that it was the first time in her life that Monica hadn't called her Olivia. That was the moment she knew that her mother wouldn't last much longer.

Though her memory skills were not quite in the same league as her mother's, she was quite adept at swiftly memorising short items like the contents of the note. How long she would remember it for didn't seem very important as she crammed it into her mouth.

As Graham entered, he caught only her last act and stared at her in disbelief.

"Christ, Liv, you must be damned hungry if you're eating paper," he observed.

Liv, tasting the blood as she chewed the last morsel of deeply unpleasant paper, simply spread her hands. Because, even without a mouthful, what could she possibly say?

"Anyway, they've stopped arguing and they're on their way up," he warned, as he gently shut the door. "I only saw three of them."

"Great," sighed Liv, "except, there's only one and two halves of us..."

Whilst Graham took up the most exposed position facing the door, Liv left Monica and stumbled over to the corner opposite. From there, when the door opened, she would have a clear side-on view of anyone who entered. Though she tried to focus on the doorway, the insistent throbbing in her left arm was a constant distraction. She was also feeling a little light-headed which she assumed was caused by losing some blood. With one arm now almost immobile, all she could do was throw a knife with her right. Though she had several blades left, she was certain she would get only one attempt.

Hearing doors being opened, as their opponents checked each first floor room in turn, she prepared herself. They would come to the master bedroom, furthest from the stair head, last. But of course, Charles Grey and his cronies were not fools and they were hardly going to allow themselves to be picked off as they entered the room one at a time. Thus, Liv concluded that, having reached the last possible hiding place on the first floor, they would rush in together. The one person they would not want to hurt any further was Monica, so Graham would be taken out first. But what about her? Might they want to keep her breathing just a little longer to persuade Monica? If they hesitated, she might just get a second blade in the air.

Outside on the landing there was silence. No more floorboards creaked as rooms were explored. Their assailants would now be standing outside the bedroom, gathering themselves for a charge. Maximum impact, so no slow opening of the door. Just a sudden crash as they smashed their way in. Liv was inclined to aim for Grace unless another was nearer. But now she tried to steady herself, breathing deep and slow, as she stared across at Graham. Would he crack under the pressure, because he would be the first person those rushing in would see? But, that moment, he caught her eye and smiled. In a reckless response, she blew him a kiss because, what did it matter now? He would never have the chance to get into her knickers. Not, of course, that she wanted him to...

The blade she had been holding for the past few moments in the fingers of her right hand was slippery with sweat. Hastily, she wiped both fingers and knife on her T-shirt before gripping the blade once more. Just one throw... one chance. Don't overthink it, she told herself. But she needn't have worried because, when the door caved in with a splintering crash, instinct kicked in. Liv's eyes flashed wide and she hurled her knife as gunfire exploded around her.

In such circumstances, each tiny spark of action hurtles by, but not for Liv. Whether she wanted to or not, she absorbed every last pixel of it. She watched her blade plunge into Grace's neck, severing the artery in an instant. Graham fired twice at the third figure who entered the room. The first bullet wounded him and, though he got one round off in reply, it flew astray and Graham's second shot killed him. She hoped the spurt of Grace's blood next to Charles Grey would unnerve him. It didn't, because he loosed off a shot at Graham, who was struck in the head, and collapsed onto the bed.

The moment Liv let fly, she reached for another blade, but she wasn't quick enough. Grey's bullet caught her on the side of the abdomen, just above her waist. As she landed on the deep pile bedroom carpet, the blade fell from her fingers. Mentally she checked off the possible organs which might have been damaged.

Right hand side, low down. So... liver, kidney... Shit, a whole shedload of things...

A furious Monica had emptied her weapon at Grey and must have hit him at least once. But, though wounded, he was clearly desperate to spare Monica long enough for her to reveal the final account details. As it turned out, it didn't matter because a stray bullet had found a home in Monica's chest. She looked down in disgust at the second wound welling with blood beside the first.

Liv managed to persuade her compromised left arm to press against her new wound though she doubted she could apply enough pressure.

"You bloody fool, Monica," stormed Grey. "Give me that last account, or it'll die with you."

"Works for me," groaned Monica.

While Grey was raging at her stricken mother, Liv's right hand groped behind her for the fallen blade.

"Give me that account, or I'll shoot your daughter again," snarled Grey, moving across to Liv and pulling her injured left arm away from the wound.

"Thank you," breathed Liv. "I don't think I could've thrown it that far..."

"What are you mumbling, woman?" snarled Grey, who had no idea what she was talking about, until she reached up and drove the blade through his throat. Blood smothered her arm, as her stunned victim dropped down upon her and proceeded to bleed out, his blood mingling with hers.

Struggling to heave him off her, Liv crawled towards Monica.

"Mother," she urged. "Just stay alive. It's over."

"Oh, I wouldn't say that, exactly," said a voice from the landing.

43

Liv exchanged an astonished look with Monica because both recognised the new voice.

"How did he get out of that plane?" gasped Monica, her voice a whisper. "There was only one parachute... for the pilot... and I'd already knocked Henry out."

"Wild guess," muttered Liv, leaning back alongside her stricken mother, "the pilot didn't make it..."

"You got that right, at least," confirmed Henry Fisher, standing on the threshold.

"Not that it matters much now," scoffed Liv.

"No," agreed Henry, "it doesn't. So, what's that last account number, Monica?"

With an effort, Monica lifted her head. "The numbers are only in my head, Henry," she breathed. "Nowhere else..."

"Oh, that's right, the woman with the photographic memory who couldn't remember to take a lousy contraceptive with her lover."

"I didn't forget," sighed Monica. "But Liv's got nothing to do with this."

"Oh, but she's got everything to do with it," retorted Henry. "Because that's why you wanted out, wasn't it? Because of her. Because of your maladjusted bastard. But, you know what, Monica, if you don't give me that account right now, I'll take this malignant little piece out of the game forever."

Ignoring his threat, Liv reached out to grasp her mother's hand and gently squeeze it. In those last moments, the two exchanged a look that had never before passed between them: an admission of love. Only when the light faded from her mother's eyes, did Liv release her hand.

Henry turned to Liv, his face twitching with anger, as it used to in her youth, when she particularly annoyed him. But this was worse. Far worse. In his rage, he struck out with his foot, kicking her so hard in the stomach that she could only curl up into a ball. Already bleeding from the gunshot wound, her midriff was a sea of agony.

"I should have strangled you at birth," he snarled, "because I knew even then that you couldn't have been my daughter."

It was Henry, Liv now realised, who had been trying to kill her. The station, the beach, the wine bar and so on... that was all down to him. Because, of course, he was the only one who knew her mother was still alive. And if, Monica was still alive, he didn't need her daughter – especially a daughter who was someone else's bastard. Henry Fisher had been cleaning house and Liv was part of the trash.

Now, with his wife finally dead, Henry levelled his pistol at Liv and snarled: "I hope you enjoyed your little moment of bonding, you scheming little bitch."

Liv had one blade left but it was out of reach. It might as well have been in Reading. With Graham slumped on the bed and Monica dead, her only weapon was brazen defiance.

"Do it then," she urged. "Finish off the rest of your family."

Pointing his gun at her head, he scoffed: "Family? I never wanted a family. Family brings weakness and the very idea of it sickens me."

In the brief, still moment before he fired, they both heard a creak from the landing outside the bedroom. Though Henry turned to look, he was too slow and before he could redirect his pistol, the first bullet entered his body. Even as he reeled from the blow, a second struck, somewhere close to the spine, Liv reckoned.

"Family!" roared the stranger who stormed through the bedroom doorway. "That's for my family, you piece of shit - for Alice and Brad."

Even before the third and fourth bullets hit home, Liv decided that Henry Fisher was well and truly dead.

When her saviour fell silent, Liv stared up at him in amazement. "Who the fuck are you?" she cried.

"Not the best greeting I've ever had," replied the stranger wearily, as he leant against the door frame.

"Sorry," said Liv. "I could say I've had a bad day but you can probably see that for yourself. Anyway, I don't really care who you are, but I've never been so pleased to see anyone in all my life - unless, you plan to shoot me next..."

"I'm Hal," he said, "and no, I'm done shooting people... period."

With that, he collapsed to the floor and passed out. Liv, who in the past few hours had observed enough wounds to last her a lifetime, suspected that his blood-soaked leg was not good news.

"Shit, Hal," she muttered, "and I thought you were the cavalry."

44

For a few moments, Liv just stayed where she was on the floor. The bullet wound and whatever damage Henry had inflicted with his boot seemed to have fused into a single wall of pain. She wondered vaguely whether anyone else was going to burst into the room and, only when it appeared that no-one was, did she decide it might be safe to move. Leaving Monica, she crawled to the window and levered herself up on the sill, though every movement tore her tortured flesh a little more.

Peering down at Graham on the bed, she was relieved to see the rise and fall of his chest. Bending closer, she observed that a bullet had scored across his temple and left blood all over his face. So, had that caused him to fall unconscious? Was that a thing? She didn't know.

"Graham!" she cried. And, when he did not respond, she wondered if he had suffered another wound that she couldn't yet see. What if his blood was slowly seeping into the mattress beneath him?

"Oh, shit," she groaned. "I'm sorry, Graham, but if you're not actually dead, then I really need you to wake up."

With her only functional arm, she reached down to gently tap his face. Well, that was certainly her intention but, losing her balance, she lurched forward and ended up giving him quite a substantial slap before she landed on top of him. A fresh wave of pain engulfed her.

"Liv, did you... did you just slap me?" muttered Graham, staring up at her.

Stifling another groan, she murmured: "People do odd things when they're dying... apparently."

Graham slid out from underneath her, unwittingly sending a further lance of pain through her. Sitting on the bed beside her crumpled body, he gripped her hand.

"You can't be dying," he said, aghast. "Where are you hurt?"

"Everywhere," she moaned. "Help me sit up."

"Are you sure that's a good idea?" he said.

"Don't know," she muttered. "Let's try." And, for once, she let him hold her.

Surveying the room's carnage, he gasped: "Shit, Liv, what happened? Isn't that... Henry Fisher?"

In a breath, it seemed, he was trembling and shaking, with tears of regret rolling down his cheeks. "I should have been here for you," he lamented, ashen-faced.

Liv, fearing he was going to have one of his moments, pleaded: "Not now, Graham... Don't leave me now, because I really need you."

"This is... a lot, Liv," he murmured.

A throbbing wave of torment suddenly gripped her and she sank down on her back, gasping for breath. And, moments later, she was weeping... for her mother and all else that was now lost. It was the pain itself though, the persistent agony, which brought her to her senses.

Snatching away her tears, she growled: "Fuck it. We're not dead yet, are we?"

In a rare moment of empathy, she tried to wrap her good arm around the anxious Graham · because who didn't respond to a hug? Well, she didn't for one, but she desperately hoped that he might. It was a relief when he wrapped his arms around her in response. Until he squeezed against her left arm · with a bullet still in it somewhere · and the urge to scream was just too great to resist.

"I'm sorry, Liv," he cried at once.

From the floor, Hal cried: "Hey, what gives?"

"Oh shit, you're still alive," muttered Liv, waiting for the throbbing in her arm to subside.

Graham turned his attention to the wounded man near the doorway who had managed to haul himself to a sitting position. "Who are you?" he demanded.

"That's Hal," explained Liv. "He's on our side."

"Bigger question," groaned Hal. "Can I stand up?"

Graham went to help him up and the pair of them sat down on the bed beside Liv.

"Three not very wise monkeys," remarked Liv, feeling very light-headed..

"Shit, that doesn't look good," said Hal, staring at his own leg.

"We should get some help," said Graham.

"Yeh, about now would be good," cried Liv, almost fainting from the pain. "In fact, right now would be fucking great..."

"You curse a lot," observed Hal.

"Yeh, I do," she admitted. "I do. But can we talk about that later..."

"I've got field dressings in my pack," offered Hal. "So, I could patch you folks up a bit."

"Great," sighed Liv, her head swimming again. "Where's your pack?"

"Outside - about fifty metres away."

"Terrific... can you give me a slap please?"

"What?"

"You know, a slap in the face?"

"Why?"

"Because Graham won't. And, if you don't, I'm going to pass out..."

"Well-"

"Just hit me, please," she mumbled.

When he did, he almost knocked her off the bed. "Not that hard," she protested.

"Jeez, I'm so sorry," cried Hal, his remorse almost tangible.

Reaching out to grasp his hand, she explained: "Sorry, I was kidding. Grim British humour, you know... laugh in the face of death...."

"Right, British humour," he acknowledged. "Yeh, well we need to get out of here and find a hospital."

"Yeh, I suppose," agreed Liv. "My phone's somewhere..."

"I'll use mine," said Graham.

But as he took out his phone to call an ambulance, a low rumble started to erupt from beneath them – almost imperceptible at first and then growing ever louder.

"Jeez, what was that?" whispered Hal. "Felt like a quake."

"Er, no," murmured Liv. "That was the sound of this house falling off the cliff."

"More British humour?" suggested Hal.

"Sadly not," said Liv.

"We need to get out," urged Graham, wrapping an arm around Liv. For once, she decided a slap was not an appropriate response and leant on him. Even so, it was still a struggle for her to stand.

Hal's wounded leg, she observed, was a mass of blood and bandage. She wasn't sure he would make it down the stairs, let alone out of the house. A sudden graunching shudder made the whole building shake and brought a look of shock to Graham's bloodied face.

"Got to go, guys," murmured Liv.

Hal gave a shrug. "I'm not going to get far."

"Well, you got up the stairs, didn't you?" argued Liv. "So, it should be a breeze going down."

But still, he looked a beaten man. "I've just watched my brother being shot," he muttered."

"So?" she snapped. "That's my mother lying there. You must have something – or someone else – that's worth trying to live for…"

After a moment, Hal replied: "Yeh, maybe…."

"Only one way to find out," said Liv. "Just get moving."

"You go, Hal," urged Graham, "and I'll help Liv."

"Yeh, OK," agreed the American, though he did not move.

When Graham put an arm around her again and lifted her to her feet, she shuddered from the pain and feared she'd pass out. But then the house gave a sudden lurch and she clutched his arm more tightly. Only then did she realise that he must still be feeling the effects of the gunshot to the head because he was far from steady on his feet.

"Alright then," said Hal. "Gotta go. Now or never, eh?"

With a grunt of discomfort, he staggered up from the bed.

"Yeh, you get going," Liv told him. "We'll follow. Don't worry about us."

Hal limped across the room to the door, accompanied by what was now a continuous groaning of cracking bricks and splintering timbers.

For a moment, he paused in the doorway. "You're coming?"

"Working up to it," retorted Liv. "Just go."

So he did, without a backward glance, and Liv felt somehow relieved because the American clearly had someone who might be waiting for him. Neither she nor Graham fell into that category because, if they both perished at Sunrise Heights, no·one would give a shit — or even notice. She had no·one left. No future either. And he was alone too, after losing his friend, Mark and Barbara — whoever she was. Unless, in his abject loneliness, he'd just made her up...

"Come on," said Graham, because she was just leaning against him and hadn't yet taken a step towards the door.

Damn, she was tired. Her stomach had stopped aching but she wasn't entirely sure that was a good thing. Blood was still seeping from her abdomen and her left arm wouldn't move. But beyond all that, she was just so... weary. So, maybe that was how she ended.

Her eyes were suddenly drawn to her mother who was sitting upright, grey-faced and blood spattered, against the wardrobe. In that moment, Liv could have sworn that she saw Monica move.

"What the fuck," she gasped. "Mother..."

Though Monica had been shot twice in the chest, to Liv's bewilderment, she slowly leant forward.

"I'm coming," cried Liv as, in her reckless haste, she slid from Graham's arms and dropped down to her knees. Belatedly, she recalled the deep cut in her knee and, by the time the shooting pain subsided, she saw that her mother was no longer moving. Only when her eyes strayed to the wardrobe behind Monica, did Liv understand that it was the whole wall itself that was leaning forward. A moment later, the window beyond the bed suddenly shattered as its frame twisted out of shape. Fragments of glass spun out in all directions, showering both Liv and Graham.

And that was the moment Liv decided that, if she was going to die, it wasn't going to be in her parents' house as it disintegrated around her.

"Graham!" she cried. "Are you OK?"

"Yeh, course. Come on," he said, lifting her to her feet once more, careful this time, she noticed, to avoid her wounded arm.

He still looked dazed, however, and when she saw his face had been pierced by several slivers of glass, she sacrificed a few precious seconds to remove them. Then she looked into his eyes and fixed him with a determined glare.

"We're going to get out of here," she assured him.

"Yeh," he muttered, "But shit, Liv, you look terrible."

"Save the compliments for later," she scolded. "But I say fuck Henry Fisher - and fuck this house!"

As a ten centimetre wide crack opened up across the ceiling, Graham complained: "Now you've really pissed it off. We're not getting out of here, are we?"

"I am - and so are you," she snarled, daring him to disagree.

After that, there was so much noise around them they couldn't hear each other's words and, with lumps of plaster starting to fall from the ceiling, he put his shoulder under her good arm and hauled her out of the collapsing bedroom. The instant they set foot on the landing, the balustrade splintered and the floor was suddenly slippery wet from water gushing out of the bathroom pipes. As they made for the stairs, every wall seemed to sway and lurch.

Walls contorted under the stress. Protesting timbers creaked and twisted as the entire rear half of the house suddenly broke off and slid away down the steep slope. Bricks, glass and all kinds of shit flew in every direction. On the stairs, they found the treads beginning to disappear from under their feet and slid down on their backsides, screaming and clinging onto each other.

Their abrupt arrival at the foot of the stairs winded Liv but, with Graham beside her, she managed to scramble through the tangle of debris, heedless of water spouts and sparking electrical wiring. Moving as if welded together, the pair stumbled along the hall towards the front door, accompanied by sounds reminiscent of the death moans of some giant, wounded beast. Half the house had already gone and the rest appeared to be imploding around them.

"Keep going," she railed at him, though with every step she was struggling just to keep hold of him. Their limbs simply didn't want to move anymore but somehow they dragged themselves out into the porch. As they paused there, Graham released her gently so that she could lean against a wall while they got their breath back. A moment later, the opposite wall of the porch flew abruptly upwards and disappeared behind them as the remainder of the house pivoted down into the sea, leaving them marooned together on a square plinth of concrete.

They heard, rather than saw, the house crash onto the sea shore below. Before them, a few yards away, Hal, with a rucksack at his feet, was a more than welcome sight.

"Hey, time to patch you two up," he said with a sheepish grin. "Jeez, I thought you weren't gonna make it. You guys left it damned late."

"We did," croaked Liv, unearthing a wan smile from somewhere.

"Come on," said Graham, offering her his hand. "We'll soon fix you up."

But as she reached out to him, the concrete plinth slid out from under their feet.

45

Liv was dead.

Or… she had her eyes shut and was holding her breath.

She wasn't sure which.

All she did know for certain was that, dead or alive, her right hand was clamped around Graham's wrist. As an experiment, she tried to move her legs and was thrilled to discover that she could. Not dead then.

"Don't do that!" cried Graham. "Just stay still, Liv, please."

Liv's eyes flew open and she didn't much like what she saw so she swiftly closed them. But when, a moment later, she eased her eyelids up a fraction, she saw the same grim scene beneath her. And, when she peered upwards, she found herself looking into a pair of eyes filled with despair. It took her just a second to understand that the strain evident in Graham's bleak gaze was only partly caused by the woman clinging desperately to his wrist. For Graham was also dangling over the sheer drop, restrained only by Hal's strong arm.

"Oh, shit," she muttered.

"Just hold on and keep still," Graham told her. "We'll figure a way out of this in a minute."

A minute? Liv knew that, before that minute was up, she would have slid off his wrist. Graham might need a minute to figure it out, but it took her less than five seconds. Because there was really only one way out.

Staring below her, she studied how the strewn debris of Sunrise Heights had arrayed itself across the shore. The tide was right in, so the house had just piled into the water and splayed out in all directions. With every successive wave, the sea was steadily distributing the heap of wreckage in an ever-broadening swathe. Her sharp eyes picked out lumps of brick and concrete which would have no trouble splitting her skull. And there were pipes of gleaming copper and lengths of dull steel just waiting to impale her. A washing machine stood proud amid a tangle of window frames, with shards of jagged glass still fixed to them.

"Liv!" Graham called down. "Are you OK?"

Casting her eyes all round her, she drank in the shimmering blue sky where the white-chested gulls soared across and dipped down towards the water.

"Yeh, I'm great," she cried, releasing her grip on his wrist.

She decided to fall head first because the last thing she wanted to do was break a leg. Aiming for a long sheet of corrugated plastic, upon which water cascaded down from the twisted mains supply pipe, she reckoned her chances were about 30/70. But, back when Henry was pointing his gun at her, she would have bitten off the hand that offered her a 30% chance of survival.

The plan was to slide effortlessly along the plastic sheeting and dive off the end into the sea - unless, of course, she bounced... Then, either she would hit the water head first, or she'd hit something else... Endgame, right there...

46

Bournemouth Hospital, January 3rd in the late evening

Graham was tired of answering questions but he suspected that he was only spared a shedload more by the sheer scale of confusion within the local police force. The reappearance and the fresh demise of Henry and Monica Fisher had rather stunned everyone.

Graham's situation was undoubtedly also helped by the death of Charles Grey, which enabled his contact at SWROCU to offer his superiors immediate access to all but one of the cartel's accounts. Taking the win, SWROCU quickly absolved Graham of any wrongdoing. Clearing Hal would have been a little more problematic had Graham not claimed that he brought in the American twins, Hal and Brad, as backup after his colleague, Mark, was murdered.

After finally shrugging off the most persistent police detectives, Graham went to check up on Hal. Well, he had to do something, and there was nothing he could do for Liv. Hal was wide awake and looked up when Graham entered.

"I'm surprised you're even conscious," remarked Graham.

"Not my first rodeo," said Hal, giving him a faint grin.

Graham thought that, had another man used the cliché, it might have jarred with him. But not with Hal.

"I'm sorry about your brother," said Graham. "That was bloody tough…"

"Sure was," agreed Hal. "And I led him into it all. That'll stay with me forever, I guess."

Graham nodded, unsure what he could possibly say but, of course, there was nothing to be said, so he settled on: "How's the leg?"

"The leg's looking alright," Hal told him ruefully. "I was lucky. The doc said the bullet nicked something called the posterior… tibial… artery – at least I think that's what he said. The Israeli dressing I put on applied just about enough pressure to hold it. I won't be doing active service again, but I didn't plan to anyway. Still, I reckon you look worse than I do."

Whilst it was true that Graham was sporting a fresh dressing on his head, he felt a bit of a fraud compared to Hal, without whom, he would most certainly be dead.

"And what about your girl?" enquired Hal.

"My girl? Oh, she's hardly my girl."

"Olivia? Liv, is it?" said Hal.

"She's still in surgery," murmured Graham, who wanted so much to talk about her, but couldn't bear to think about what she'd done.

"Tough lady," observed Hal. "She sure took a hell of a beating…"

"Yeh, typical Liv," said Graham. "She managed to catch a couple of bullets, neither of which hit anything vital. So, she decided to dive head first off a sodding cliff and smash her skull to pieces on an iron pipe."

"That's..."

"It's crazy," said Graham, who had struggled for many hours already with the bitter cocktail of guilt and grief. If he was honest, it was only having to deal with the authorities that had kept him from falling apart completely.

"But, if she hadn't let go," murmured Hal.

"We wouldn't be having this cosy little chat now," said Graham.

"That's for sure," agreed Hal. "It was a ballsy call... I'd never have pulled you both up. I'm telling you: I was done and struggling just to hold your weight. Your girl took one for the team, Graham, that's what she did."

"I didn't think Liv even knew what a team was," confessed Graham.

"Really?" said Hal. "You only have to watch her for a minute to know that's not true."

Graham nodded absently and reflected that perhaps he should have watched more and said less.

"Did you manage to call Lisa?" asked Hal.

"Yeh, she's on her way."

"Really? She is? She wanted to come?"

"Yeh, even before I told her what a hero you are," said Graham. "She seemed to like hearing that you saved our lives and foiled some criminals. You're lucky you've got someone like that."

"Didn't think I'd ever see her again," admitted Hal. "I'm not even sure what to tell her."

"I'd keep it simple and truthful," advised Graham. "You and your brother went looking for your lost father and, when you found him, it turned out he was a criminal. You got into a fight and helped us out."

Hal nodded and Graham realised belatedly that the poor guy was probably exhausted – especially after the surgery to repair his torn leg.

"I'll let you rest till Lisa comes," he said.

But Hal's rest was short-lived because, next moment, Lisa was standing in the doorway. She looked very hesitant though, Graham thought, as she waited there, looking from Hal to Graham and back again. She was clutching her winter coat tightly around her, even though the hospital room was warm.

Then, staring at Hal, she said, her eyes sparkling with tears: "Well, you haven't left me so, that's a first."

"I want to stay here... in England... with you," Hal told her.

"OK," she said, walking slowly over to him. "Let's get you patched up first," she said. "But, if you want to stay, you'll need to tell me everything."

"It's bad," he confessed.

"OK," she replied, "but let me decide just how bad, alright?"

"I'll see you guys later," said Graham, heading out, though he was pretty sure neither of them noticed him leave.

There was genuine affection in her words, he thought. And, in the hand that gently cradled Hal's face, there was love. Those two at least would be alright, he decided, as he walked away down the corridor. What he wouldn't give for such a gesture...

47

Bournemouth Hospital on 5th January at noon

Liv was drifting down towards a shining patch of blue light, but she couldn't be certain what it was. Opening her eyes seemed to be inordinately difficult, though she didn't know why. But her head hurt – of that she was certain. The ache seemed to extend all over her scalp but, when she attempted to lift her hand to examine the head, her arm wouldn't move. Prising her eyes open, she achieved some blurry vision – enough to take in something of her surroundings. The first part was easy: she was in a hospital room and the machines at the outer edges of her limited peripheral vision suggested she was plugged into several tubes and wires. Or were they plugged into her?

Shit... How did she get there?

A few moments later, she woke up again to find some stranger sitting in a chair watching her. The cheeky bastard must have snuck in the instant her eyes were closed.

"Who are you?" she slurred.

"Liv?"

"Shit," she muttered. So, not a dark, handsome stranger after all...

"Liv?" prompted Graham again.

"Who are you?" mumbled Liv.

"It's me, Liv," he declared. "It's Graham."

"Who's Graham?"

"Don't you remember anything?" he gasped. "Don't you remember me?"

A trace of a smile must have crossed her lips before she groaned: "Had you going there... but I couldn't be arsed carrying through with it..."

"Christ, Liv, you're a bloody idiot," cried Graham. "Why would you do that? Don't you know how worried I've been?"

"Obviously not. I'm guessing I've been out for a while. What time is it?"

"Try: what day is it," said Graham, a little more gently.

"Oh shit, how long have I been out then?"

"Two days, give or take a few hours," he replied.

"Why?"

"Why? Because you fractured your stupid skull diving off a cliff..."

"Seems like they must have put me back together though," observed Liv, whose eyelids were feeling heavier by the moment.

"Only just," he conceded.

"You alright?" she murmured.

"I'm fine."

"What about the American?"

"Hal's fine. We're both fine. We're all fine, Liv..."

"You sound cross," she breathed, closing her eyes. "You need to work on your bedside... bedside... whatever..."

"And you need to rest," he said.

"According to you, I've already had two days' rest," she grumbled. "So, talk to me. What's happened?"

"It's all OK," he told her.

"How can anything be 'OK'?"

"You're in the clear..."

"What, for being shot at?" she growled.

"Don't get worked up, it's over, Liv."

"Worked up?" she groaned. "Piss off."

So, he did. And that shocked her. She thought he would stay with her for a while longer... be sympathetic... ask her how she felt... how she was coping with her mother's death - not to mention losing her father and uncle without ever knowing them. And why was he so angry with her? Hadn't she saved his life?

Setting aside thoughts of Graham, she began to consider his bald statement that 'it' was 'over' - whatever 'it' was. Their life and death struggle, she supposed, was what he meant. But why then did she feel as if her entire life was over? Perhaps because she had no job, no money, no parents and no place to live... Had she left anything out? Oh yeh, her fucking head hurt...

When the nurse came in to tell her that they had stopped the morphine, she told the woman to piss off. It probably explained though why her head was now throbbing as if it was going to burst. No more morphine, which was a pity. But life was a bitch like that. After a few hours, her headache felt worse but oddly, she had to concede that she was beginning to think more clearly. She was surprised to discover that she could remember every detail of what had happened at Sunrise Heights.

It made her weep a little, which was to be expected, she supposed, since they'd just rebuilt her head. But she felt no desire to move on, or look ahead. What was the point?

Graham came to see her again the following day and, though she deduced, from his sheepish grin, that he regretted how he had been with her before, she could tell that he had erected some sort of barrier between them. Several more days passed, however, when he did not come at all and she had never felt more alone. Hence, she was overjoyed when the American, Hal was wheeled into her room by a blonde woman who seemed about her age – only better looking.

"So you're the one Hal wanted to stick around for," she said.

"Lisa," said the blonde.

"Without your man, Lisa, I'd be dead · simple as that."

"But you took a fall for me and Graham," Hal reminded her.

"Yeh, we're all heroes, aren't we?" said Liv. "You should really hold onto this guy, Lisa. He shows definite promise."

For a few moments they exchanged some polite platitudes before Lisa announced: "Hal's been discharged. So we're just here to... you know..."

"OK," said Liv, facing abandonment again. "But Graham told me why you were there at Sunrise Heights – who you were looking for... and found."

"No pot at the end of the rainbow though," said Hal ruefully.

"Maybe not," agreed Liv, "but you could try Winthrop and Hall. They're my late mother's lawyers. They don't represent Henry, but you could ask them to advise you on what to do about claiming his legacy."

"Now I know what the bastard was, I'm not sure I want anything from him."

"Well, perhaps there isn't anything anyway," said Liv. "But at least you might be able to find out."

"Thanks," said Hal. "I'll think about it..." Then glancing at the woman at his side, he added: "We'll think about it."

Liv wanted to reach out and clasp the hand of the man who had saved her but, even if her arm hadn't still been bandaged, it just wasn't what Liv Fisher did.

Instead, she said what others said: "You should keep in touch."

"Forgive me, Liv," replied Hal, "but you don't seem a sort of 'keep in touch' person."

Clearly Hal was an excellent judge of people.

"Yeh, well, I guess I've never been great at small talk," she agreed. "So, just put your number in my phone and piss off."

48

It was another week before she saw Graham again, loitering at the door to her room.

"Come in then," she muttered, "I don't bite."

"I think we both know you do," replied Graham, with an attempt at a grin.

"You've not been for ages," she complained, though secretly pleased that he had come at all. "I thought you'd... moved on. So, why have you come?"

"To see how you are, of course."

"I'm on the mend and desperate to get out of here."

"You've lost weight in hospital," he said.

"There was a time I'd have kissed you for saying that."

"I live in hope."

"Hope's overrated...."

"I suppose it's goodbye then," he said.

"You said it was over but... how can that be?" she asked. "Surely the cartel will be coming for us."

"There is no cartel. It seems that when Henry Fisher took Monica to the States, he'd already been busy undermining his bosses working with Charles Grey. When Monica told him she'd cleaned out the cartel's old accounts, it gave him the perfect opportunity to take over."

"But the accounts were always in my mother's head..." she murmured.

"Yes, but I don't think he realised that until the end."

"So, no more south coast cartel."

"Oh, I dare say, a new group will take up the slack in the south – and perhaps they have already. But I doubt they'll be interested in you or me. So, you're free to do whatever you like. How did you get on with your mother's lawyers?"

"Oh, that didn't take long. It seems Monica had no assets in her name. No bank accounts and no pile of ill-gotten cash either. All she had was the house. So, lucky me: I'm homeless again. And to cap it all, the doctors won't let me out yet unless I've got somewhere to stay."

"Well, don't look at me. My flat's in Hammersmith – or at least it was. Turned out it was in Barb's name."

"How could you not know that?" she said, with a shake of the head.

"Because I didn't pay attention, Liv, alright? No bloody attention at all to people who might possibly care whether I lived or died. So, yeh, I'm an even worse fuck-up than you – and that's saying something..."

"Well, you're a real dose of good cheer," she grumbled.

"Just sharing how I feel. It helps me to work things out. OK?"

"Well, since we're sharing, it does nothing for me."

"This little reunion isn't going as I planned," he muttered.

"Nothing goes as we plan, Graham."

"Yeh, anyway, I was thinking..." he began and then hesitated.

"Oh, spit it out!"

"Well, I thought now that the whole multiple murder scenario is sort of... over, perhaps the two of us could-"

"No, Graham," snapped Liv. "There's nothing between us."

"But there could be," he insisted.

A young nurse, who had unwittingly wandered into their exchange, now stood open-mouthed.

"Piss off!" said Liv and Graham together, sending the poor girl speeding from the room.

"We've got to stop doing that," murmured Liv.

"Yeh, it's almost as if we're occasionally on the same page..."

"Look, just because we helped each other out, doesn't mean I have to sleep with you."

"No, of course not," agreed Graham. "But what I was going to say was-"

"So, just leave it," advised Liv, not entirely sure why she was being so abrupt with him.

"All I was going to say was, do you think, maybe after a bit more dust has settled-"

"No, not even then," insisted Liv. "We're not exactly made for each other, Graham. I told you: you're not my type."

For a moment he fell silent before muttering: "All I was asking, Liv, was to be your friend. That's all. Because, you said you couldn't ever remember having a friend. So, I'd like to be one... if that's OK."

"A friend?" said Liv, as if encountering an entirely new concept. "Yeh, well, I suppose we could be *friends*."

"Good," said Graham.

"But only if you can get me out of here..."

"I should've known there'd be conditions," he grumbled. "But OK. I'll go and see what I can do."

"Thanks," she said, favouring him with a rare smile.

He had reached the door when he stopped and told her: "And who are you trying to kid? Because you haven't got a type."

Somehow Graham managed to negotiate her release which was nevertheless accompanied by dire warnings of a medical apocalypse if she strayed even slightly from her doctor's instructions. They took a taxi to Graham's hotel – well, a local Travelodge, in fact.

"You've no money, Liv," he explained. "And I've not got much more. So, at forty quid a night, it'll have to do."

"It'll be great," she replied, "because it's not a hospital."

"And we're only sharing a room because I've been given strict orders to literally keep an eye on you. Though it is cheaper of course... They're worried you're not taking your head injury seriously enough. Twin beds though, as you see."

"Thanks," she murmured. "I do appreciate you getting me out."

"So, you should probably lie down and rest now."

"No," she told him. "We're going for a little walk first."

"And so it begins," he groaned.

"I think it's only a short walk."

"But you've not been out of bed for weeks," he protested.

"Well, that's not quite true," she confided. "I spent most nights this past week wandering around the wards and that was a sobering fucking experience, I can tell you. Because there are some really sick people in that place. And the kids... they made me think what a waste of space I've been. Anyway, my head might still hurt and my left arm's still a bit numb, but at least my legs are strong enough."

"Your legs are fabulous," he murmured.

"Don't start," she warned.

"So, where are we going then?" he enquired.

With a grin, she said: "The only honest answer to that is, I don't know exactly. But it's only in the High Street."

"What is?"

"You said it was all over, Graham, but it's not – at least not quite."

It was one of those moments in Liv's life when she just thought: sod it, let's just roll the dice and see what happens. Past experience told her that what happened was that even more shit hit the fan. But she knew that she had one last act to carry out before she could even hope to get past all that had happened.

Graham offered her his arm as they walked out into the High Street. She hesitated for a moment before taking it but did so because, after three weeks in hospital, she'd forgotten how much her eyes processed every couple of seconds. It was a shock... too many distractions... So, she better go back to keeping her eyes hooded, she decided glumly.

The address she had memorised from Monica was a place on Christchurch High Street which she expected must be a small flat. An old bolthole of her mother's, perhaps. To her surprise, it was actually a small office, though presumably there were rooms above it. Since a blind covered the broad front window, she couldn't see what was inside. So, awkwardly, she just stood staring at it, wedging her hands in the pockets of her jeans ‐ which she suddenly realised still bore traces of her mother's blood.

The combination lock on the door looked rather upmarket but staring at it with hostile intent failed to open it. By the look of it, it had been installed quite recently ‐ a few months ago at most. So, what might the combination be? Since her mother hadn't told her, she must have assumed that Liv would be able to guess it or work it out easily.

"Wild guess: you don't know the combination," observed Graham.

"No. And, shit, you were right. I'm too tired to stand here doing this all day. Walking was alright, but standing... not so much."

For so long, she had hated her mother, yet even now that she was aware of the dark business in which Monica had been embroiled, she couldn't help feeling something for the woman. Having said that, why had her mother bequeathed her a vacant office? The lawyers had made no mention of it at all.

"I don't think you need a code," remarked Graham. "It's a biometric deadbolt."

"Speak English," growled Liv.

"You just need your fingerprint."

"That can't be right, because surely it would be Monica's fingerprint. I mean: how would she have mine?"

With a sly grin, he said: "remember you saw Mark near your Reading flat? Well, I doubt it was the first time he'd been there."

She nodded and placed her forefinger on a small half-shielded pad beneath the combination. Nothing happened. No clicking or whirring of a lock.

"Try the other index finger," he suggested.

And though she did so with little hope, she did then hear the door lock disengage and, when she turned the handle, the door swung open.

Once inside, she realised that the premises were not entirely empty because there was a desk, two office chairs and a filing cabinet. Not that any of it made much sense because she didn't need an office. A cursory examination of the filing cabinet revealed that it was completely empty so, no clue as to why her mother had sent her there. Passing to the rear of the property, she climbed the stairs, wincing as the movement pulled at the wound in her abdomen. Upstairs was a small flat – even smaller than her Reading one.

Another, slimmer and multi-drawer, filing cabinet had been squeezed in between a lumpy-looking bed and a long wooden chest. A layer of dust covered every inch of it apart from the bed which she surmised Monica might well have used just before she came to Sunrise Heights for the last time. An inspection of the chest yielded nothing of interest other than bed linen, which only left the filing cabinet. Resting her hand upon its scratched and tarnished grey metal top, she stared down at it. Why have a filing cabinet in the bedroom?

Monica had quite explicitly told her that this place was her legacy, but what did she mean by that? As Liv gripped the handle of the top drawer, she wondered whether she even cared what her mother meant. With a sigh, she pulled open the drawer and discovered that she truly *did* care. The drawer was completely empty. No secret account. No great stack of used notes. Not even a grubby tenner wedged into a corner. Liv slammed shut the top drawer, raising a tiny cloud of dust, and then turned her attention to the remaining shallow trays, trying each of them in turn.

She should have known. Fuck-ups don't suddenly inherit wealth – even the dirty money her parents might have bequeathed her. And it was drug money anyway, so she probably would have flushed it down the loo. Yeh, like hell she would...

In the bottom drawer, there was, however, a single manilla envelope. Hardly worthy of note because it was disappointingly thin. No wad of cash stuffed in there. Breaking the seal, she drew out a single sheet of paper with a yellow post-it attached.

"What is it?" enquired Graham, who had followed her upstairs.

The hastily scrawled note on the post-it was in her mother's hand.

"Olivia - if you're reading this without me, then my hope of a reconciliation has come to nothing. We must have talked at least – because you're here. This office was mine a long time ago. Now it's in your name to keep or sell as you please. My friend, Mark will call and tell you anything you need to know. Love, Monica."

Attached to the note was what purported to be the deed of the property in which they stood. Sure enough, it was in her name and dated four months earlier. Monica must have been preparing this for some time. So, it was official. She wasn't inheriting it because she already owned it. No rent to be paid - thanks to the local drug barons. So, rent free, if not exactly guilt-free.

But still, what was she supposed to do with an office – or a shop? She had no money, so she'd have to sell it anyway. Shit, more hassle. And, of course, Mark wasn't going to be calling her - ever.

Graham, who had been reading over her shoulder, said: "Well, on the bright side, you've got a place to live and a bed to sleep in – and you could rent out the premises. This will give you a place of your own and an income. It won't give you a life though, Liv. That you'll have to work out for yourself."

Still processing, she nodded.

"Do you want me to leave you alone while you work things out?" he asked.

"No, why would I want you to leave?" she replied sharply. "You're my friend, aren't you? Let's go back to the hotel."

When she closed the shop door behind them, they stood for few moments on the pavement.

"What now?" she murmured.

"Looks like you've become a landlord," he said, with a grin.

"Yeh, but I hate landlords…"

Author's Note

Eyes Like Blades has been in my head – in one form or another – for several years and it's good to finally get it published. I hope readers feel that the effort has been worthwhile.

Much of the story is set on the south coast of England where I live, though I have changed some placenames and also taken a few liberties with the local landscape.

The sequel, ***Death In The Water***, which will be out later in 2025, will also take place in the same area around Christchurch.

To find out more about my books, go to my web page: **http://www.tomhadleyauthor.com**

My alter ego, Derek Birks, has written quite a number of historical fiction books. If you are interested, there is a list of them overleaf.

Tom Hadley
2025

Historical Fiction by Derek Birks

The *Wars of the Roses* series [in order]:
Feud
A Traitor's Fate
Kingdom of Rebels
The Last Shroud
Scars from the Past
The Blood of Princes
Echoes of Treason
Shadow of Doubt – a novella
Crown of Fear

The Last of the Romans series [in order]:
Aquileia – a short story published in the *Imperium* collection.
The Emperor's Sister – a short story in *Triumphs & Tragedies*
The Last of the Romans
Britannia: World's End
New Dawn – a novella
Death At the Feet of Venus – a short story
Land of Fire

To find out more about the books and Derek's other work, you can go to his website:
http://www.derekbirks.com